THE SHATTERED SHADES OF CRIMSON

THE SHATTERED SHADES OF CRIMSON

A HUES NOVEL
BOOK THREE

J. L. JACKOLA

Tivshe Publishing

Library of Congress Control Number 2023903360

Paperback ISBN 978-1-954175-97-6
Hardback ISBN 978-1-954175-98-3
Electronic ISBN 978-1-954175-99-0

Distributed by Tivshe Publishing
Printed in the United States of America

Cover design by Dark Queen Designs
Map design by Worldwyrm

Visit www.tivshepublishing.com

ALSO BY J. L. JACKOLA

Even the naughty ones deserve love.

AUTHOR'S NOTE

Dear Reader,

You've made it to book three! This is Crimson's story, but don't worry, Mark and Skye are still essential to this story and the series. You'll see plenty of them again in book four and five.

As with the first two books, book three consists of characters who are mature and sexually confident. Please be aware of possible triggers. This series contains intense and explicit sexual scenes, language, non-consensual sex, abuse, reverse harem situations, violence, and death.

Get ready because everything is about to change!

J. L.

KANTENDA
DRANTH MOUNTAINS
FETTERRED FOREST
CHENTHOM

ELTANDER
NENOCHIN
APENDIA

PETE

Pete leaned against his car and stared at the house. The structure looked no different than it had ten years earlier —the last time he'd seen it. It still looked as if it had stepped out of a 1930s movie. The two-story white building with its old-fashioned well in the front yard and two small cottages in the back held fond memories, yet he was still hesitant to return to his childhood home before now.

When he'd left ten years ago, he'd never returned. Refusing to even visit. A scattered number of phone calls had been his only connection. His father had inherited the house from his parents, they from Pete's great-grandparents, and so on.

He fiddled with the key in his hands. Now the house had come to him. No one had expected his father to die suddenly. The heart attack had taken him quickly, his body found at the forest edge where he'd died.

Never go into the woods at night.

Those words had been ingrained in him since he could remember. He glanced at the forest, which stretched for miles. His family owned two-hundred acres, all of it untouched forest. Beyond the oak trees, he could see the towering white trees in the distance. Their limbs stretched high in strange, twisted shapes as if they were reaching for some unobtainable object. They looked innocent enough now but, at night, their shadows cast far over the other trees in eerie movements.

Pete never understood why his father kept the house, but he had no intention of doing the same. He looked back at his loaded car, questioning his decision to sell his penthouse apartment and most of his belongings, and quitting his Wall Street job if his intent was to only stay until he'd fixed this place up enough to sell it.

He shook his head as he got back into the car and drove it down the long, steep driveway until he reached the back of the house. Gripping the key to the house, he made his way up the back steps, turning to look at the woods once again. There were two Adirondack chairs set in front of the firepit to the right of the woods. A dilapidated shed stood in the distance, in need of more repair than he'd be able to provide. He wondered if his father had sat there at night, drawn to the woods as Pete had always been.

"What did you do, Dad?" he asked, still puzzled as to why his father had been found where he had.

Sighing, he opened the front door and took a step into his childhood home. The house hadn't changed. Cabinets lined the back wall. They had been his favorite go-to when playing hide and seek with his sister. The master bedroom sat to his left, where his father's belongings were already cleared out. He walked into the kitchen with its antique metal table; the paint chipped in the corners from age and wear. It was a small space, but one that held many memories. He let his fingers drift along the cool metal, remembering the bingo games his grandmother used to play with him when he'd visit. That had been many years before his mother had died, the cancer ripping so viciously through her body. Years before his father had packed them up and moved them all into the small home, running from the truth that she was really gone.

"Leave the memories in the past, Pete," he scolded himself.

He checked the lights, thankful his sister had left the power on, then peeked in the fridge, smiling at the six-pack she'd left him. He'd need more than beer, but it was late afternoon on a Sunday. He'd make a run to the store in the morning and deal with a growling stomach for now. He wondered if anyone delivered this far from town and made a mental note to check as he headed to the car to start unloading before the sun set.

PETE DESCENDED the creaky wooden stairs to the basement. He raised a brow in surprise at finding that his father had installed better lighting than the last time he'd been here. Although neglected, the rest of the house was in fairly good shape. Other than the sitting room and kitchen, it didn't look like his father had ever used any other rooms. His sister had left their father's things in different spots throughout the house, unlike the bedroom. Pete guessed she had either run out of time or emotional stamina.

Curious about the basement, he'd decided to head down after he'd settled in. The basement had been his grandfather's wood shop. The smell of must and wood shavings was a large part of his childhood. Now it only smelled of must. Someone had cleared the stone cellar of most of the woodworking tools, only a scattering of projects remained—a few frames, some small objects, and the large workbench. He walked to the workbench, which was covered with writings. A large notebook lie open, his father's scribblings on the page.

He moved closer, his eyes drawn to a sketch of a robed figure. The robe had been shaded in, giving the figure a menacing appearance before the tall eerie trees sketched behind him. The bottoms of the trees were sketched with dark gnarly spots that faded to white with the height of the tree.

He put the sketch down and picked up another. The paper

on this was newer, and he wondered if there was a difference in age between the two. He brought the sketch closer, intrigued by the beautiful woman with the haunted eyes his father had drawn. He didn't recognize her. His fingers traced the features of the sketch before he put it down and looked through the papers. He found more sketches of her, some side profiles, some that made her look ephemeral, as if she were a spirit.

He wondered who she was, unsure if she was real or a figment of the imagination. His father had always been a talented artist, drawing dragons and all sorts of creatures for Pete and his sister when they were children. But this didn't look like an imaginary woman. His eyes were drawn to her again. Whoever she was, his father had been obsessed about her.

He looked at the notebook. It was an incoherent mess of his father's ramblings And thoughts about spirits and screaming. His finger stopped at the word *screaming*. No, it wasn't screams that echoed through the forests; it was wails. He remembered that night, ten years ago. The wails that would forever haunt him. As a child, he would occasionally be drawn to a sound that faded too fast for him to clearly identify it. But that night...that night it had echoed for hours. Terrifying cries that haunted one's dreams. And then there had been the one distinct scream. It had cut through the cries, bursting through the forest. He'd gone to run, knowing a scream like that only came from true pain, but his father had stopped him.

"No one goes to those woods at night."

He'd argued, but his father had refused to let him go. It was the last time he'd seen his father, the last time he'd come home to visit. The scream haunted him to this day. He dropped his eyes to the sketch again and those eyes which seemed to see straight into his soul.

A creak from above startled him from his thoughts.

"Why are you hanging in the creepy basement?" he heard his sister say as she descended the stairs, balancing a pizza in one hand

and two beers in the other. Courtney's face peeked out from behind the pizza, her mop of black curls cut into a bob. Her blue eyes evaluated him seriously as she placed her pizza and beers on the table, shoving the papers carelessly out of the way.

"So, the reclusive big brother does live."

"Hey, Court," he said, looking away from her perceptive stare, knowing the guilt he harbored was easy to recognize.

"Couldn't even come to the funeral?"

"I..." He stopped, knowing he had no excuse.

"Yeah, that's what I thought."

She walked to him and gave him a hug, then a kiss on the cheek. "Good thing I'm a forgiving person, or perhaps I just know my brother well enough now."

"Court."

"Don't '*Court*' me, Pete. I had to handle everything myself. Do you know how hard it was to clean out his bedroom? To find his body that day? To make funeral arrangements and handle everything else?"

"I sent you money."

"Yeah, you did, as always." She sighed and pulled the stool out, sitting and crossing her arms.

"I don't have any excuse, but I'm here now."

"Long enough to clean it out and sell it for a profit?" she asked, raising a brow.

"Long enough to fix it up and then...I don't know. I sold my apartment."

Her eyes widened in surprise. "Moving home finally? It's been a long time, Pete."

"I know, but I'm here now."

"So you are. What happened to your fancy job and your fancy girlfriend?"

"Dana? We broke up three years ago."

"That's the last time I saw you. Bo and I came to New York for the weekend, remember?"

"Yes, I remember."

They sat in silence as he looked at his hands, not sure what to tell her about why he'd never come home.

"So," she started, breaking the silence, "rummaging through dad's crazy notes?"

"Just starting to."

"Well, don't. He started going a little off the rails, babbling about spirits and crazy things." She grabbed the pizza box. "Come on, bring those and let's get out of this dungeon before we both lose it, too."

He grabbed the beers, glancing at the sketch again, the woman's eyes seeing into his soul.

"Catch up, you always were the slower one."

"Nice, Court. Guess I deserved that," he responded, drawing his eyes away and following her.

Instead of stopping in the kitchen, she headed out the back door. He continued to follow her until she plopped the pizza onto the ground between the two Adirondack chairs and threw some wood into the firepit before lighting it. She grabbed a beer from his hand and dropped into a chair.

"You just going to stand there all night?"

He drew his eyes from the woods and sat in the chair, staring at the fire. They went on to chat about irrelevant things, about their lives over last few years, skirting the thing that sat heavy on Pete's chest.

Finally, he asked, "What was he doing in the woods?"

Courtney was silent for a few minutes. It took all he had not to press her. "I don't know."

"We were always told, Court, the family saying it, over and over. Do not go into the woods at night."

"We don't know that he was there at night."

"You found him on the edge of the trees."

She shuddered. "I was on my way to work, heading in early to do inventory. The sun was still rising. I don't know what prompted me to come to the house that morning, he wasn't an early riser." She paused, as if remembering that day. "He was over there." She pointed to the tree line. "Like he'd been running from something. They said his heart gave out."

Pete's eyes drifted to the woods.

"He'd been losing it, Pete. Ever since you left. Every year, he slipped a little more."

"He was already a little off."

"Aren't we all?"

He chuckled, his eyes still fixed on the woods. After a moment, he said, "Did you ever hear it?"

"What?"

"The wails. The cries that drift in the air." He felt her eyes on him but continued to stare at the woods as if answers would come. "When we were young."

"I heard them. All the time. That night before I left, I heard them. And there was this one distinct scream that was distinct above the wails. It was a gut-wrenching sound."

"That's why you left?"

"I asked him about it. He acted like it was nothing. I heard what I heard. That scream will stay with me forever. It was haunting." Drawing his eyes from the trees, he asked, "What secrets has our family been protecting in those woods?"

"I don't know," she whispered.

Silence followed. There was nothing more to say. Neither had answers, but he was determined to find them even if it meant they found him facedown at the edge of the woods like his father. He needed answers, needed to know who that scream belonged to, who the beautiful, sad woman in the sketch was.

As he settled into his father's bed that night, her face filled his mind, her haunting eyes searing into his soul and stealing it from him.

CRIMSON

Crimson watched as the embers of the fire burned down. Life had returned to the house on the edge of her forest, and with it had come a man. Not the old crazy man who had tried to catch her, stealing glimpses into her prison despite her efforts to scare him off. She hadn't wanted to hurt him. She'd been curious about him. But he was old, wandering her woods, rambling as if he knew she was there somehow. The thought had frightened her so that she'd kept closer to the grove. He hadn't returned in some time. The last time she'd seen the old man, he had run off. One of her souls had broken from its prison and terrified him before Crimson could wrangle it back in. That soul was a handful, and it had taken a great deal of seduction to lure him back. She didn't know how long it had been since she'd last seen the man, time was irrelevant to her. But she knew it had been some time since he'd finally left her and her souls in peace. Well, as much peace as a prison of trapped, restless souls could offer.

Now there was a new man, a beautiful man from what she could tell from the shadow of the flames in front of which he'd been sitting. Flames that had danced in his blue eyes. His dark hair had waves that begged to have fingers run through it, and she'd imagined what it would feel like against her own fingers.. He'd looked right at her, seeing into her woods as if he could see her.

She'd watched the man and the woman he'd been with. Curious that lights had shone once again from the house, she'd snuck past the comfort of her trees and into the edge of her prison of trees. He and the woman had talked as if they'd known each other forever. There was a comfort there, one that came from old lovers, but she didn't get that sense from them. She knew enough about lovers to know the difference.

Her body tingled at the thought. It had been a very long time since she'd felt the touch of a man. Markhem had been the last. Though a good one to end with, no matter that deception marred the memory. She'd fallen for him, his touch, his taste, the feel of him when he came. Markhem had been good, one of the best, but he hadn't belonged to her. None of them had. No matter how much she'd given them.

She watched as the lights went dark in the house before she turned back to her forest, wondering at the man with the blue eyes she'd seen shimmer in the firelight. She imagined his touch, need sweeping through her as the spirits sensed her return. The low rise of their wails assaulted her ears as she felt them reach for her.

"Hush," she murmured stroking the black bark of the one who had escaped that night. The trees imprisoned each spirit, but the spirits still had the ability to stretch beyond the bounds of their prison. Mostly, they stretched upward, the black of their bark rising to ground them back to the Shadow Realm as they stretched toward the white bark that always lay just beyond their reach. There were times she could see their spirit forms like mist that seeped into the shape of a body. They longed for freedom and that longing gave them shape. This tree, although her most unruly, was her favorite. As the black of his bark rose, she felt his phantom hands reach for her. She turned and leaned against him, imagining the spirit was the beautiful man as her own hands massaged her breasts. The pressure of the spirits hands joined hers, her body shivering in response..

She arched her back as more ephemeral hands touched her. The touch wasn't quite physical but the desperate need they had to feel mortal flesh lent a tantalizing feel to it that drove her desire. Her dress lifted, the feel of the hands rising along her legs. Moving her hand to accompany them, she let her fingers touch her wetness, stroking as the spirits did until she plunged her fingers deep. As she imagined the man's swollen erection entering her, his image changed to Markhem's face, and her orgasm rose then crashed through her. The souls joined her cry of release as she drifted down from her peak. She missed the true feel of a man, and desperately craved the thickness of one within her, missing how it burned her to the core. Markhem had been the only man who'd ever brought her to the edge. She didn't think there would ever be another. Her sentence was eternity. An eternity fantasizing about a man who had turned her on enough to bring her to climax without her own touches.

"Fool," she told herself, pushing the hands back and fixing her dress. "He was never yours."

Her eyes glanced back toward the house far beyond her trees, then she returned to her endless duty as the Keeper of Lost Souls.

PETE

Pete stood, looking out the back door, drinking the remnants of his cold coffee. He'd risen early that morning to head into town. It had been years, yet the small town remained the same, like he'd stepped into the scene of a Norman Rockwell painting. He'd stopped at the local hardware store to pick up some supplies he'd need to start renovations. He'd always been good with fixing things. It was in his blood thanks to his father and his father before him. However, he'd bulked at the calling and gone to a college as far away as possible, intent on finding a high paying white-collar job.

Even then he had struggled to ignore the call. After college he'd delved into odd jobs, women, alcohol until he'd finally severed ties with his past life and stepped into the world of Wall Street. Eventually, he worked his way to where he was today, a far cry from the life his father had led.

After the hardware store, he'd stopped at the market, knowing beer and pizza may have worked as a staple in his twenties, but in his early forties, it no longer sufficed. When his errands were completed, Pete had left town and headed back to the house.

He'd tried to keep thoughts of his findings in the basement

from his mind as he'd unpacked his groceries and grabbed a snack, but it hadn't worked.

Now he stood, staring into the woods, drawn to it. There was something he couldn't shake. It was the same feeling he'd had the morning he'd turned his back on the forest ten years prior. He'd stood by the forest edge that morning as he'd said his goodbyes to his father, his eyes fixed on the trees as if waiting for the owner of the scream to emerge.

He turned from the door and headed back to the basement. Leafing through his father's notes, Pete took in his ramblings about ghosts and spirits that haunted the forest. The wails that woke him at night, had since childhood. Pete looked up from the notebook, his eyes falling to the sketch. His father had heard them, too. Courtney had found him at the edge of the forest and Pete couldn't help but think he'd gone out there. Whether it was to search for the woman in the sketch or for some other reason, there was no way of knowing. Pete lifted the sketch and carried it up the stairs with him, placing it on the table and leaning over it.

Whoever she was, she had something to do with the forest. He was certain of it. He looked at his watch. It was only eleven. He could finish unpacking this afternoon. He dug his water bottle from his bag, filled it, then headed out the back door.

He passed the two small cottages behind the house. One was filled with miscellaneous things his father had never cleaned out after Pete's grandparents had passed, the other still held a menagerie of children's things—dolls, stuffed bears, a small table, all layered with dust and cobwebs. He made his way to the tree line and froze, suddenly doubting himself. He was going against everything his family had ever taught him about the woods. No one went into the woods. But his father had, he was certain of it.

He glanced back toward the house, the mountain across the road casting its shadow over it. Pete remembered the story of the mountain that his grandmother had told him. That of the woman who had cast herself from its peak after her lover had been killed.

Her love for him so strong that she couldn't live without him. He had always doubted love like that existed, but the story had stuck with him, as had the warnings about the forest. He shook his head at the memories and turned back toward the trees.

"There's nothing in there but bugs and animals, Pete. Let's get this over with so you can move on."

He stepped in, double-checking that his phone was in his back pocket. He had a pretty good sense of direction, even when the way held no path, and he walked on for about a half a mile. The sun faded the further he moved into the forest, but the canopy of branches allowed small streams of light to shine through. He'd never realized these woods were so thick.

Eventually, the dense feel dissipated, and he stood before an open grove of trees. These weren't the maple and oak trees he'd walked through earlier. These were different. They were two toned—darker on the bottom and white toward the top. He looked up, his eyes following the smooth white bark further than his neck could reach. These were the trees he'd always seen from the distance, stretching as if to reach the heavens.

He'd always assumed they were beech trees, but they weren't quite. No leaves adorned their branches, yet it was still early fall. Their stumps were black and gnarled, the ebony climbing as if to pull the stretched limbs back. It was a fascinating dichotomy, beautiful and eerie at the same time.

As he stepped into the grove, a wave of emotion swept over him nearly knocking him from his feet. He took a step back, trying to steady himself. The sensation had been unexpected—a strange mix of pain, regret, and hopelessness.

Composing himself, he put his foot back in, slowly feeling the onslaught again, bracing himself for it this time. It didn't help, and as he took the full step, it nearly doubled him over. The hair on the back of his neck stood, and he had the strangest feeling he was being watched.

This place was unlike any he'd ever seen. It gave him an unsettled feeling. He'd always questioned why his family had kept the property for generations and why it was in the will that it could never be sold. That stipulation was something Pete had decided didn't matter, planning to turn it and get rid of it. Closing the door on the memories, on that scream that still echoed through his head at night. But now, he wasn't so sure that this space wasn't the reason behind the requirement that everyone inheriting the property before him had heeded.

His eyes dropped to the ground, seeing that a fine coat of white layered it like a covering of snow. He bent and touched it, feeling the soft delicate texture of the substance. It wasn't snow. It was slivers of bark, like fine shavings. His eyes went to the closest tree, the way the black seemed to have clawed its way up the trunk. A shiver went through him.

"What the hell is this place?"

He dropped his gaze, and in that movement, he saw it. A lone footprint—small, bare, delicate against the shavings. A woman's foot. He thought of the sketch, the woman's distant look, hollow and sad.

"What did you find, Dad?"

He stood, searching the trees for her, for any sign of life but he was unable to step further, something holding him back. His phone rang, causing him to jump. His heart raced, the sound of it nearly carrying through the silence along with the ring. He pulled his phone out to answer it, still scanning the area as he talked.

"Where are you?" Courtney asked. "It sounds like you're in a tunnel."

"Just outside working. What's up?"

"Bo and I are heading to the bar after work for a drink. Join us. He says he forgives you for being an ass to me and wants to catch up."

"How nice of him."

"Come on. We'll be there around six-thirty."

"Fine."

"See ya."

Hanging up, he studied the grove again. He wanted to go further, but it was like an invisible barrier was pushing against him. Instinct told him he didn't want to go beyond that barrier. He stared at the footprint, unsure of who could have made it. He was tempted to say that it belonged to the woman in the drawing, but that didn't make sense. There was no one living out here. She could have been a spirit his father had seen but he didn't think spirits made footprints, which meant she was real.

He had more questions now than when he'd entered the forest but still had no answers. A shadow fell upon the footprint, and he scanned the grove to find nothing, yet the shadow remained.

That's your sign, Pete, he told himself.

He backed out of the grove, the feeling of being watched growing stronger. Only when he was far enough from the grove did he turn to find his way back, the same sensation following him as he walked away.

CRIMSON

As night fell, Crimson woke. Stretching, she prepared for her shift of waking the souls from their daytime slumber. The moon was full as it peeked through the branches. She still didn't quite understand how this prison worked. During the day, she would sleep, waking at the last sliver of sun, her cycle now nocturnal for eternity. She was alive yet not alive. No sustenance was needed to survive, as if the Death God fed her as she slept.

She laughed at the thought of the Death God. Once she had been his toy, lapping up his attention, his body. She'd had him wrapped around her finger, taking him for her own pleasure just as he had taken her. A god had been her lover before Skye had ruined it for her. It annoyed her that men couldn't seem to resist Skye. Both Markhem and Derrant had chosen Skye over her.

"Bitch," she mumbled as she slumped against one of her trees. The souls had yet to wake, and she was glad for the quiet.

"Talking about me again?"

Crimson cringed and looked to see Skye emerge from behind a tree. She was annoyingly beautiful as always, much to Crimson's dismay. Her thick brown hair was loose, enhancing the lush blue eyes that were so unique to her. She wore a flowing blue dress that sat perfectly on her curves. What Crimson wouldn't do for a new dress, something with color, instead of the drab black she had no choice but to wear. If she ever had the chance, she would never wear black again.

"Skye. Can't get enough of me, can you?"

Skye sat against the tree opposite her, elegant and graceful, as opposed to how Crimson was currently feeling.

"How's life with the souls, Crimson? Still dreaming of my husband to keep you satisfied?"

Snarky bitch, she thought. "He makes me come every night. Are you keeping him satisfied for me? I doubt it."

Skye laughed. "You have no idea how satisfied he is."

They sat in silence for a few moments. Every visit with Skye was always like this. She couldn't remember how long Skye had been visiting her, but she came randomly. Sometimes just to sit with her; other times to talk. The first visit had been unsettling for her, and she suspected Skye had felt the same. Crimson had been stunned by it, not knowing what to say. Since then, they'd developed a rapport. One that danced around the tension, the dislike that still sat under the surface. There was a history between them that had scarred them both, yet there was something shared between them. Other than Skye's husband, that is.

Crimson had no regrets. Markhem had been the best man she'd had, aside from Derrant. Sure, she'd forced him most times, but it had been worth it.

The first time Skye visited, Crimson had asked her why she'd come to her, after all she'd done to hurt her. Skye had answered honestly that she didn't know why. Despite Markhem telling her not to go, she'd felt the need. Over time, Crimson realized that it was curiosity. A way to satisfy Skye's question about why Markhem had caved, why he'd taken Crimson. Oh, she knew most of the times had been to turn her own deception on her, to gain his freedom and his way back to Skye. But that first time had been unrestrained.

"Why are you here, Skye? To remind me of what I've lost?"

"Nah, I do that each time I visit you."

Crimson laughed.

"Does the Death God know you pass through his realm and his brother's to get here?"

"You leave Derrant to me."

"Ahhh, still pleasuring him?" she asked with a raised brow. She knew of the sentence—the deal Derrant had forced Markhem to strike in exchange for Skye's life. "You know Markhem is probably lonely those five days Derrant has you. Why don't you send him here and let me remind him how it's done?"

"Good try. If you remember, it's your fault he's forced to give me up for that time each year. To spend those days knowing the Death God is taking his wife's body."

"Over and over again. Derrant has the sex drive of an animal. I know how many times he takes you. Markhem had quite the sex drive—" Bands of black wrapped around her throat, cutting her words short. The trees grew restless, a few wails escaping at her duress.

The hues faded, and the grip dissipated.

"I wouldn't do that again, Skye," she said, glaring at her. "My souls don't like it when I'm upset."

"Then I suggest you leave my husband's sex drive off the table. Besides, I wouldn't bank on having your head attached long enough to even reach his dick. He holds quite a grudge against you."

"I do like it rough."

"You're a piece of work, Crimson."

"I know." She crawled to Skye. "You know, when Derrant had you, you and I had quite a good time."

She draped her fingers down Skye's arm, brushing her breast. Skye pushed her hand away. "I was under his spell."

"That doesn't mean you didn't enjoy it. It's been a long time since I've touched flesh. Ages since I've felt its touch. I would settle for a round with you."

Skye pushed her away. "I've told you before, Crimson. I have enough shared hands on me. I doubt adding you to the list would make Mark happy."

She pushed herself back against the tree, caressing the bark as she might a lover. "You never know, he might find it quite a turn on."

Skye rolled her eyes. "Why do I bother?" She rose and called her magic.

"No," Crimson cried, desperation in her voice. It killed her to admit, but she looked forward to Skye's visits. Even with how infrequent they were. They'd developed a friendship of sorts, even if it teetered on the edge of resentment. "Please stay. I'll behave, I promise."

Skye eyed her, then sat back down.

"It gets so lonely here," Crimson said, casting her eyes to the ground.

"You really need a man, Crimson," Skye joked.

"Can you ask Derrant to send me one?"

"See, that's your problem. You take what you find—"

"I take what I want," she corrected.

"I'm aware. But doing that always left you empty."

"Since when did you start reading my mind?"

"You're easy to read, Crimson. It's desperate."

"It satisfied Markhem enough."

"Really?" Skye asked with an edge to her voice.

"Sorry. Well, in case you didn't notice, there are no men in the Forest of Lost Souls. Just the souls and none of them have dicks."

"Gross."

"You take what you get when you're stuck here for as long as I've been. How long has it been now?"

"Ten years."

"Ten years?" It hurt to even say it. Such a long time to go without interaction. She wondered if she was losing her mind. Maybe Skye wasn't even real; maybe she was a figment of her imagination.

She scurried over and pinched Skye's leg.

"Ouch! I swear you're insane."

"Nope, you're real, so I haven't lost my mind."

"Jesus, Crimson."

"Still have no idea who that is."

"It doesn't matter. Look, I didn't come here to chat." Crimson wondered at her sudden change in demeanor. It was authoritative. She'd finally become the queen she was meant to be. A worthy adversary. But then, she always had been.

"Why are you here, then?"

"Your cousin has fallen ill."

"Cousin? Oh, you mean that usurper who has my throne?"

"I mean the boy we chose to take your throne when the Death God deemed you unfit to rule."

"Unfit to live because your husband tricked me."

Skye sighed. "Because you tricked us, killed Mechon, invited the Death God to steal me, then kidnapped my husband! Need I go on and do we really need to rehash this?"

Crimson sighed as Skye's shoulders relaxed, her face growing sad.

"You're not the only one punished by the repercussions of your actions, Crimson."

"A few days in the bed of the Death God is pleasurable compared to this."

"Not when you love someone else, not when you're ripped from the man you love. If you'd ever taken the time to make your-self vulnerable enough to love someone, you'd understand."

They sat in silence for a few moments until Crimson finally said, "Why do I care if the usurper...cousin is ill?"

"Because if he dies, there is no one left of your line. Your father made sure of that."

Skye had told her of her father's actions before he'd died. How he'd killed anyone with even a trace of royal blood, guaranteeing his throne would never be contested. All but one small child he'd missed.

"So what? It makes no difference to me. I'm stuck here, anyway. What happens there will never affect me again."

"But it affects our world. There are already rumblings of unrest in your realm. Theodore is rallying his own troops—"

"What? That bastard is going to make a play at my throne? How dare he!"

"Exactly."

"Well, get the novice mages to heal the boy."

"It's beyond their abilities. They've tried everything. It's only a matter of time before the boy dies."

Crimson sat back. She hadn't thought of her kingdom for a very long time, not since she'd first been trapped here. But the thought of Theodore with his greedy hands and sore excuse for a dick getting his paws on her kingdom—on her crown—angered her.

"If Theodore doesn't make a move, which we believe he will, one of the rebel groups that have formed will."

"Non-royal blood on my throne?"

"Yes."

"Why are you telling me this, Skye? There's nothing I can do from here. I'm cursed for my lifetime, then for eternity once I finally die."

Skye ran a hand through her hair. "I can't believe I'm saying this...we think you're the only one capable of ruling Apendia, of stopping the unrest, and keeping Theodore in check."

Crimson had no doubt her mouth was agape. "Have you lost your mind? The Shadow Realm finally getting to your sanity?"

"I'm serious. Mark and I have talked this through."

"Markhem? I thought he wanted me dead. Does he still crave me after all?"

"He only craves to kill you, but he knows what unrest will do to your kingdom, especially since you so greedily took the Digremile Kingdom when their queen was killed."

"It was sitting there for the taking," she said.

"My ass it was. Anyway, Mark definitely doesn't want Theodore getting his hands on it. I think he hates Theodore almost as much as he hates you."

"And Revina? I'm sure she has an opinion."

Skye's expression grew sad. "Revina has distanced herself from us. The Eltander Kingdom has become more reclusive. They rarely respond to our messages, withdrawing from the world further than they already were. Revina is the least of your worries."

Leaning her head back against the tree, Crimson let herself imagine being queen again. Imagined being home, holding power again, sleeping in a bed, wearing gowns of the finest material, bathing in luxuriously scented bath water. It was something she hadn't allowed herself to think on in a very long time.

"It sounds grand being home again, but"—she met Skye's eyes, their blue almost as dark as the night—"I'm cursed here, Skye. Nothing can change this. It's my punishment."

"Punishment for being a foolish child."

"I'm older than you," she snapped.

"Okay, a foolish old lady."

Crimson couldn't help but laugh. "Yes, I suppose I was."

"Would you make the same choices, Crimson? If given the chance to do it again?"

She thought about it. It was a question she'd asked herself countless times.

"I don't know," she answered honestly. "I was a different person then. Ten years stuck in this wretched place changes you. It's hard to believe it's been that long. I can't say if time were reversed that I wouldn't. Giving up the memory of Markhem's body would be hard." She gave her a wink, but Skye only scowled and crossed her arms. "If I knew this was my fate, I wouldn't have repeated history, but that wouldn't mean I'd have stopped my scheming. What I thought was important then is...well, it's different from what I find important now."

Skye stood, drawing her hands as if to call a portal.

"You're leaving?"

"Yes."

"What was all that about, then? A tease? See how poor, pitiful Crimson will react if we tell her there's hope?"

She stood suddenly, clenching her fists in anger at the hope she'd felt at what Skye had told her. She knew it wasn't possible and hated that she'd let herself even contemplate returning home.

Skye's response gave her pause and she relaxed her posture.

"No, it was a test to see if we should bother finding a way to free you."

Crimson wasn't certain how to react. They were testing her. The hope wasn't a false one. "What do you mean?" she pressed.

"Mark doesn't think you've changed. He hasn't been here—hasn't talked to you."

"You're always welcome to bring him. Like I said, I'm very willing to occupy him when you're with Derrant."

"Crimson," Skye scolded.

"Did I pass your test?"

"Yes. Now I just need to convince him."

"You're really going to help me?" she asked in a whisper. "To free me from this place?"

"Yes, I just don't know how yet. I need time, but I'm not sure we have time."

Crimson stepped closer to Skye, her words swimming through her mind. Freedom.

"Please don't give me false hope. Hope can crush a person. Trust me. I've been the bearer of that false hope."

"I won't."

"Why are you helping me?"

She furrowed her brow. "I hated you for a long time. What you did to us, it ate at me. Every time Derrant pulled me from Mark. Any time my mind wandered to Mark sleeping with you. You brought so much harm to us. I almost let that hate bury me before I saw the good that came from it. Mark and I are closer now, inseparable. Eliana is back. Derrant is happy. The Shadow Realm no longer consists of only shadows and things that lurk in them. And the dragons have returned. When I took the time to open my eyes to all of that, I decided to visit you. I needed to move past the hate, needed to..." She paused and looked down at her hands. "To understand why it happened—why you were so irresistible. How you could break something I had thought was unbreakable."

"But I didn't break you and Markhem, Skye."

Skye's blue eyes met hers again, their color a startling cobalt. "No, you didn't. You almost did, but you didn't. I think there was a bit of curiosity there, too. Mark has a past littered with women he used to chase away his need for me when he couldn't have me. I could write those off, tell myself they were simply fillers, that they didn't matter, but I couldn't do that with you. He had me already, so there was nothing to ease the pain. So, I came to you to find out why he broke."

Her honesty was surprising. Crimson had always suspected that was the true reason that Skye had been seeking answers she couldn't find, an understanding of why he'd faltered that one time.

"Did you find what you were looking for?"

Skye laughed. "No, if anything, I made it worse. You're annoyingly beautiful and sexy, and those boobs are unsettling the way they just rest there, even in that drab outfit."

"You think Markhem fell for me because of these?" She lifted her breasts with her hands to emphasize them. She wasn't certain what to make of the fact that Skye thought she was beautiful and that was why Markhem had strayed. Skye was breathtaking. "He fell because I tricked him, Skye, that's all. I break men. It's what I'm good at—what I *was* good at. Trust me, my breasts had nothing to do with it. Although he did give them quite a bit of attention once he loosened up."

Skye's eyes deepened a shade, then she sighed. "Maybe this is the wrong decision—"

"Please, Skye." Gods, she sounded desperate, but the hope Skye had given her was the first she'd had, and with it came a warmth in her chest, one with which she wasn't familiar.

Skye searched her eyes, looking for something. Crimson felt the weight of her stare in her very core.

"As much as I still hate you for all of it, there's a part of me who likes our visits, who thinks the person underneath the foolishness deserves friendship and love. That's the reason I'm helping you."

Crimson didn't know what to say as Skye pulled the shadows to create a portal. A part of her wanted to hug her, but that would have completely ruined her reputation.

"I'll return when Mark and I have a plan."

She stepped through the portal and was gone, the grove strangely quiet as Crimson stood staring at the space where Skye had been. Skye had offered her hope and it was something Crimson hadn't expected coming from her. The idea that her enemy might become her savoir was an unsettling one. That thought would have irked her in the past. She'd never needed saving. She'd always been strong, knowing what she wanted. She was born to be queen, her title and power guaranteed by her father. He'd sold her soul to the Death God for it, with no thought, no regard to what that might do to her. To know she was not her own person, that her father had sold her for power, to the Death God no less, had left her feeling powerless for a long time.

She'd accepted her fate as a child. She'd been sentenced to an eternity in the Shadow Realm. There was no reason for her to be anything but a naughty girl. It made no difference, her fate was sealed. Her body belonged to the Death God, so she might as well give it to him. As a young girl, she'd called him that first time and offered her body to him. The pain was still as fresh in her mind as the tears she'd hidden, and the blood that had stained the sheets. He'd been rough with her, and she'd been innocent, but she'd changed that, quickly. She'd made her body and her sexuality her own, claiming it from him and learning all she could to become the woman she was. She'd taken older men, soldiers, husbands, men on whom she could practice until she was ready to call him again.

And when she did, she'd controlled him, driven him, owned him. That was when she'd discovered her power: sex and pleasure. She had dominated it and she'd loved it. Men were hers to control, to take, to manipulate, and that included Derrant. But she'd gotten greedy with Markhem, and she'd let her guard down. He'd shown her the possibility that there was more to it, something deeper, and she'd fallen for him and his tricks.

She envied Skye from the moment she'd seen her. There was something otherworldly about her. She was beautiful, powerful, confident, and she had Markhem. A man who loved her so much that he'd faced the Death God for her. Crimson sat wondering what it would be like to have someone love her like that, to love her so deeply that nothing else mattered, not even his own life. And what would it be like to love someone that hard, to put her own life on the line for him, for their love?

She felt the tear build and let it slip down her cheek. Skye's words came back to her. The idea that she deserved love was a foreign one. She didn't know what that meant, didn't think she ever would.

She wiped the tear away, pulling herself together. Skye's visits always left her rattled. There was work to do and she needed to focus even if the spirits were strangely quiet this eve. She stood, wiping her hands down her plain black dress, her eyes wandering in the direction of the house. She could see lights on with the strange Keeper magic that let her see the distance of her forest, an awareness of life outside the grove to guard from potential intruders.

There was a ward around the space, letting no one enter...only one had ever succeeded and he'd died as her unruly soul had escaped his tree and chased him. That man's presence had left her shaken. Mortals weren't able to reach her grove or even see it, so she didn't know how he'd found it She'd found no answer, but it had left an unsettling feeling that perhaps the ward was damaged. She'd always suspected she could allow access to the grove, but that had not been the case that night.

Since her souls were quiet, she slowly made her way through the grove and into the forest, standing at the edge and staring into the home. The beautiful man approached a window, his eyes seeming to see her. Her body tingled, her breath catching in reaction. She wanted to touch him so badly it hurt.

Then he was gone, and her excitement dropped until the door opened, light pouring from it. He was walking out into the night.

Everything in her told her to leave. Keepers were not meant to be seen. But she didn't leave. She wanted him to see her, wanted him to know she was there, and she wanted to feel his touch. As he drew closer to the forest edge, she froze, unable to take her eyes from him. Too enraptured by the temptation, she stepped as close to the edge of her prison as she could, feeling the moon on her skin as his bright blue eyes met hers. In that moment, she lost herself to him.

PETE

Pete had returned to the house even more confounded than he had been. If he made the assumption that the footprint and the sketch were the same woman, then she was real. But it made no sense that she was real. There was no reason for a random woman to be in those woods.

He'd rubbed his face as he'd entered the house. Questions—too many questions. He'd warmed up his coffee, grabbed half of a bagel, and turned his attention to the dining room where he'd discovered layers of wallpaper lay below the faded yellow paint.

"So much for a quick touch up," he said, wiping the sweat from his brow a few hours later. His phone rang, redirecting his attention at just the moment his patience was ready to tip.

"Hey, dork," Courtney teased when he answered.

"Court."

"What are you doing to our family legacy today?"

He laughed. "Fighting wallpaper and getting defeated."

"Oh, the dining room."

"You knew what was under there?"

"Yeah, Dad thought about touching it up when he took over

the house but was too lazy to peel the wallpaper. Don't you remember?"

"No, I must have blocked that from my memory."

"I think you were at school."

"Maybe," he replied, flicking a piece of wallpaper from his shirt.

"Up for a break?"

He checked his watch; it was a little after six. He hadn't realized it had gotten so late. He looked back at the wall that reflected what looked like he'd only done an hour of work. "Shit."

"Forgot we were meeting?"

"No, lost in work."

"That's why I called."

"I'll hop in the shower and head over."

"Good. I'll see you soon."

"Okay," he said before hanging up.

"Damn," he mumbled to himself, taking his shirt off and heading to the shower. He hadn't meant to lose track of time. His focus had been on the wallpaper, blocking out thoughts of the woman in the forest.

He showered quickly, the water was warm and soothing on his sore muscles. The woman entered his thoughts again. Part of him wished he'd seen her and wondered what it would feel like to touch her. He closed his eyes, imaging her hands on him, feeling himself growing hard, then cursed himself because he didn't have time to alleviate it.

Turning the water off, he cleared his head, pushing thoughts of her away. He tried to calm the throb of his erection as he lifted his jeans around it, knowing Courtney would bitch if he was any later than she expected him to be.

He threw on a shirt, adjusted himself, and headed out, casting his eyes toward the woods before driving off.

He met Courtney and Bo at the small bar, putting up with Bo's incessant jibes about leaving Courtney with all the work, about his jet setting life, or at least the one Bo imagined Pete had. He didn't defend himself, didn't disagree that the life they had envisioned was nothing like the one he'd had. Bo and Courtney had been a thing since high school, and Pete knew he was just protecting her. He let it slide, his mind not really present.

He had a few beers and some wings, then headed home, making the excuse that he'd spent too much time peeling wallpaper and needed sleep. Bo had always grated on his nerves, but he was good for Courtney. They'd never married, but Pete knew he'd step in front of a moving vehicle if it meant saving her. So, he put up with the jokes, let them slide for Courtney's sake, even though he really wanted to punch him.

As he pulled into the driveway, his eyes went straight to the trees. He was tempted to enter and make his way to the grove, but the warnings flooded his head. *No one goes into the forest at night.*

Instead, he went inside, turned on the television and tried to relax. His attempt to redirect his attention failed and after half an hour, he wandered the house, finding himself at the window that overlooked the forest. He felt the eyes on him, as if someone was out there looking in as he looked out. A slight movement caught his eye, and his heart hammered in his chest.

He moved from the window and ran to the door, pausing, his hand on the knob. There was no certainty that the woman in the sketch was out there. The movement could have been a wild animal. Worse, it could be a woman but one who would devour his soul or rip his organs out for some satanic ritual. He'd seen enough horror movies to know he was the foolish main character the audience tells to run the other way.

"Shit, Pete, you're losing it."

He turned the knob and walked out, not bothering with his flashlight. Having convinced himself that it was the woman, he didn't want to scare her off. With every step he took closer to the tree line, his family's warnings screamed in his mind.

But then he saw her. Her figure blended with the trees, but he could make out her outline and her eyes. They were a green that stood clear against the night, and they met his. He felt the wind knocked from him, and he didn't care if she was a ghost or a witch who would torture him, then sacrifice him to a demon. He wanted her.

He stepped into the trees. Her eyes grew wide, but she didn't move. His heart was pounding so hard it drowned out any other noise. Reaching out, he grabbed her hand. It was soft and warm as she pulled it from him.

"You're real," he said.

She took a step back, whispering, "You can see me?"

"Yes."

"You shouldn't see me. Gods, you need to go back now."

Gods? It was an odd thing to say.

"Who are you?"

She hesitated, then turned and ran. Her movements were soundless, as if she weren't more than a spirit and for a moment, he was stunned. He ran after her, not caring if it led to his death. He needed to see her, to touch her again, the feel of her hand in his still fresh.

"Stop!" he yelled. "Please wait."

The woods grew brighter with moonlight, and he could see flashes of her as she ran. Until she stopped. She stood in the moonlight of the grove. He drew a breath. She was exquisite. Her rich red hair lay in long waves down her alabaster skin, her eyes a dark green that bewitched him. She looked both broken and brave.

He stepped into the grove, ignoring the strange sensation he'd felt earlier.

A startled expression overcame her lovely features, and she said, "No, don't. You'll wake them."

Ignoring her, he moved toward her as an eerie chorus of wails filled the sky. He disregarded it and reached his hand into her hair, feeling the silkiness of it as he pulled her close and kissed her.

There was no explanation as to why he'd been so rash. No reason why nothing seemed to exist in that moment but her. But as she relaxed and the noise around them settled, he knew it had been the right thing.

Her lips parted, her tongue meeting his as his body came alive. She moved closer, pressing into him and he wrapped his arms around her waist. There was no way she was a ghost, she felt too real. Her hands touched him as if she'd never touched a man, but with the knowledge of a woman who had. He let his hands slip along her curves and as he did, she reached behind her; the dress fell from her shoulders, the material bunching at his hands until he removed them, and it fell the rest of the way.

"Jesus," he breathed, stepping back, his eyes taking in her body as her lithe legs delicately lifted from the dress that now lay at her feet. He moved his hand to catch one of her legs as she brought it down, then traced her skin up past her hips. He followed the path over the curve of her stomach to reach for her full breasts. A soft cry escaped her as he caressed them, softly running his fingers over her nipples and loving how they responded to his touch.

God, he was going to take her here, and she was letting him like she was as desperate to touch him as he was her. He'd never done anything like this. He'd taken women home from a bar, had one-night stands, but this was different. And he didn't care. His eyes met her hungry ones, and he took his shirt off, then pulled her against him, relishing the feel of her skin against his.

Her kisses were desperate, and she reached down to his erection, grasping it firmly. He groaned as she tried to undo his pants, unhooking the button, then acting like she'd never dealt with a zipper before. Once he helped her, her hand reached right in and stroked him. He inhaled at her touch, pushing his pants the rest of the way down so that they were both naked.

She continued pulling at him in confident, seductive moves. Her touch was like magic on him, and he knew if she continued, he would come right in her hands. Grabbing her waist, he pulled her against him again. His need for her was beyond anything he'd ever experienced, and he pushed her so that she backed into the nearest tree. Her kisses stirred a part of him, waking a fire that he didn't think anyone but she could calm. With a desperation, he touched every part of her body. Dropping his mouth to suck on her breasts, he teased her nipple with his tongue, hearing a deep purr from her before she guided his lips back to hers. She tasted of berries and moonlight, if one could taste moonlight. Either way, he was lost to her taste.

He brought his hands to ass, running them over the soft curve of it before he lifted her. The move brought his length to press hard against her stomach and he heard sharp inhale in response. Those stunning green eyes studied him even as her legs wrapped around him. There was a moment where they simply looked at one another, lost in each other's gaze. The moment was more intense than anything he'd experienced, and part of him knew, without a doubt that this woman belonged to him.

"Take me," she demanded, her voice holding a breathless quality. "I want to feel you inside of me."

His heart thudded, and his dick twitched at her command. The seductive smile she gave him was almost enough to make him break right there. Instead, he kissed her again then indulged her request without hesitation, lifting her so that he sank into her. Her warmth greeted him as her cry escaped. She felt amazing, and he took her there, reveling in every sigh, every quiver of her body. The feel of her was too much and it had been so long since he'd had sex that his orgasm grew too quickly, cresting, then crashing over him as he clung to her. As he calmed, he chastised himself for being too fast, embarrassingly fast.

To his relief, she didn't seem fazed and pressed her lips to his in a kiss that told him she was still hungry for him. Her pelvis continued to move against him, coaxing him back with her rhythm, his reaction building quickly. She stopped her kisses, and dropped her legs, pushing his hands so that he released his hold on her. There was a glint of excitement in her eyes before she slowly moved down his body with her mouth. She started with small kisses to his neck, then draped her tongue along his chest, making her way down his stomach.

His muscles quivered in anticipation, his mind having no question what her intention was. Her tongue slid along his shaft and a moan rumbled in his chest. His dick jerked in surprise when her mouth enveloped him, and he couldn't suppress his groan. The feel of her mouth sent a myriad of sensations through his body, and he grasped her head with his hand as she took him—all of him like no other had. Her tongue danced along his shaft, and he threw his head back as euphoria whipped through him. He let the magic of her mouth overtake his senses. The way her hand was working in tandem with her mouth was tantalizing. Currents of electricity burst along his skin with each touch of her tongue.

He hadn't had anyone go down on him in years. The women he dated now were too prissy, never giving him the satisfaction. But this woman took him as if she owned him, as if she was waiting for him to explode in her mouth. The thought sent him building again, and he grabbed a handful of her hair. Holding her head tight, he thrust further into her mouth until his climax washed over him.

He'd expected her to pull away, but she didn't. Instead, she drank him down like he was her sustenance, licking every last drop of what he offered.

He tried to catch his breath, but she rose quickly, smashing her mouth against his and pressing into him. He didn't care that she tasted of him; he kissed with a fervor that matched hers, needing more of her.

She pushed at him so that they walked away from the tree, and he thought he saw a strange white mist reach for her as they moved. She clearly wanted more, pulling him down to the ground so that he was atop her. He'd never been with a woman who'd wanted more, and it aroused him. His erection returned but, this time, he wanted to take his time touching her. He kissed her neck, tasting the sweetness of her skin, before taking one ample breast into his mouth. Her nipple was taut, and he let his tongue dance around it, enjoying how the skin around it pebbled with her arousal. With his other hand, he cupped her other breast, teasing the nipple with his fingers. She writhed below him, her moans filling the space. Leaving a hand on her breast, he made his way down her stomach with his mouth. The softness of her skin was lush and delicate. She had curves that demanded to be touched, ones that he kissed and licked.

He spread her legs, the dampness of his first orgasm still sticky on her thighs. With his heart racing, he drifted his tongue over her clit loving how her back arched in reaction. Needing to taste her further, he plunged his tongue into her. She cried out, her pelvis pushing against him. Bringing his fingers to her, he drove them deep, working her until he felt her legs tighten. He sank his tongue in their place, her scream of pleasure like strokes to his own arousal. Within moments, her body convulsed with her orgasm. The feel of her breaking below him stoked the fire within him but he continued tasting her as her arousal flowed into his mouth.

He licked it up, the taste of her making his erection throb as her body continued to shake. She pushed at him as she squirmed, then she yanked at him, drawing him over her body again. Wrapping her legs around him, she guided him into her until her body enveloped him. She fit perfectly against him, as if she'd been made for him. Everything about her was perfect.

She brought her legs up and he hooked them around his neck, plunging as far as he could, the sensation heaven. With every move, he took more of her in, falling for her further. Her body rose and fell with his like they were one until his arousal was like a climbing wave, his need for release at its cusp. Her body clenched against his, tightening around him as her own climax swept through her, sending him over the edge. She clung to him while the waves continued to crash through him, her body quivering below his until it finally calmed.

When he was able to move again, he picked his head up and looked at her. Her green eyes were lush in the streams of moonlight.

"Who are you?" he asked, brushing the hair back from her cheek.

She turned and kissed his hand. "No one you should worry about."

"But I will," he said, turning her head back to look at him. "You're in my head. You're everywhere I look and now that I've had you—"

"You have to let me go."

"What?"

She brought her finger to his lips. "Shh. The night is short. Take me again before it ends."

She smashed her mouth against his, kissing him as if she was ravenous for him, and he couldn't resist her, no matter how many questions he had. She was too addictive. He made love to her again, to the low hush of what sounded like whispers around him. All the while he prayed he could keep her forever, but feared she would disappear when he woke from this dream.

CRIMSON

As the man drifted off to sleep, Crimson laid against him, listening to his steady breaths, feeling the rise and fall of his chest as his arm held her tightly. She traced the black ink on his chest to the biceps of his arms, drawn to the unique markings she'd never seen on anyone before. She felt safe in his arms, comfortable. Too comfortable. Eventually, she forced herself to rise, working her way out of his embrace. She stood over him, taking in the strength of him, the muscles that lined his chest, the arms that spoke of his strength, the beauty of him, his peaceful and relaxed face.

He was gorgeous, like one of the gods. Her eyes perused the rest of him, tempted to take him again, but knowing she couldn't. Not yet. She left him sleeping to walk among the souls. While he'd kept her distracted, they'd stretched higher, trying to escape their prisons.

"Tsk, tsk," she muttered, calling them back down, the black of the bark growing to drag them back to their prisons.

The murmurs became wails, but she quieted them, rubbing their bark and cooing to them as if they were fussy children. As the night waned and dawn threatened to take her to her slumber, she walked back to the man, wondering at him.

He had kissed her before she'd even known what was happening. There had never been a time when she hadn't been the aggressor. She'd always taken her men, whether they were willing or not. She controlled them, manipulated them, but the man before her had kissed her first, claiming her as she'd always wanted to be claimed.

The space between her legs burned with desire. She wanted him once more before she had to leave him. She let sleep drift from her fingers, ensuring he stayed in his state, the same as she did to her trees in the early morning. Then she kissed him. His mouth responded in his dream state, his hands entwining in her hair, drawing her closer. She'd intended to just take him as she had the others in her past, but even in his dream state, he wanted her.

Her hand reached for his length, feeling it grow until it was ready for her. Enveloping him, she tipped her head back as he filled her with his hardness. She moved slowly, enjoying the feel of him and memorizing it. His hands tried to bring her closer, but she pushed back on her knees to rise and fall with a rhythm that sent a fire through her. He reached for her breasts, teasing them and pulling at them, sending flames burning through her with each touch. Dropping his hands to her hips, he held them firmly and she couldn't contain the moan their feel caused. She wanted to stay here forever with him, to never leave his hold but his hands began to move her, encouraging her to quicken her pace. With each thrust of his pelvis against hers, waves of bliss assailed her. His touch alone was enough to send it crashing over her, which it did as he tightened his grip. Within her ecstasy, she felt him release, his body growing still as his own climax joined hers. She dropped against him as it receded, reveling in the spasms that shook them both.

She'd found him—the second man to bring her to ecstasy. Markhem had been the only one who'd done so without her help.

But what she'd felt for him had never been real. It had been a desperate attempt to know what Skye had. But this man—this man sent her heart racing, her body melting.

She lay there as long as she could before she sensed the morning coming to take her. Hesitantly, she rose, a sadness overcoming her as the night faded, knowing she would lose him with it. She kissed him quickly, and his body relaxed back into his deep slumber. Rising, she grabbed her dress just as the cycle took her away.

PETE

Pete woke suddenly, sleep falling from him like a heavy curtain. He looked around, taking in the grove, the morning sun casting long shadows. Last night hadn't been a dream. He sat up, finding that he was still naked.

God, she'd been real.

As if he still didn't believe it, he touched himself, the remnants of their lovemaking still fresh—still damp, like he'd just taken her. The dream...he'd dreamt of her atop him, taking him another time, his body shaking with the force of his orgasm. He wasn't certain if that hadn't been real, too.

He stood and looked around the grove, eerie silence encompassing the space. Even birds avoided this place. Dressing, he glanced around for her, but found no trace of her other than the remnants from their lovemaking. He wiped his face, taking one last look around before leaving the grove to make his way back to the house. Images of the prior night filled his mind. He'd never been with a woman like her. So sexual and secure in her body and sexuality, aggressive even. It turned him on, and even as he stepped into the shower to wash the traces of her from him, his erection grew. He couldn't help it. She drove him crazy. Flashes of her body, her mouth, and sounds of her cries echoed through his head.

He gripped his hardness, envisioning how her mouth had taken him, and groaning as he imagined her lips around him. His hand replicated her movements as his mind filled with images of her. He leaned against the shower wall until he came again, thinking of how she had swallowed him in his entirety. The groan rumbled through his chest while his orgasm rocked him. His legs shook as he coaxed out the last of his release, his eyes watching the water take his mess away.

She had lit something in him, a fire, a sexual need that had been dormant. He'd always been content with one or two rounds of sex at the most when he'd been with a woman. Never had he taken one as many times as he had last night. He wasn't even sure how he'd had the stamina.

He finished washing and made his way to the coffeemaker, needing caffeine—anything to take his mind off her. As he stared out at the forest, he wondered why she hadn't been there when he'd woken. She hadn't felt like a spirit. Nothing about her led him to believe she was anything but human. He ran a hand through his hair and shook the thoughts away, frustrated at the lack of answers. Diving back into the wallpaper fiasco in the dining room, he tuned out the images of her, an act which only allowed more questions to enter.

He'd had the best night of sex in his life with a woman whose name he didn't even know. A woman he had no way to reach. There was a connection between her and the grove, that much he knew instinctually. What he didn't know was why or how.

The questions went round and round to the point that he lost track of time, ignoring the pings from his phone until the sun had started its descent. With the loud grumble of his stomach, he realized he hadn't eaten all day. Putting his tools down, he grabbed a piece of leftover prize and a beer from the fridge, then wandered to the window.

He stared out at the woods as he mindlessly ate his pizza. She was out there somewhere. His heart raced with the thought. He needed to see her again, to touch her again. He chugged the rest of his beer before wiping his mouth with the back of his hand. Grabbing his phone, he headed out of the house.

Never go into the woods at night. The words echoed through his head as he stepped into the forest, knowing the sun was almost ready to set, and he was taking a risk once again.

He thought of his father. Whatever had happened to him had something to do with the woods, and he had a feeling the woman knew. His glorious woman. He would find her again. And this time, he was going to get answers.

He needed them.

Reaching the edge of the strange grove, he paused, taking in the empty space, the trees that eerily reached to the sky, the black of them appearing to have receded.

"You shouldn't be here," he told himself.

But she was here somewhere, and he needed to see her again. He stepped in, feeling the chill that ran down his spine. Forcing himself past it, he moved further into the grove scanning for her, yet finding nothing but shadows. The air was heavy, making it difficult to breath but he pushed past the discomfort more easily than he had the first time he'd entered. When he'd been with her, the feeling hadn't been there, and he wondered if she had some kind of control over it. If she had given him some kind of permission to enter that he didn't have now that he was without her. The grove seemed to go on forever, like a forest within a forest. As the final glow of sun drifted below the horizon, he saw a shimmer of light, and there she was.

The woman from the sketch, his woman from the prior night. Her hair was a fiery red in the lingering rays of sunlight, and for a moment he stared at her, too stunned to move.

Her eyes met his, then grew wide with fear. A cacophony of wails berated his ears, and a movement to her right drew his eyes from her. A massive cloud of mist filled the space, taking the shape of a man.

"Good God," he muttered, stepping back. He ran in the woman's direction to block the thing from her.

"No!" she yelled as it let out a ferocious cry and lunged toward them. Pete braced himself, but she pushed him aside and a flash of dark wisps flew from her arms at the spirit, banding around it like chains and dragging it back toward the tree.

"I told you not to escape your binds again!" she screamed. The grove fell quiet, save for the echo of her voice. The thing roared, but she didn't flinch.

Something touched his arm, and he jumped, moving away from a line of mist that crept from the tree nearest him.

"Dammit," she muttered. In a strange language, she softly spoke as if she were singing a lullaby.

The line next to him drifted back, the beast in front of her receding to the tree it had emerged from. She stopped speaking and walked to the tree, placing her hand upon it. The black spread further, as a scream of agony, faint but discernable, echoed through the space.

"I warned you," she said to it.

The black spread to the branches, which no longer reflected white in the moonlight, and bits of the tree flaked to the ground until it was no more. Low wails emitted from the other trees and Pete could see the black clawing at the white of their bark, pulling it back.

"Shh," she said, her voice drifting over his ears like satin.

The wails quieted and the claw-like effect disappeared.

Pete stared at her. "What the hell was that?"

"That was something you should not have seen. You foolish man, never under any circumstance are you to enter the grove if I am not here!" Her eyes were full of rage, her hair seeming to grow a shade darker.

"Who are you?" he asked. She didn't answer him, instead evaluating him with a cold stare. He grabbed her arms roughly. "Who are you?"

There was a twinkle in her eye. "So, you like it rough? I can do rough."

"What? I... That's not why I'm here."

He could see the disappointment in her eyes.

"Then why are you here?" she asked, freeing herself from his grip. She crossed her arms and waited, a stance that accentuated her cleavage. The thought of kissing her crossed his mind. She must have sensed his thought, a slight smile forming on her lips.

"Why are you here?" she asked, her tone softer. "No one enters these woods at night and now two of you have within a matter of moons."

"Two?"

"Yes, an older man, moons ago, but I couldn't tame that one in time. By the time I reached the boundary of the prison, it was too late. I should have sent the violator to the Death God then, but I didn't."

Pete didn't know what a Death God was or to what boundary she referred, but he knew the man. "My father."

Her face fell. "I'm sorry. I tried. They aren't supposed to escape. They know better; it seals their fate."

"His heart gave out. That's what they said."

"An easier fate than some. The Death God tore my father to pieces when he judged him. Oh, but you didn't come here to hear that."

Peter stared at her, unsure of what to say.

"I'm not sad," she went on. "I felt no pity for the man who sold my soul before I could talk. He deserved what he got and what he still suffers to this day, no matter how he says he did it for me."

"Who the hell are you?" he asked, unsure why the woman of his dreams was talking like a crazy woman. She did live in a forest, and she had appeared from thin air, then defeated some sort of spirit demon. Maybe he was the one who'd gone mad.

"My name is Crimson. I am the Keeper of Lost Souls. Since we're finally exchanging names, who are you?"

"I...I'm Peter. Well, Pete. What's a Keeper of Lost Souls?"

"Me. An eternity of punishment."

He rubbed his hands over his face.

"Wishing you had just come to fuck me again?" she asked with a sly smile.

Her question was bold, but there was something about her confidence that turned him on.

"Maybe," he admitted.

"Well, you didn't and so now that's ruined."

"What? Why?"

She studied him, her brow creasing. "Because I'm me."

He laughed. "I don't know what that means, but you'd have to do a lot more than this to make me leave without fucking you again."

She drew a breath, and he realized he sounded like a line from a dirty movie. It was the truth, though.

"Now tell me why you're out here in the middle of the forest, what that thing was, and why you'd think I'd ever walk away from you after last night."

"Gods, you're too good to be true," she said, moving closer to him. She pressed her body against him, her eyes searching his. "Take me first. I want to feel you inside of me again."

His erection swelled, and he knew there was no way he was turning that invitation down, regardless of the strange things he'd seen and heard. He thought of his father and that thing. He needed more answers, but she was nibbling at his lip. Sliding her tongue along it, her hand reached into his pants, distracting him.

There was no denying the need he had for her. Nor was there any stopping her. He took her again, pulling her down atop him this time, and watching as her body moved over him. Her face was a reflection of the desire that was tearing through him. She was demanding, greedily taking him, her rhythm smooth as he glided in and out of her until he could take it no more. He held tight to her hips, forcing himself deep within her as he climaxed, her own moans joining his.

Unable to resist the temptation of taking her again, he flipped her, letting his hands caress her body before he took her from behind. His eyes perused her curves as she slammed back against him with every driving move he made. Her body was hypnotic, addictive. Gripping her hips, he thrust deeper, watching her ass move. He couldn't pull his eyes from her. The way her hair cascaded as she threw her head back, and her arms moved as she played with herself only further excited him. She was uninhibited, and he was hooked. He pushed her hands aside, stopping his movements and brought her up against his chest. Caressing her breasts with his one hand, he relished the way the fullness of them felt in his hand. He imagined he could play with them all day and be tantalized simply with how they responded to his touch. The thought of resting his length between them caused him to twitch, and he heard her resulting moan. He wanted to hear that moan again, so he pulled her nipple softly and dropped his other hand between her legs. Still nestled deep within her, he began to move his pelvis again, circling her clit with each thrust.

Her head dropped back against him, and he could feel her arousal building, the slickness growing around him until she cried out. Her body spasmed with the intensity of her orgasm, squeezing tight around him. Each quake of her muscles brought him closer to his own release. He pushed her back down and grabbed her hips, thrusting with a force that sent his climax tearing through him. He released the firm grip on her as she coaxed the last of his essence from him and leaned back to catch his breath. Too soon, she slipped from his grasp, moving so that her mouth caught the small drips that lingered on his tip. The act was so stimulating that his length responded, much to his surprise. She remained there, working him with her tongue until he felt the need for release building once more. His eyes rolled back as he tangled his fingers in her hair, knowing he'd never been with a woman who had effect on his body. She was unbelievable. As her mouth continued its magic, his climax crested, and she finally broke him. His orgasm shook him to his core, and he could do nothing more than collapse onto his back, drained completely.

Crimson sprawled over him, resting her head on his chest and he drew an arm around her. He held her close, saying her name, liking the way it sounded from his mouth. "Crimson."

"Mmm."

"Where did you come from, and where have you been my entire life?"

"That's a long story summed up in sex with too many wrong men, a lifetime of mistakes, of greed, and of guilty pleasure that culminated in my eternity in this prison."

"Prison?" he asked, running his fingers through her hair.

She picked her head up and leaned her chin against his chest.

"If I tell you who I am, you'll never come back to me."

He searched her eyes, wondering why she'd say such a thing.

"I told you. I'm not going anywhere. I'm addicted to you. How any man could give you up is beyond my comprehension, but I'm glad they did."

She sat up and, as she did, he noticed the wails he'd grown accustomed to.

"Shh," she said. "I'll be back."

He watched as she walked around the grove. She would stop and lean her hand on certain trees, the wails diminishing, before she'd continue walking. She disappeared deep into the grove for a while and when she returned, they were silent.

Finally, she sat, not hindered by the fact that she was naked. She was unabashedly unreserved. He turned on his side, letting his fingers drape down her breasts, watching as her nipples responded.

"If you want answers, then you shouldn't tempt me to ignore your questions. The night is fading."

"Why does that matter?" he asked, rubbing her nipple between his thumb and finger.

She moaned, her head drifting back, and his limpness faded. She was right. He needed to let her focus before taking her again. He dropped his hand to her leg, his fingers tracing the softness of her skin.

"All right, talk," he said.

"I should ask you about who you are, Peter Well Pete."

He laughed at her confusion over his name and replied, "Pete is just fine. There's not much to tell. I inherited the house and this land from my father. It's been in our family for generations. I decided to leave my life in the city and move home to conquer my fascination and fear of these woods."

"Why have I never seen you before?"

"I was away. I stayed away. I used to visit, then one night, ten years ago, I heard this haunting scream. No one else heard it, but it was the kind of scream that stays with you, so I left and never returned." He stopped, realizing he sounded crazy. "I know it doesn't sound sane. Although none of this seems sane."

Her eyes were a rich sage. "Ten years ago?"

"Yes." He furrowed his brow, unsure why she'd become so serious.

"That scream was me."

CRIMSON

Crimson couldn't believe he'd come back. She'd even told him who she was, and he hadn't left. He'd seen her calm the souls, sending the one back to Derrant as punishment. But Pete hadn't left. Instead, he'd taken her again, letting her have her way with him. Every time he sank into her, her body screamed, needing him more. She ached to have him fill her, to feel his body tense, then relax as he spilled into her. She'd joined his release so many times, her orgasms flooding her with sensations she never wanted to forget.

Now he was telling her he'd heard her scream. Skye had told her it had been ten years. Ten years ago—she remembered the moment Derrant had cast her into the forest, the scream escaping as the understanding of her punishment hit her.

"You?" he asked.

Peter. Pete. She loved the way it bounced through her head and left her breathless.

"Yes. That was the night the Death God cursed me here."

He was quiet for a moment. She watched him, his blue eyes serious.

"That was you? For ten long years that scream has haunted me and it was you all along?"

She nodded, not really knowing what to say.

"Tell me about yourself—why you're here, what curse this is."

He looked expectantly at her, and in that moment, her confidence faded. For the first time in her life, she felt vulnerable. There was no way of knowing what he would think of her. And if he left and never returned...she didn't think she could bear it, although she wasn't certain why. This man was a stranger. She didn't know him, but there was a part of her that seemed to.

"I don't think you want to know me," she said, rising and walking to where her dress had fallen.

"Are you kidding?"

"No. Trust me, you don't. I think you should go before the dawn comes."

He sat up and watched as she pulled her dress on. She'd always been proud of who she was, who she'd been, never shying from the fear her subjects held of her. There had been intention behind every one of her actions, and she owned them without hesitation. But suddenly she felt ashamed of that past, and it baffled her.

He rose and picked up his pants, his eyes showing the hurt she felt from her own words. Turning her back on him, she cursed the tears that welled behind her eyes. Tears she never shed. Crying was weakness, and she was no fragile girl. She wrapped her arms around her waist, waiting to hear him leave.

"Dammit," she heard him mumble. "No, I've thought about you for a decade and every waking minute since I've been back." She felt his hands on her arms, soft but secure. "I don't care what you've done in the past. You're not pushing me away."

"I could make the spirits push you."

"Is that really what you want?"

She thought about how lonely her nights had been, how long and mind shattering. Derrant had known exactly how to break her when he'd cursed her.

She shook her head. Wrapping his arms around her, he kissed her head. "Now, tell me who you are, Crimson."

Hearing her name from his mouth sent a tingle through her belly.

"I'll tell you, but you may not like what you hear."

"I promise you, it won't sway me from you," he said, holding her tighter.

Being in his arms gave her strength, so she pushed aside the fear and summoned the courage to tell him who she really was. Closing her eyes, she let herself be that woman again—not the lonely, cursed woman formed from ten years in this prison, but the unrelenting, powerful queen she'd once been.

"I am the queen of Apendia," she started, her confidence returning with that statement. "I am not from your world. I live in a world of magic and gods. I've done a lot of things for power, for land, and self-gratification." She turned so that she could see his face. His chest was still bare, and she rested her hand upon it. Somehow, just that simple act fortified her. "I am not a good person and I've never claimed to be. My father sold my soul to the Death God at my birth. His deal with the Death God gave me power to steal magic from the mages of our world and to seduce and control them. With that power, I started a war between the kingdoms. I brought down the kingdom of Digremile, manipulating my mages to kill theirs and strike down their royal family. Countless innocents died because of my deeds."

His blue eyes were still on her, but he hadn't flinched at her words or given any reaction. A pensive look remained on his face, but it held no judgement. She dropped her eyes to his chest and continued. Confessing her deeds was something she'd never fully done, and she was finding it freeing in a way that she didn't understand.

"I have lied, I have manipulated, I have cheated. I have murdered kings and queens, subjects who were disloyal and loyal. I took the Death God as my lover and even handed him the queen of Kantenda. As my last act, I tricked her and her husband, Markhem. I lured them in, and after stealing her power from her, I called the Death God to take her while I kept Markhem as mine. I did all of that because I wanted something that didn't belong to me. I took what I wanted. I had my way with him while the Death God played with Skye. And I didn't care what it did to either of them."

She laughed, hearing how absurd it all sounded, but she couldn't stop her confession now that she'd started. "I was naïve, cruel, thinking I could make him my king, that I could steal their kingdom, and control all the mage power in our world. With it, the kingdoms would be mine for the taking.

"But Markhem was my downfall. I was foolish enough to think he'd want me when he loved her. I didn't know what love was, and I paid the ultimate price. The Death God sent me here as punishment for leading Markhem to the Shadow Realm, where he rescued Skye. I thought we'd just have a good time, the four of us." She laughed again. "Gods, I was stupid. And now, I am Keeper of the Lost Souls, bound to spend the rest of my days followed by the eternity of my afterlife guarding them. An endless cycle of ensuring they stay silent as they suffer. An eternity of bondage, of loneliness that began ten years ago."

Finished with her story, she realized she was lighter, as though she'd carried the shame and guilt of what she'd done for the past decade. Never noticing that each day the weight of it burdened her more. That with each passing year, she'd changed from the woman she'd once been. She wasn't remorseful, she'd been who she'd been. She wasn't a good person and perhaps she never would be, but she saw her mistakes now—saw the web she'd weaved and how weak it had been. The web that had collapsed with the weight of her deeds and pulled her under, crushing everything she'd been.

His eyes had never left hers but had grown more creased the longer she'd spoken.

"Now, do you see why you don't want to be here?"

"You really did all those things? You stole another woman's husband?"

She gave him a sheepish grin, then a shrug.

"Huh. There are so many parts of that story that I don't understand and, to be honest, if I hadn't seen the things I saw earlier, I might be tempted to say you're insane."

"I am a bit mad."

"You wanted to rule your world and had people murdered for it." He rubbed his hand over his face. "You know that sounds like something out of a movie, right?"

"What's a movie?"

He looked at her. "You really aren't from here, are you?"

She shook her head.

"So, do I look past the colorful history, or do I walk away from you?"

"You walk away. I'm certain if the soul I sent to the Death God talks, he'll gladly talk about the mortal I had in the Forest of Souls. It's forbidden for anyone to enter this part of the woods. You should go."

She couldn't read him, and the silence that followed was overwhelming.

"How do I break the curse?" he finally asked.

"What?" she asked, having clearly misheard him.

"How do I free you from the curse?"

"You can't. No one can. Only Derrant, the Death God, can and he will never."

"What is a Death God?"

"The one who judges your worthiness, then passes your judgement if deemed unworthy. There are several gods in the Shadow Realm, but Derrant is the supreme one. He is the Death God. If he deems you worthy, Eliana—now that she's back—guides your soul to their brother in the Upper Realm. If you are unworthy, you spend an eternity of torment in the Shadow Realm with the shadow gods and their demons."

"Heaven and hell."

"What are those?"

"Heaven sounds like your Upper Realm, a place those who do good things in life go. Hell is the devil's land—fire and brimstone, an eternity of torment."

"Hell...that's connected to the Shadow Realm. I passed through it when Derrant sentenced me here. It's where I travel to when I sleep. Derrant's brother rules it. It's extremely hot there."

His mouth had dropped, and she closed it gently.

"I warned you."

"That you did. So, you know a god? The equivalent of our devil? And they're real?"

"Yes, and I don't just know him. I was his lover."

He stepped back.

"Although there was only sex involved, I'm sure Eliana would not allow that to happen again now that she's returned."

"And Eliana is a goddess?"

"Yes, Death's Mistress."

"And you slept with a god?"

She nodded.

"How do I compete with a god?" he asked.

Her heart did a strange flutter. "Why would you compete with him?"

"Because I don't want anyone else to have you again. I'm not one for sharing."

"Are you claiming me?" she asked, raising her brow.

"Is that what you call it in your world?"

"Sometimes."

"Then yes, I'm claiming you, Crimson." He drew her to him.

"Are you certain you want to claim me? I'm quite broken," she said in a whisper, her mind in a daze at the idea that he'd claimed her.

He brushed her hair back. "I like broken. It's more interesting."

"And you think I'll allow you to claim me?"

"Will you?"

Her heart fluttered uncontrollably. "Yes."

He kissed her and the fluttering resounded through her body.

"I want you, Crimson, no matter what it takes."

The words made her heart swell with a sensation she'd never experienced. She wasn't certain she understood what it was but it felt too perfect to ignore.

They made love—slow and intentional, her heart filling with each move—until their bodies climaxed as one. She clung to him, afraid to let go, afraid of the coming dawn in a way she hadn't been for a long time. Pete didn't sleep. Instead, he stayed with her, talking with her, holding her, making love to her once more before her Keeper duties forced her to dress and put the trees to sleep, to cease their never-ending stretch to the Upper Realm. When she finished, she returned to him to say goodbye. His arms held her close, sending her a bit of strength before the darkness claimed her again.

PETE

Pete had stayed with Crimson, holding her as she disappeared from his arms. As the sun rose below the tree line, nothing but a white mist remained. He'd stood there until sunlight lit the grove, casting long shadows of what he now knew were sleeping souls, seduced to sleep by Crimson.

Making his way back through the forest, his mind raced through everything he'd learned and done that night. He didn't know what he'd gotten himself into. There was no certainty that she was even real, but she had felt real. Everything about her felt real. What she'd told him was unbelievable. Curses and kingdoms, gods and magic. Her story had sounded like an episode of *Game of Thrones*.

Whether it were real or not, it didn't matter. He was in too deep. Tempted to say he'd fallen for her, but that sounded just as ridiculous as her story. No one fell in love after only two nights. Perhaps it was only infatuation. No, it was much more than that.

"Holy shit! There you are!" Courtney yelled, rushing to him from the house as he broke through the tree line.

"Where the hell have you been? Were you in the woods at

night?" She was screaming at him now, her voice rising with each word.

"I took a walk, Court. Settle down."

"Settle down? You haven't answered your texts all night. I tried to call, and you didn't answer. Then when you hadn't texted back, I came over worried something had happened. I was here all night!"

He didn't know what to say, so he remained silent. His mind was too frazzled to even try fabricating something.

"You were in the woods?"

"Yes."

"All night? Did you get lost? You know we're not supposed to go in at night."

"Dad did."

"And look what happened to him!"

"I'm fine. Nothing happened to me."

She grabbed his arm as he went to climb the stairs. "There's something in those woods, Pete. You know that. Dad knew that."

"Yes, there is."

She dropped his arm, her eyes wide. "You saw her?"

Her words took him by surprise, and he furrowed his brow at her. "Who?"

"The woman. Dad rambled about her, a shadow woman in the forests."

"She's not a shadow. She's very real."

He moved up the stairs, leaving her there. He needed a shower and some sleep, but first, he needed to search the scribblings in the basement. Inside, he threw a coffee pod in the Keurig and impatiently watched the mug fill.

"Pete, what's going on?"

"You'll think I'm insane like dad."

"Dad was crazy."

"Then why did you ask me about her?"

"Her? She—"

"She's real. Dad wasn't crazy and neither am I." His coffee finished and he grabbed the mug, pushing past her and heading down the stairs.

"Maybe it's the house—"

"It's not the house!" he yelled back at her.

"Peter!"

He turned around to face her. "What, Courtney?"

"What the hell is going on and why are you down here?"

He grabbed the sketch and shoved it at her. "This is why I'm down here."

"A drawing?"

"That's her. She's alive and trapped in that forest. I'm going to find a way to free her."

She stared at him. "Are you insane? You are. You've lost it. There is no woman in that forest."

"Then why have both dad and I seen her?" She remained silent. "She's real. I've seen her, I've talked to her, touched her. Trust me, she's very real."

"Touched?" she said with a raise of her brow. "Did you sleep with a woman in the forest?"

He hesitated. "Yes—"

"Oh, my God. I can't." She put her hands up and walked backward, dropping the sketch. "You need to get away from this house, from whatever fumes or chemicals you're unleashing with all your peeling and painting. I'm going to work. Come with me. Spend the day there. You can help me."

"I can't. I need some sleep, a shower—"

"Then do those things and then come. Leave the house, Pete. I expect you for lunch. If not, I'm sending you to a shrink like I should have sent Dad." She turned and stormed up the stairs. He listened as the door slammed shut moments later.

Sitting on the stool, he stared at the sketch on the floor. For a moment, he questioned his sanity. She had to have been real. All of it had felt too real for it not to have been.

He leaned down to pick up the sketch, then turned back to the workbench to find answers, some clue as to what his father knew, and others before him. He didn't know what he was looking for, but he hoped he would find something that would lead to her freedom.

AFTER A FEW HOURS OF SLEEP, Pete rinsed and drove to the café his sister owned. It was small but busy, especially at lunch hour. He sat in the car, hesitant to go inside, knowing she would drill him further.

He'd spent an hour weeding through his father's notes, finding more than he'd bargained for. The papers he'd found dated back to the original tribes who had settled that land, ones his family had descended from. He never considered himself Native American; the family's blood had been watered down too much for him to feel any connection. But it was there in the land he now owned and in the writings he'd found.

He grabbed the book and headed to the shop, waving to Courtney as he entered. She was busy helping the line of customers, so he found a corner spot and waited. She'd told him she'd bought the shop where she'd worked since high school, but this was the first time he'd been there since he was young.

She'd always loved to cook, so it was no stretch that this was where she'd been drawn to. He had fond memories of her helping their mother in the kitchen when they were younger. Courtney had continued to cook and bake, saying it helped her remain connected to their mom.

He looked around the cozy café, seeing the touches of Courtney's personality through it, from the pops of rich color to the books that lined a small bookshelf in the corner. A picture of her and their mother adorned the bookshelf, and he smiled, knowing it was a piece of her that kept Courtney happy.

"Hey," she said, walking over with a sandwich and iced tea. She placed them in front of him and took a seat, resting her arms on the table.

"Hey. Don't you need to work? I can wait."

"Nah. Bo's got it."

Pete looked up, and Bo nodded to him.

"Look, I'm sorry," she said. "It's just, with Dad, I never knew what to believe. He really did sound crazy near the end. But you, you're the sanest person I know, so grounded and realistic. If you say there's someone out there, I believe you."

Relief rippled through him. "You do?"

"Yes. Now tell me about this mystery woman and why she lives in the forest."

He thought about Crimson. How to describe her. "She's stunning. She has this red hair and these green eyes. I've never seen eyes so rich in color; it's like looking into the forest itself."

"Okay. What's her name?"

"Crimson—"

"Crimson? That's a new one. No last name, or did you not bother to get one?" she asked with a devious smile.

"I didn't ask."

"How many times have you slept with this woman, Pete?"

More than he could count, and the thought of it threatened to make him hard.

"I don't know, quite a few."

"You've been to those woods... Wait, you've only been here a few days, Pete."

"I've been to the woods two nights."

She sat back, her eyes growing wider. "Oh, wow. That's too much to think about. Why did I ask?"

Laughing, he said, "Don't ask what you don't want to know."

"I'll keep that in mind now that I can't burn the image of my brother having multiple rounds of sex with a stranger in the woods from my mind."

He gave her a crooked grin.

"God, that's gross. Okay. So why does she live in the woods?"

He went through what Crimson had told him, while Courtney listened, her expression never revealing any judgement. When he'd finished, she remained quiet.

"I think I have proof," he said, unsure how to take her silence.

He put the book on the table and pushed it toward her.

"What's this? It looks ancient. Did you dig this up in the basement?"

"Yes. It's a history, our family history. It's supposed to be handed down to each generation that takes the house."

She flipped it open and began looking through the book, the notes, the sketches, the details that supported part of Crimson's story.

"So, you're telling me that this woman is some queen cursed to spend eternity in our forest guarding souls—"

"She called them lost souls."

"Lost souls. And our family has protected this place all this time."

"From as far back as they could remember. Look"—He flipped back to the beginning—"it says our family protected the land. That a spell from the gods keeps it from the outsiders. We must protect it always and vigilantly or suffer their wrath."

"That's crazy, you know that, right?"

"Think about it, Court. The will specifically states that we cannot sell the land, that it must pass to the next generation."

"If whatever this is, is this old...Pete, I don't think you should go into the forest again. If this is true, you're dealing with something much bigger than us." She leaned over and whispered, "Gods? The devil? Don't go back there."

"I have to."

She scrunched her lips. "Oh, my God, you're in love with her."

"I don't know what I am."

"You are. Jesus, Pete. If a god really has cursed her there, what if he finds out? What if he kills you for finding her? This book says we are not to go seeking the Forest of the Damned." She pointed to the line on the page.

"I can't leave her there."

"You don't have a choice. A god sent her there to pay for her crimes. A god, Peter!"

"What would Bo do if you were trapped there?"

"He...he..." Her eyes grew sad. "You really are in love with her."

"And I'm going to free her."

"And if you can't?"

"Then I suppose I'd better adjust to living at night because I won't live without her, and I won't leave her there alone."

PETE RETURNED to the grove that night and every night after. He couldn't stay away from Crimson, and he didn't want to. They made love repeatedly. He took her in each time, memorizing every curve, every sigh, every quiver as if each night were the last. And he fell deeper in love with her until there was no one else who existed.

He checked in with Courtney each morning, assuring her he was safe and that he was still alive.

"What will happen to them?" he asked Crimson as they walked through the grove. The space was too big for him to traverse in its entirety, but he still walked as far as he could with her. Countless lost souls were bound here, and magic allowed her to attend to each, ensuring no one beyond the grove heard their screams, calming them to minimize the wails. She was a keeper, but also a mother to them, coaxing them to calm their struggles. In some, he would see the white bark extend downward as she did it, in others the black trunk would climb.

"They eventually earn their freedom, most. The truly lost souls do—those who were taken by Derrant's demons and never passed through for judgement. As the ivory stretches, that soul is nearing the Upper Realm and Eliana will greet them, guiding them to the Upper God as it becomes a full white tree, the tree fading, and leaving room for another."

"And if the black wins?"

"Then she will gather them back to the Shadow Realm to spend their eternity in subservience to the Death God and his shadow gods."

Scratching his head, he tried to twist his brain about those facts. A goddess who shepherded souls to realms like heaven and hell. Souls that spent the afterlife locked in a prison as they struggled to escape damnation. It all sounded like mythology to him.

"If the grove is this massive, do any ever reach their destination?" he asked, giving up on trying to comprehend what she'd just told him.

"Not many. The damnation they suffer is a long, brutal one. Souls fear the forest for a reason."

He glanced around, seeing the different states of the trees, hearing the slight echo of the wails to which he'd grown accustomed.

She took his hand. "Let's not talk anymore."

Her mouth brushed his, and he wrapped his arms around her waist, bringing her closer. "That's fine with me."

They'd made love when he'd returned to her, but he had no limit when it came to her.

As he grew more excited, he pushed her against the closest tree, drawing the sleeve of her dress down and kissing her neck before he cupped her breast. Scooping it from below the dress, he brought it to his mouth. He let his tongue drift along her skin, circling her nipple before he sucked it in. Her back arched in reaction, and he teased her nipple further with his tongue.

She moaned, clasping her fingers in his hair as his other hand lifted her skirt and spread her legs. Finding her warmth, he let his fingers sink into it, her wetness driving his erection to throb. She tipped her head back as his fingers penetrated her. His lust for her intensified, leaving him with an ache only she could calm.

Her hands worked his zipper down, stroking him in a way that sent a flame of need scorching through him. He continued to plunge his fingers into her, ignoring the urge to replace them with the length she was so wonderfully tormenting. His thumb slid to her clit, stimulating it as he tugged at her nipple with his teeth. Her body lurched in an erotic way, and it took everything he had to not come right in her hand. She was magnificent in the way she reacted to his touch, and he wanted to feel her fall apart before he found his own release.

As if knowing, she pulled his head from her breast and pressed her lips to his.

"Take me, now, and come with me," she murmured between kisses.

His length jerked in her hand like it was trying to answer for him. Removing his hand from her warmth, he gave her a mischievous smile and brought his fingers to his mouth. Slowly, he licked them clean. Her groan was feral and stirred the flames within him so that they soared. His reaction only grew when she pulled his hand away and brought his fingers into her mouth in a move that almost broke him.

Her eyes were sparkling with seduction as she dropped his hand and then her gown. Grabbing her, he lifted her. He didn't bother to even pull his pants down his hunger for her was so great. He took her there, sliding into her with an ease that sent his dick pulsing. Her legs gathered around him, forcing him to drive further with each thrust. She was soaked and he could feel how close she was to release. There was a quiver in her thighs that ran through her body and with each thrust it grew until she cried out. Her body spasmed around him as her climax hit, sending his own over the edge. With a heavy grunt, he joined her, holding firm to her hips as his release burned through his body.

After what seemed an eternity lost in passion's grip with her, he relaxed his hands and let her body down, her legs unwrapping from his waist. Kissing her neck, he lifted his head and met her eyes. They held the same depth of emotion that he felt in his heart. It was there, shining clearly in her the sage of her eyes.

She brought her hand to his cheeks, softly running her fingers down it. "Where did you come from?" she whispered. "And why didn't I find you years ago?"

He turned into her hand and kissed it. "Because we weren't meant to find each other until now."

She smiled a small, sad smile. "That would imply we're meant to be together." He felt her heart race. "I can't love you, Pete."

"Why not?"

"Because it will hurt too much, and it already hurts too much."

"Because you love me," he said with confidence, gently brushing a strand of her hair back.

"I don't know what love is."

He smiled. "Does your heart flutter each time you think of me? Do I fill your mind nonstop? Is every breath you take for me now?" She nodded, her eyes glossy. "Then you love me as I love you."

Tears welled in her eyes. "That's love?"

"Yes. It hurts, but it's worth every bit of hurt."

A tear slipped from her eye, and he brought his finger up to wipe it.

"You deserve to be loved, Crimson."

"I don't think I do."

He kissed her passionately. The knowledge that she loved him sent his heart soaring. He took her into his arms and kissed her more deeply, bringing her to the ground and making love to her among the white and black flakes of bark. Overwhelmed by his love for her, his desire mounted. With each move, each touch he became further lost in her. She took control and forced him to his back, stopping his movement just as he was close to climaxing. He grunted in surprise. She'd stymied his impending release, frustrating him. He gripped her waist, trying to move her pelvis, but she put her finger to his mouth and pushed against him.

Pete groaned as need ached inside him.

"Do you really love me?"

"Now you ask that?" He complained. "Did I not make it clear enough?"

"Tell me again."

"I love you, Crimson. More than I've ever loved before. I love you with a fire that eats at me when I'm not with you, one that will consume me if I'm ever forced to be without you."

"Is that what that feeling is? That burning in my body and between my legs?"

"No, that's me inside of you waiting to come."

She giggled, kissing him as she began moving her hips again. He sighed as she moved and drew back to watch him. His need increased again with the rise and fall of her body. The movement was something from which he couldn't draw his attention. She was beautiful, and she was his. Every curve was his to touch, his to love, his to hold. She leaned forward, pressing her hands against his chest. Her lush hair fell in waves across her breasts, and he watched as the locks swept over her nipples so that they were just peeking from below them. The sight lent another level of seduction to her. Tearing his eyes from them, he reached his hand up and cupped her cheek before drawing her down for a kiss.

The act lit the flames that had been licking within him, sparking a reaction that scorched him. "I need you, Crimson," he said against her mouth. "And I love you."

She stopped his words with her kiss, the passion within it clear and intended. Leaning back, she met his eyes, never drawing them from his as she sent him over the edge. He broke just as she did, their cries resounding through the grove in unison. Holding tight to her waist, he forced her quivering body down as his climax drowned him with its intensity. Even when the last of his release had fled his body, the waves of it were still sweeping through him like residual tremors. Crimson lowered her head, brushing her lips across his ear, and whispered, "I love you," as her own body trembled against him.

They lay entangled with each other, their breaths as one. He was fighting the sleep that threatened to steal his time with her when a bright circle formed across from them, a spectrum of colors within it.

"You've got to be kidding me," Crimson mumbled, sitting up.

A woman emerged from the circle, beautiful and tall, her long auburn hair flowing in waves down her chest. Her eyes were the deepest shade of blue he'd ever seen. She wore a long loose dress of the same shade of blue. It hugged her curves, accentuating the breasts that were enhanced by the material. She was breathtaking.

"Always impeccable timing, Skye," Crimson said, standing, her demeanor changing. Her expression hardened, wiping away the soft, delicate woman he knew.

"Better than that time I caught you masturbating with the help of your trees. At least you're finished this time, and I don't have to wait."

The woman's eyes perused Crimson's body, then moved to him, taking in his nakedness with a satisfied smile. "When I told you to find a man, I had no idea you'd find one so fast. Nice to know you've got your mind off my husband and found a man as well-endowed as he."

Pete grabbed his pants and covered himself while Crimson crossed her arms.

"Did you get a good enough look?" Crimson asked her.

The woman's eyes hardened, and Pete could see that she was more than she appeared. Her eyes had a lethal aspect to them, but Crimson didn't flinch.

"You had more than a look at my husband. I think that gives me every right to take my time."

"Well, I certainly took mine with Markhem," Crimson bit back.

They stared at each other, and Pete wondered if they were about to have the world's sexiest catfight in front of him. The thought threatened to increase the erection the woman's appearance had stirred.

"How is Markhem? Not satisfied with you these days, Skye?" Crimson pushed. "This is twice you've visited me in a matter of days. Has he wandered? I guarantee he wouldn't stray with me. Oh, but then he strayed *in* me, didn't he?"

Pete thought his mouth had dropped to the ground. There was an undeniable sexiness to this version of Crimson. A bad girl side that turned him on in ways he wouldn't have thought possible. Streams of black burst from the forest, cutting his arousal short. The ebony joined streams of red that were seeping from Crimson's hair, surrounding her in a torrent of motion.

He hopped up, but something held him back.

"Always so touchy, Skye."

"Don't make me bleed the color from that pretty hair of yours, Crimson. I'm not sure gray would be as flattering on you."

"Don't make me call my spirits, Skye." A wail filled the air. The streams around Crimson receded, and she relaxed, the forest calming.

"Put some clothes on, both of you," the woman said with a frustrated tone.

"You don't command me, Skye."

"I do now. You're crownless for the moment, Crimson."

"Don't remind me."

Crimson walked over and snatched up her dress as Pete tried to discretely pull his pants on.

"Don't be shy. She's seen plenty of my husband's dick. I can see a bit of yours."

"Wait, you're the one?" he said, pulling his pants up, as the realization settled in him. She was the one Crimson had sold to the Death God, whose husband she'd stolen.

She raised a brow, and he couldn't help but notice how it accentuated the blue in her eyes.

"She told you about her past, yet you still want to fuck her? Oh, Crimson, you are a naughty girl. Did you figure out how to spell a human?"

"No, I did not," she snapped back.

The woman creased her brows. "You willingly came to her? No pun intended, of course."

He couldn't help the snicker that escaped before he answered her. "Yes. She has a past, so what?"

"Interesting. I wish I could be so nonchalant about it but since her *so what* shadows my happily ever after, I can't quite let it go."

"Why are you here, Skye? And why are you bitchier than normal?"

Skye sighed, a sound he found strangely arousing. "Your cousin has died. Mark and I have been arguing the past few days about what to do."

So, Mark was the one Crimson had stolen, seducing him. Pete looked between the two, both beautiful in unique ways, powerful in their stance and commanding. They oozed sexiness, and he could see why the man had strayed. Crimson hadn't said as much, but there was something underneath Skye's tone that told him it had happened. He couldn't blame him. Crimson was irresistible, but everything he observed about Skye told him she was as well. He imagined it would be hard to stray from her.

"And what does dear Markhem say?" Crimson asked.

"That I should leave you to rot and let your kingdom fall."

There was more to those words below the surface. He couldn't help but think it confirmed that her husband had strayed willingly to Crimson at some point. His hatred of her fueled not only by what had happened to Skye but by the guilt he still carried. Crimson may have stolen him and instigated it, but Pete had a feeling there was quite a bit to the story that he'd not heard.

"Some thanks for all the satisfaction I brought him."

"Enough, Crimson. This is serious. Your kingdom is under siege, two regimes are fighting for power, the stronger of the two is winning. Their violence is spreading to Theodore's kingdom, and there's fear they may vie to overthrow him as well. They're brutal and determined."

Pete listened in awe, all the pieces of Crimson's story now gaining support with every word he heard.

"That pisses me off. They'd better not damage my castle or…if they touch my wing, I will have their heads."

"And that's the Crimson I remember. Going to tie some up in your dungeons for later?"

"No, those don't deserve pleasure."

"Wait, why would prisoners get pleasure?" he found himself asking.

"Oh, he doesn't know what a whore you are, does he?"

"Was," Crimson corrected, not denying the accusation.

"What's your name?" Skye asked him.

"Pete."

Her eyes perused the bare chest he'd yet to cover before she met his eyes again. He found it hard to draw his eyes from hers, the navy in them seductive. "Cute and human. If we get you home, Crimson, you can't bring him."

His heart fell, and Crimson's face dropped.

"Don't tell me…has someone finally broken you?"

"Shut up, Skye. Did you find a way to get me out of here?"

"I'm not sure. Mark and I argued for days, but I finally convinced him that I needed to go to Derrant."

"An extra night with the Death God isn't a bad thing."

Skye glared at her. "Do you know what that cost me? Do you have any idea what it costs me each time I'm forced to go to him?"

"It's five nights each year and Derrant is as good in bed as Markhem is. It should be a pleasurable respite. He even makes you come; he never did that for me."

"How do you like spending the day without your lover? To be torn from him each morning? Try five days and nights knowing he's with another woman and you might know Mark's pain. Try being forced to have sex with a man you don't love for that time, being touched by him when it's your lover you really want. Then you might come close to knowing my pain, Crimson, and understanding just why Mark thinks of nothing but ways to kill you as punishment each time the Death God calls me back."

So that was why the man hated her so. It wasn't only what Crimson had done to Mark, but what harm her actions had brought to Skye. Pete was speechless. The thought of another man touching Crimson, even hearing her talk about other men, sent his jealousy rising. He couldn't imagine going through what this guy was experiencing.

"I'm sorry, Skye. I didn't know—"

"Didn't know?" She let out a sharp laugh. "You turned me over to him while you took Mark for yourself!" She turned, and he saw lines of color seep from around them—grays, blacks, whites. He stared at them in wonder. "I don't know why I even came here," she muttered.

"Skye, don't go, please. I'm not that person anymore."

Pete felt like he needed to say something, but he had no idea what. Everything he'd seen and heard left him completely confounded. He was out of his element and not certain where or if he fit into any of it.

"Don't go," he begged Skye.

She dropped her hand and the streams hung in stasis. Turning, she said, "You'll lose her if we free her."

"Maybe. But she deserves to be free."

"Does she? After all she's done? Things I'm still feeling the repercussions of, that my husband still feels the repercussions of?"

"Things for which your Death God has punished her."

"Ten years? I have a lifetime to suffer, as does my husband."

"Look, nothing can take that back, but she's not that same woman."

Skye stepped closer, her navy eyes evaluating him. For an instant, he was lost in them again, their beauty entrancing him. "You know all this after how many nights of screwing her?"

"Yes."

"God, you're in love with her. She's psychotic."

"Hey—" Crimson started.

"She's beautiful, sensitive, smart, calculating, determined, driven, but she's not psychotic."

"Huh." She looked between them. "You managed to get someone who will stand up for you, who barely knows you, to vouch for you, even though he will likely lose you?"

She looked back at Pete. "Welcome to the wild ride, Pete. Crimson," she said, backing up, "I've done what I can. I've pleaded your case to Derrant. I traded an extra night in his bed for it—you're welcome. I have Eliana's ear, she has his. That's the best I can do."

"Thank you. I know what that cost you."

"No, I don't think you do, but you will the moment you're forced to leave him behind. I pity you both because I know the pain."

She turned back to the colors, and they moved again, forming a portal. Glancing back, she said, "Derrant knows about him, Crimson. Don't let him catch you with him. He may bring you back, but he still harbors his anger. He still thinks you deserve punishment. Punishment he may very well place on your lover's shoulders in your stead."

She stepped through and disappeared, the portal closing behind her with only a faint shimmer of color that the dark of the grove quickly shrouded.

CRIMSON

Crimson couldn't take her eyes from where the portal had been. She didn't know what to think. Happiness filled her, bringing a lightness to her body as if the weight of eternal damnation had been lifted. There was a chance she might be allowed to return home, to have her sentence forgiven, but she was devastated by the idea of losing Pete. The thought made her heart ache.

Skye's final words lingered in her mind. There was a possibility that Pete was in danger and that frightened her. She considered sending him away to keep him safe from Derrant in case the Death God did come take her home. But she didn't think she could. It was selfish, she knew, but she didn't want to let Pete go.

"So, that was the woman whose husband you stole?"

She pulled her eyes from the empty space and met his.

"Yes. She's beautiful, isn't she? And powerful. Everything I've always wanted to be."

He took her in his arms. "You are beautiful, Crimson, and powerful. I've seen you work your magic here in the grove, and you said you had magic in your world. For Christ's sake, you ruled a kingdom!"

He talked funny with his strange terms like Skye did, which Crimson found odd. Markhem had used strange terms as well.

"That magic never belonged to me. I stole it. I can take another's magic, but it fades. It was enough to keep my kingdom under control."

"What did she mean about that five days' stuff? What else did you do to them?"

"I didn't do that to them," she said, her tone defensive.

"Crimson..."

She cringed, knowing that even though she hadn't orchestrated it, the fault had been hers.

"All right, maybe I was the catalyst for it. I'm not sure of the entire story but somehow Skye's soul ended up here with the lost souls and, to help Markhem get her back, Eliana had to make a deal with Derrant's brother, who rules the place you called Hell."

"A deal with the devil?" He laughed as if there were a joke she didn't know.

"Yes. She promised him five days each year, away from Derrant, sharing his bed instead. Derrant was pissed when he found out and as punishment he made Skye his for those five days."

"What?"

"He takes her to the Shadow Realm to share his bed. It's not that terrible. She slept with him when he stole her before when I had Markhem. Derrant is quite the lover if you stay on his good side."

"You're serious?" he asked, astonishment clear in his tone. "You really think that's not that bad?"

"Well—"

"Crimson, that's horrible. Her husband has to send her to another man, knowing that man will be having sex with her that entire time. That must be torture. I can't even imagine you with another man."

"You can't?" Her heart swelled at the protectiveness in his voice.

"No, all this talk of you sleeping with them before we met is bad enough."

"So, does that mean you change your mind about me? I told you I have a past. A naughty one in every sense of the word."

She was afraid of his answer, afraid he'd had enough of her past and he would turn and walk away. There was a vulnerability to her that she hid below her confident demeanor, one she rarely showed. She knew she was revealing it to him, that her fear showed in her eyes, in the expectant way she awaited his answer.

Sighing, he said, "No, but it makes me think you need to fix that if you do go home. You owe them that much."

"Fix it? There's no swaying Derrant once he's made a decision, especially when it comes to Skye."

"They're swaying him to free you."

She chewed her lip. Skye had said it had cost her another night away from Markhem. She'd given herself to Derrant once more for Crimson's freedom. After all the visits, she'd known Skye long enough to know what that had truly cost her.

"So, if I keep you around, are you going to continue being my voice of reason?"

"Damn right I am."

She would have laughed, but then she realized she would likely not have him there. She'd have to leave him. The idea hurt too much to dwell upon.

She smiled. "I need to calm the trees before the dawn."

He gave her a kiss before she forced herself to walk away. "Don't bother putting that shirt back on. I plan to take you once more before I sleep."

He arched a brow. "You're going to take me?"

"Definitely."

Laughing, he replied, "I'll be right here waiting for you."

"Good, think dirty thoughts because I want you nice and hard."

"Jesus," he muttered, running his hand through his hair.

She smiled as she worked her magic on the trees, weaving her sleeping spell. In the back of her mind, she thought perhaps she shouldn't have been so selfish. That she should have sent Pete back. If Skye was right and the Death God knew she'd given a mortal entry into the forest, he would be irate. It could even cost her the chance at freedom. Something she would gladly give up to keep Pete safe.

That thought gave her pause. She'd never worried about anyone but herself. Never put anyone before her own needs. Now, here she was, willing to give up the one thing she'd dreamed of for a decade.

She hurried through the last of the souls, ready to return to him, when something grabbed her internally, taking her breath away. It seared within before black shadows engulfed her.

Derrant.

The space disappeared, and a force thrust her to the ground. Raising her head against the pain, she looked to Pete, who was now across from her. The Death God had forced him to his knees, and he was struggling. Fear shadowed his eyes. She looked to the Death God, who now stood before them. He was in his terrifying state. She'd forgotten how horrifying he truly could be. The portal behind him remained open, flames licking out around his shadows.

"So it's true!" he bellowed, stepping forward.

"Derrant—"

"Dare not use my name, whore! You brought a mortal into my forest!"

"It gets quite lonely here. Can't a girl have some fun?"

He lifted her with his power, and the air squeezed further from her lungs.

"Don't hurt her!" Pete grimaced out.

Foolish man, she thought.

Derrant's head snapped to him, and he walked closer to Pete, who held his stare. His head tilted as he studied Pete.

"And not just any mortal. You brought a Guardian into my forest?"

"I don't know what a Guardian is De—my lord."

He looked back at her, and she dropped to the ground with a grunt. "Do you not? Every Keeper knows inherently what a Guardian is."

She stood, rubbing her neck. "I don't know."

He towered over her. "Think, Keeper."

"It's hard to think when you're in that state. Where is the beautiful god I know?" she said, trying to calm him.

"Your charms won't work on me, Crimson. Not anymore."

"Oh, I know. You are quite satisfied now, aren't you?"

"As are you, it would seem."

Relieved he'd calmed some, she dared, "Please transform, so it's easier to look at you."

He shifted to his mortal appearance, and as it always had, that part of her deep within stirred. Whatever claim he had on her soul craved his touch again.

He walked closer, letting his hand graze her body, then he smacked her. Pete struggled, anger in his eyes at the move and she prayed he kept quiet.

"Tell me what he is, Keeper," Derrant growled.

She held her cheek and thought back through the knowledge that had come to her when Derrant had sentenced her here. Digging for the word guardian until she found it. Her eyes grew wide with understanding.

"The Death God sent the Guardian here when the lands first became populated. He was sworn to protect the Forest of Lost Souls, to keep the land untouched, and ensure the sanctity of the Keeper's domain."

Her eyes met Pete's. He wasn't a random man. He was connected to their world, to her.

"And what is the one rule of the Guardian?"

It was Pete who answered. "To never enter the forest at night."

"The forest is off limits to a Guardian. A Keeper and Guardian must never meet, they are to remain always separate."

"Why?" Crimson asked.

"That is none of your concern."

Derrant walked away and began pacing, the flames of the portal licking across his skin as he moved. Rubbing his forehead, he said, "Your kingdom is under siege. Skye has pleaded your case, although I do not understand why. Eliana has pleaded on her behalf. It is not in my nature to ever free one I've punished, but the situation is out of hand."

Her hope rose, a feeling like butterflies flapping through her chest, but she didn't want him to see the hope. "I would think you of all the gods would be happy for unrest."

"Yes, that is usually the case, but this is beyond what even I enjoy. Too many dead, too many for Eliana to ferry, and so she is away from me too long."

"Gods, how many have died? I thought it just started."

"It has, but they were prepared. The dead arrive in droves daily as they move through your realm and the one you so greedily stole. Now they march to battle Theodore's kingdom, and Skye refuses to help him as punishment for his involvement with you. The last time things were this busy was during the Mage Wars."

"What will you do?" she asked, her eyes glancing to Pete's.

"I am conflicted." He stopped, turning. "Although now I have a solution." He released Pete and Crimson ran to him, only to be stopped by Derrant's magic. "I do not forgive, Crimson. I will release you from your duties, return you to our world, but you will still be punished."

She felt the weight of her imprisonment as Keeper lift from her. The connection to the souls was severed as they wailed in misery, but she ignored the sensation as she awaited her punishment, praying he didn't hurt Pete.

"A Keeper is always required."

"No!" she screamed, realizing what he was planning to do.

Pete's clothes changed, a black shirt appearing, along with a long black cape that shimmered in the moonlight donning his shoulders.

"You dared stray into my forest and break the Guardian's covenant. You will now serve me for eternity."

Pete's face filled with recognition as his eyes filled with fear.

"No!" she cried. Derrant's grip dragged her through the portal as she reached for Pete.

She heard him cry out for her as the portal sealed, tearing him from her as the flames of hell scorched her body. The dark, heavy feel of the Shadow Realm brushed her skin before she fell, landing hard on what felt like a stone floor.

"What the hell?" she heard behind her. She knew the voice and dreaded turning to see the man to whom she knew it belonged.

She rolled over, meeting Markhem's hazel eyes as he drew his weapon, pinning it to her neck.

PETE

The wails filled Pete's head in a way he'd never heard them before. They were painful, distinct cries of the souls he now felt all around him. Still, he stared at the space where Crimson had been pulled from his life by a god. Death God, she had called him. A terrifying beast until he'd morphed into the guise of a man, an astonishingly good-looking man.

A god. The concept was surreal, just as all of this was. The god of death. One Crimson knew well enough to speak to, to dare use his name, one she'd been lovers with, one who owned her soul and now perhaps Pete's. The Death God's words had confirmed everything Pete had found in the book. The forest and his family were connected.

Guardian. He'd never heard the term used in reference to him before. He must have missed it in the book he'd found. His family were Guardians of the forest. That was why the house and the land had to stay in the family. Why the family had kept it protected. Pete had been the oldest and so he'd been the one the mantle had fallen upon. But now he was more than that, he was both Guardian and Keeper.

He stared at his hands; the wailing so loud now that his ears and head ached from it.

"Shut up!" he screamed, and silence followed.

They need to sleep before dawn, his mind told him.

His mind suddenly filled with a history that belonged to the Keepers before him, including Crimson.

She was gone, sent back to her world. He left here as punishment for loving her. He walked through the grove, accessing a magic he now had and somehow knew how to use. Through it he put the souls to sleep, sensing them as they moved to their slumber. Sealing their essence in the trees.

He couldn't believe he was stuck here. Forever. It didn't seem possible. An eternity serving a god that wasn't his. Or perhaps he was. If his family was from Crimson's world, then he was a god to Pete.

"Shit, shit, shit," he muttered.

He reached back to see if he still had his phone, but his clothes were gone, replaced with this old-fashioned outfit of black. He contemplated running back through the woods. Going back to the house and sleeping whatever this was off. Letting himself believe this was a nightmare from which he could wake.

"Don't be a fool," he told himself.

He knew enough to know that wasn't an option. This was now his prison.

A glint of color bled through the forest as dawn approached, and he felt himself yanked from his spot and moved to darkness. The heat was excessive, flickers of red popping into the blackness.

Hell. He was literally in Hell. As he thought it, an unwelcome sleep took over him and everything went black.

PETE WOKE WITH A JOLT. He was standing in the grove but he didn't know if he was dreaming or awake. It was hard to tell.

Looking around he noticed that the trees seemed to be waking. They were stretching their limbs, the white of them reaching long. The black held them down, grounding them...to the Shadow Realm. As the final bit of sunlight faded, he saw how the grove glowed from the essence of the spirits. He'd always wondered why it had seemed light in this space.

His mind went to Crimson, missing her painfully—her touch, her voice, her lips, everything about her. She was gone from him, and he was stuck feeling the ache of her absence for an eternity. It was anguish enough to send him to his knees, which shook as though they might give.

"Pull yourself together, Pete. There has to be a way out."

He left the trees, their wails growing louder at his absence. Making his way out of the grove, he headed toward the house, running the closer he came to the forest's edge. Reaching it, he felt an overwhelming need to go back, but he ignored it, putting his hand out, hoping it would go through to the other side. His hand hit a barrier, like an invisible forcefield, and would go no further.

"Dammit!"

He ran to different spots, only to end up with the same effect until he saw headlights coming down the drive. He watched as the car pulled in and Courtney rushed out.

"Damn you, Pete! If you're out there fucking that woman instead of texting me back, I will have your balls!" she groused as she stormed toward the door.

"Courtney!" he yelled.

She paused and looked over her shoulder.

"Court!"

She continued to look, then turned and proceeded to the house.

"Dammit."

He waited as she turned the lights on. He could see her walking around, looking for him. All the while, the souls complained, their cries echoing through the forest.

She exited the house, then stopped, looking around as if she'd heard them, too.

"Courtney!" he yelled again.

She came down the stairs to head back toward her car. Desperate, he ran to that section of the woods, hoping to catch her eyes, which were still peering into the trees.

"Court!" he yelled as loud as he could.

She paused, her hand on the car's door handle, then took a few steps closer to the forest. "Damn, Pete. I am not looking in there for you. Why couldn't you meet a nice girl in town? No, had to be some mysterious spirit woman in a dark, creepy forest."

She continued to mumble as the clouds shifted and the moonlight hit part of his skin. She gasped and took a step back. "Pete?"

"It's me. You can see me, Court?"

She acted like she hadn't heard him. "That's not funny, Pete."

He tried again, but she still didn't hear him. She took her phone out and turned her flashlight on. "What the hell? Are you doing some kind of role play? If you're into the kinky stuff, that's all good, but keep it to yourself. I'm not into that kind of stuff."

He rolled his eyes and gestured for her to step into the forest, hoping she could hear him if she did.

"Are you serious? I've seen enough horror movies to know you could be some shape-shifting demon luring me to my death."

He wanted to strangle her, but she was too far away, so he gave her the finger instead.

"Okay, maybe it is you."

He gestured again, impatiently waving his arm for her to move closer.

"If you kill me, I will haunt you, evil spirit," she said, walking into the trees.

"Can you hear me now?" he asked.

"Yes. What the hell are you doing? And why haven't you answered your phone?" She shoved him. "We made a deal!"

"I don't have my phone. Look, I need you to listen to me. Something happened."

"With that woman?"

"In a way. She's gone; they sent her home."

"Home?"

"Back to her world."

"Pete, you're scaring me." She took his hand and started dragging him back to where the tree line ended. "Come on, let's go inside and have a beer. I'll order Chinese."

She walked through, but the wall to his prison prevented him from going further. She looked back and tugged.

"Pete, stop playing," she said, stepping back through.

"I'm not. I can't leave the forest. Their god, the Death God, replaced her with me."

She dropped his hand, and he raised it to push against the barrier. "I can't go any further."

Fear crossed her eyes. "What's going on, Pete?"

"I'm stuck. He said we were Guardians. Does that sound familiar?"

"Guardians?"

"Yes, we are the Guardians of the forest. She was the Keeper of Lost Souls. Because I stepped into the forest, because I...I fell in love with her, he cursed me to take her place. The souls must always have a Keeper."

Her eyes searched his, looking for any sign of doubt.

The souls grew louder, their struggle increasing.

"Do you hear that?" he asked.

"Yes." Her voice was shaking. "What did you get yourself into, Pete?"

"Something huge. Something I don't know how to get out of. Listen, I need you to search that book, search dad's notes, find anything you can on Guardian or Keeper. He said our family was sent here from their world to protect the forest."

"Their world?"

"Yes, the same one she's back in now. I need to get out of here and find her, Court."

"I'm so confused."

"I know. I need to go and settle the blasted spirits before they wake the entire town."

"Those are spirits?"

He nodded. "Trapped souls trying to claw their way to heaven and escape the hell that awaits them if they fail. Their version of those things, anyway."

"You sound insane."

"At this point, I wish I were. Find everything you can, then meet me here tomorrow after sunset."

"But, Pete—"

"Just do it, Court, please. I have to go. Something tells me if I don't do my job, there's a price to be paid."

He backed away, leaving her in the darkness of the forest until it swallowed her and he could see her no more.

He didn't think she was his way out, didn't know if there was a way out. But she was all he had. He needed to escape this sentence and somehow find Crimson.

Thinking of Crimson, he wondered where she was. Where the Death God had sent her. He was inclined to think the god had sent her back to her kingdom to reclaim her throne. The thought was a conflicting one. He wanted her to take back her crown but he worried that she'd forget him and leave him here to suffer.

He prayed she wouldn't, that she'd find a way when she could. He had no way of knowing how long that would be or if he'd still be alive when that day finally came.

CRIMSON

Crimson stared up at Mark as his weapon dug into her throat. She held her breathe, the pressure of it uncomfortable.

"I've dreamed of this day for ten years, Crimson, and now it's finally here," he growled.

"You've been dreaming of me, Mark, after all this time?"

The tip dug deeper, no humor in his dark hazel eyes. He was still as beautiful as she remembered—lethal, but beautiful.

"I dream a lot of things, and each one involves your head severed from your body."

"That's a bit kinky, even for my standards."

His eyes narrowed and she could feel the hatred.

"If you're going to kill me, then do it."

"Mark?" she heard Skye's voice. "Holy shit."

She rushed over and stood looking down at Crimson with an expression of astonishment on her face. "He did it. He actually freed you."

"I don't think his intention was for your husband to kill me."

"Mark, let her up, please," she said, her hand on his arm. His muscular arm made her think of Pete. An overwhelming sadness washed over her, accompanied by a numbing pain in her chest.

"Mark."

"Skye, she's the reason we still suffer."

"I know," she whispered, turning his face to hers. "But nothing can change that. Killing her won't take it away."

"But it will satisfy me."

"I have plenty of other ways I could satisfy you," Crimson purred.

"Really, Crimson? I'm trying to help you and that's what you say?" Skye said.

"Sorry. I can't help it and that opening was there. I don't know any other way."

"Well, it's time you learn another," Skye said, crossing her arms.

Markhem still hadn't moved.

"He imprisoned him," Crimson murmured, bowing her head.

"Who?"

"Derrant. He made Pete Keeper of the lost souls." A strange sob-like sound slipped from her throat as she said it.

The weapon drew back from her throat.

"He exchanged you? For your freedom he took Pete?"

"Yes." She brought her hand to her chest. "Gods, why does it hurt so bad?"

Skye's eyes saddened as Mark put his weapon away.

"Because love does that," Skye said.

"Damn, I can't believe I'm doing this," Mark grumbled, extending his hand.

She would have made a comment about his touching her again, but the pain hurt too much, so Crimson took it and allowed him to help her up.

Mark took his hand away quickly, as if touching her too long might scald him.

"I suppose now you get a taste of your own medicine," he quipped.

"Crimson, what did Derrant say?" Skye asked.

She noticed the tension in Mark at the mention of Derrant's name.

"He said the fighting is keeping him from Eliana and he wants it ended, so he would bring me home but that a Keeper is always needed..." She couldn't say the rest, for fear of breaking and the last thing she wanted was to break in front of them.

"So, he chose Pete?"

She nodded. "He's something called a Guardian. His family, sent by Derrant ages ago, guards the forest."

Skye and Mark looked at each other.

"Sent from here?" he asked.

"Yes."

"Wow—didn't see that coming," Skye muttered.

"I need to get back to him. I can't leave him there."

"You need to pull yourself together and take your kingdom back. The rebels have claimed your throne and murdered the dissenters. They've spread to Digremile and toward Theodore's kingdom. His men are preparing to fight them as we speak. It's like they were waiting for the day—everything was in place, their men already in position."

"Like they knew my cousin would die," Crimson said.

"Yes."

"If I wanted to take over a kingdom in a legitimate way, a simple poison would do the trick."

"You think they murdered him?" Mark asked.

"I'd be willing to bet my stolen crown on it."

"Well, that makes matters even more concerning."

Mark started pacing, and she watched him, his body reminding her of Pete.

"You touch him again, Crimson," Skye snarled, "and I will be the one to kill you, crown or no crown. I will let this world burn before you touch him again."

Mark looked up at Skye, surprise on his face and something else—desire that sparkled behind his eyes.

"I was thinking of Pete, if you must know. As much as I'd love another go at your husband, Skye, I don't think it would help. I want Pete."

Skye studied her, her navy eyes hard. "Fine, but my warning stands. If your bed gets lonely, don't come searching mine for company." She grabbed Crimson's arm. "Let's get you cleaned up. Mark, call the council, send word to Theodore and Revina, if she'll care."

"If she doesn't hunt her down."

"That is a possibility."

Skye paused, glancing back at Mark, a small smile forming. His eyes brightened, then hardened again as Skye turned away from him and they fell on Crimson. She turned quickly from him and walked with Skye, wondering which threat she feared the most, the usurpers or Mark.

BEING in Skye's castle was a reminder of her own, and it felt good to be close to home. Skye had a bath drawn for her and as she sank into the warm water, Crimson wondered how she'd remained clean all those years in the forest. She didn't remember bathing, but she'd always woken clean. Probably best she didn't know what went on while she was sleeping.

Resurfacing from beneath the water, she found Skye looking at her.

"Did you not get enough when you interrupted my time with Pete? Or perhaps you want to join me? I promise I won't invite Markhem." She patted the water, gesturing for her to join her in the tub.

"Is that all you think about?"

"Why is it okay for a man to think about it nonstop and not a woman? I guarantee if you were in this tub and Markhem were standing there, he would join you in a heartbeat."

A sly grin transformed Skye's frown.

"See!"

Skye rolled her eyes.

"I bet the two of you go at it nonstop. He has quite the stamina. The only man I've ever had who could keep up with my appetite was Derrant and well, he's not really a man, is he? Not hung like a man either. My gods, he's like a stallion."

Skye's mouth had dropped. "I don't know whether to hurt you for that comment about Mark or drown you for the other words."

"Oh, come on, Skye," she said, rising from the tub and grabbing the towel laid for her. "You spent moons with Derrant and now you spend time every year with him. In his bed the entire time, I've no doubt. You can't say you don't enjoy it."

"No matter how he makes my body feel, I only want to be with Mark. One day soon you'll understand that. The next time you're below a man or pleasuring Theodore as I'm sure you'll do, I want you to tell me whose touch you think of, that man's or Pete's. Tell me who you picture atop you. Tell me how it hurts each time another hand touches you, how much it hurts to have his lips on yours and not those of the man you love."

Her eyes had grown misty.

"When will you ever learn, Crimson?"

Crimson looked down to the floor, the puddles of water gathering at her toes, toes Pete had kissed just hours before, legs he'd caressed. That part of her ached for his touch, to have him by her side and she wondered if Skye was right. Would she think of him if she took another man?

"Get dressed. We have work to do."

She met Skye's eyes, not certain what, if anything, to say. She didn't like this feeling; it left her feeling powerless. Under the control of a force she didn't understand. She dried herself and perused the dresses Skye had set out for her.

"Are these yours?"

"Yes."

"You do realize I'm a bit more endowed than you."

"So I've noticed. Make it work. That's all you have for now."

She picked a loose green dress, knowing she had more curves than Skye and would need the extra room for her hips and breasts. The dress slid over her, no longer loose but hugging all the right places, her breasts pushed up and over the bodice.

"This will do," she said, sliding her hands down her body.

"I don't think I can ever wear that again after seeing how you fill it out."

Crimson smiled. "My body is my weapon, Skye. You bring men to your knees with your magic; I bring them to their knees with my body. We're not that different. Now, let's get my kingdom back, then find a way to bring my man back."

"Your man?" Skye said with a raise of her brow.

Crimson sighed. "Yes, my man, my lover. The man I love. Is that what you want to hear?"

"Nice to know you're not pining over Mark anymore."

"Oh, don't get me wrong, I'd fuck Markhem in a heartbeat again—"

The green of her dress whipped around her body, cutting her words and her breath off.

"Mark is off limits," she growled.

"I know that. You've warned me enough," she wheezed. "I was going to say that I never really loved him. I didn't know what love was."

Skye's grip loosened, and Crimson gasped for air, coughing as it filled her lungs again.

"You are quite a jealous bitch, aren't you?"

"You have no idea."

Crimson stared as the remaining mist wrapped around her hair, drying it. The stream of magic lingered in the air before returning to her dress. An idea formed as she watched it.

"What?" Skye said.

"I think I know how to take back my kingdom."

Skye widened her eyes in surprise. "Then let's go."

CRIMSON

Crimson didn't recognize anyone sitting around the table of the room. Silence ensued upon her entrance, and she gave a smirk at their response. Their reaction didn't bother her. It gave her a sense of power. Mark stood to the side, hand to his weapon. She spotted Noah on guard in the corner and remembered how she'd found enjoyment in taking him when she'd let Mark rest. He crossed his arms, glaring at her.

"Well, well, Noah. It is so nice to see you, but I do prefer you with your clothes off," she said, taking a seat at the head of the table.

His stare hardened, and she licked her lips. There were a few uncomfortable coughs.

"This room is too uptight, Skye. With as active as I know you and Markhem are, you'd think they'd be less prudish."

"It's Mark, Crimson," he said through gritted teeth, "and get out of that seat. It belongs to my queen, which you are not."

She huffed. "I could have been."

"Jesus, Crimson," Skye muttered. "Just let her sit there, Mark. What's the latest situation?"

There was a moment of quiet, then Noah spoke, pointing to a

map on the table. "Their troops have met Theodore's; the fighting has begun. Theodore remains behind the castle walls, but if they defeat his troops, he will fall."

"How did they amass troops?" Crimson asked.

"They convinced your soldiers that the only one capable of filling your shoes is Stavin."

"Stavin? That prick?"

"You know him?" Mark asked.

"Yes, he was the head of my guard. He's the one I ordered to kill Mechon."

"Well, that adds a whole new layer."

"Did you sleep with him, too?" Skye asked. "Is there a way in with him?"

Crimson noted the edge to her voice with the first question. "No, I left my guard off limits. They needed to focus on my protection, not on my ass. But that doesn't mean it's not the way in."

"How so?"

"Stavin has an appetite for women, defenseless women. I could never prove it and who was I to judge at the time? I don't think he's ever had a willing woman. I'll keep him busy; you take his army and stop the battle."

"No," Mark said.

"But I thought that's what this was about."

"We won't help Theodore. He was complicit in your crimes. And unlike you, he never received punishment for them."

"I'm confused. So, why am I here?"

"To reclaim your kingdom and stop them from taking his kingdom."

"With no help from you?"

"You'll have help getting your army back, but then you're on your own," Skye said. "I will not come to Theodore's aid."

Crimson sat back. "Huh, all right then."

Her mind worked through the dilemma. Stavin was weak-willed when it came to women. She had no doubt she could kill him, but then she'd have no way of knowing who was on her side and who wasn't. She didn't want to cut the head off the snake only to have more heads grow in its place. Stavin wasn't known for his mind. He was a brute, which had made him a force in her guard, but he wasn't the brightest. There had to be someone else.

"Who's leading the attack on Theodore?"

"Not anyone we know. A man named Bormick."

She knew of Bormick. He had not been part of her guard, but he was one to be feared. And he was cunning.

"You know him, don't you?"

"I know of him. He lived outside the main kingdom, hailing from Digremile. He's brutal and elusive. My guard hunted him for years and now I suspect I know why. Stavin and Bormick saw an opening and took it. Well, they won't see me coming." She stood and rolled her neck. "It's time I showed these boys true power. I need a way into my kingdom and a way to contact you. If I show up with any of you, they'll know it's a coup."

"We can take care of that," a woman at the table said. Crimson could sense her power. Full mage, and a strong one at that.

"When I signal, I'll need two of your strongest Elite, Mark and Noah."

Complaints erupted immediately.

"To fight!" she yelled. "I'm not doing anything with them. Now hush. I'll also need magic. I'll need the power from a full mage, and Skye, I'll need yours."

Skye narrowed her eyes.

"I can be there," a man next to the full mage said.

"You don't need us. You want our power," Skye said.

"Yes. I can bleed magic for my own use. It lasts a few hours but leaves the mage powerless for that time. You should remember that, Skye." She gave Skye a playful wink, but only received a grimace from her.

"Hell no," Mark said. "You are not draining Skye's magic again, nor anyone else's!"

There was a murmuring as the others realized what she'd been saying.

"It's the only way to win."

"Why can't they just fight for you?" Mark demanded.

"Because I know these men. I know how they work. I need to have the power to take back the throne once I kill them. But I need to work with them until that time. Once I have them vulnerable, thinking they are controlling me, I'll turn them on each other and take the two heads from the snake. The army will need to see me as untouchable, a threat they can't and won't want to overthrow."

"Replace the snake with a viper," Skye said.

"Exactly. I need to be who I was before, and that person was a magic stealer."

"Skye, you can't—" Mark started.

"She's right, Mark. Otherwise, she'll be a target for the next one to challenge the throne. There was a reason her kingdom stayed peaceful within itself. She ruled with power and control. If she does not have that, then she'll be a target. No one can question her return. "

Concern etched Mark's face.

"I don't like it, Skye," Noah said. "None of us do."

"Because we don't trust her."

"With good reason," Mark said.

Skye turned to Crimson. "I never trusted you and you proved me right back then. I have no choice but to trust you now. Prove me right on that and I will help you find a way to free Pete."

Crimson's breath caught at the hope the statement brought, and she nodded.

"Elspeth, work with the others to find a way for her to signal us when she's ready."

"Yes, Skye." The full mage and the one next to her rose and left the room.

"Noah, you may want to let your wife know you'll be heeding Crimson's signal. I don't want to blindside her. I know how she feels about Crimson. I know all too well."

"Damn, this should be fun."

Crimson had no doubt about how his wife felt. She'd brought Noah to climax enough times to know the woman wasn't nearly as capable as she. He'd given in far more times and faster than Mark had, and she was certain his wife didn't know about the details of those moments.

She bit back her smile as he walked out without looking back.

"How many days do you need?"

"I don't know. I need to find out who is still loyal to me while I convince Stavin to bring his troops back."

"And how will you do that?" Mark asked.

"There's a reason I had Theodore wrapped around my finger, Mark. Don't worry, I know what these men like. They like it rough and hard, and they always take it. When it's given to them, they tend to lose their bearings. I'm about to make their wildest fantasies come true right before I decapitate them."

"And that doesn't bother you, Crimson?" Skye asked.

"Did it bother you when you pretended to enjoy fucking the Death God? Did it bother Mark when he pretended to enjoy me?"

Mark made what sounded like a growl while Skye's eyes deepened in color.

"It's all an act, right? It's one I'm very good at."

They looked at each other.

"I still don't like it," Mark groused.

"I don't think we have any other choice if we want to stay out of it."

CRIMSON

A few hours passed before the magic was ready. They'd created a ring for Crimson to wear. Skye had imbued hues into it that held the portal magic in place. Once she broke the stone, it would form a portal and signal them to come to her aid. Mark and Noah would stay with her to fight after she'd syphoned the mage magic she needed.

The plan sounded solid, but Crimson knew how plans tended to go; they never went well, even the best laid ones.

Only Skye was there to see her off. Crimson had expected Mark to be by her side, vigilantly watching her. In the past, that behavior had angered her. She'd been jealous of how protective he was of Skye, wanting that protectiveness for herself. Now, the experience was different, as if she were seeing them in a new light —one that didn't involve jealousy or pettiness. She had Pete to fill the space she'd wanted Mark to fill, to give her what Mark gave Skye. Or at least she had Pete before Derrant had taken him from her.

"Don't let me down, Crimson."

"I won't, I promise. And you'll help me free Pete?"

"Yes, I will do everything in my power." She had no reason to doubt Skye. She'd done nothing but help her, even with all Crimson had done to her.

"All right. Then let's do this."

"Crimson…" She turned to look at Skye, hearing the hesitation in her voice, "be careful."

"Are you worried about me, Skye?" she teased.

"Just watch your back."

"I'll be on it too often for it to be a concern."

"Gross. Okay, here goes."

Skye created a portal, and Crimson smoothed down the curves of her green dress before walking through, never turning back to look at Skye. She heard the portal close behind her with a *woosh*. Nerves swirled in her stomach.

"Shake it off, Crimson, this is what you're good at."

She pushed her breasts up, thankful Skye's dress was such a snug fit. Then she peeked around the corner. She'd had Skye drop her in a rarely used wing, directing her to exactly where it was. Portal magic still amazed her, and she wondered how mages didn't drop themselves off cliffs or into the ocean more often.

Head held high, she strolled through the castle, surprised that it was so empty. No servants bustling, no guards. She was hoping to find Stavin in the throne room. He seemed the arrogant type to hoard the throne. As she approached, she heard the screams of a woman.

So, he's busying himself. Perfect timing.

Two guards stood before the door. Someone had left it cracked enough that she could see the woman struggling.

"Halt!" one guard said.

She straightened her posture, making sure her breasts protruded more. "Do you know who I am?"

"Queen Crimson?" the other guard said, his eyes wide in shock.

"Exactly," she replied. "Now, I need to see your new king."

"He's busy."

"I think I can offer him a better time. He needs a woman who can keep up with his needs, and that scrawny thing is barely a woman."

She moved their swords and walked around them. Opening the doors further, she strutted in as Stavin was undoing his pants. He had the girl pinned below him, and she was struggling to free herself. It was a disgusting sight, and if she hadn't come with a purpose, Crimson would have taken a sword from the guards and plunged it into Stavin's spine. As it was, she needed him alive for now.

"Oh my, is this what you have to resort to for sex?"

He stopped his abuse and turned to stare at her. His expression was that of a man ready to kill until it morphed to surprise, his jaw dropping.

"How..." He stood, his hard-on prominent, and her eyes lingered on it before slowly moving to meet his. "You're dead."

"Go," she told the girl who scurried away quickly.

Sauntering up to Stavin, she closed his mouth, her finger running along his bottom lip.

"Far from it. The Death God favored me and brought me back. It looks like just in time. Why is a powerful man like you forcing a scrawny girl like that?" She brushed her fingers down his arm, then along the tent in his pants. "You need a real woman. How many times did you watch me take other men?" He swallowed. She reached up and bit his lower lip, running her tongue along it. "Did you enjoy watching?"

"What do you want, Crimson? This is my kingdom now."

She wrapped her hand around his erection, stroking it tightly. "I want to give you a woman who can rule by your side and in your bed. Those others can't keep up with you, you're too much of a man—"

He pushed her hand away and sat on the throne. "The kingdom is mine."

Full of bravado like he'd always been, but she knew this would be easy. Stavin had wanted her for years, had watched her hungrily as she'd taken men, his bulge always prominent. She walked to him, letting her hips move erotically with each step. Positioning herself over him, she straddled him, feeling the length in his pants reach for her.

"You were always my fiercest warrior. You've proven yourself, taken my kingdom, freed me—"

"I took this kingdom back for me, and I certainly didn't mean to free you."

"The Death God wants me back on my throne, Stavin." She moved her lips across his face, then licked his lower lip, biting at it as she drew away. "I'm proposing we form an alliance. I know how to rule. I was born for it as much as I was born to please men. You were born to fight, as much as you were to take women. Together..." She pulled her dress over her head, letting his eyes peruse her body. "Together we can bring this world to its knees."

"I'm already doing that," he replied, letting his fingers drift across her breasts.

"No, you're meeting resistance. I don't meet resistance, ever." She worked the buttons from his pants and guided him out.

It was working. She saw his resolve wavering.

"Have you ever experienced a woman who truly wanted you? You can have me in your bed and by your side."

"So you can slit my throat?"

She lifted her hips and brought him into her, seeing the change as she slowly moved her body, further enveloping him. He grunted and grabbed her hips roughly.

"Power and sex like you've never had, isn't it worth the chance?" she asked, leaning closer and kissing him.

His resolve broke, like it always did in men, and he reached his hands into her hair, pulling it.

"I'm going to fuck you like you've never been fucked," he growled.

She had to bite back a laugh. He had no idea. This brute of a man who thought he was some sort of god. She would stroke his ego, knowing she'd once had a true god and that Stavin came nowhere close.

"Hmm, I bet you will. I hear you like it rough." She increased her hip motion as his mouth found her breast, tugging at her nipple with his teeth.

Working his shirt off, she rode him until he came, quickly, just as she'd suspected he would. Satisfied, he shoved her back, but by no means was she finished. Her intention was to bring him to his knees.

"So, you are as good as they say," she lied, moving to her knees. "Time to show you I'm as good as they say."

She grasped his deflating manhood and wrapped her hand around it. He groaned as her strokes sent his erection slowly rising again. This was her power and she reveled in how good it felt to be using it again. Lowering her mouth around him, she worked her magic until he came once more, with a grunt that had him grabbing the arms of the throne. When he was finished, she slid her hands up his chest. Years of training had left him defined and sculpted like she preferred.

Kissing him, she dropped a hand to his length and began gently tugging. She needed to show him that she was worth keeping in his bed, and she was certain no woman had ever worked him the way she was.

"So, you really are insatiable," he said with a sly grin.

"You watched me enough to know that's true. Do you want me to stop?"

She kissed him, stroking him until he was firm again. He yanked her head back, then pushed her away, rising from the throne. He was trying to assert his dominance, and she would let him. Some men enjoyed it when she was the dominant one, others needed their egos pampered. Stavin was one of those men. He wanted to be in charge, and she would let him believe he was while she manipulated him without his even knowing it. She gave him a coy smile as he reached her and flipped her over, slamming her knees against the floor before raising her hips and penetrating her with an intense thrust.

"I think I will accept your offer, Crimson." His hands squeezed her waist. He was trying to hurt her, but she welcomed pain and so she turned it on him. This was child's play compared to what she'd experienced in the past.

Throwing her head back, she moaned. "I like it rough. Take me harder."

She heard the intake of his breath, the increase in his heartrate. They were the words every man like Stavin wanted to hear. He pounded against her until he filled her once more. *Not even time to enjoy it,* she thought as he slipped out of her.

Turning, she licked him clean before she rose, scooped up her dress, and walked past him, reveling in his confused look. He'd thought he'd taken control, but he hadn't.

"You'll find me in your bed when you're ready," she said. "And make sure you're ready, because I'm just warming up."

With dress in hand, she walked through the throne room doors, proudly walking toward her wing, taking in the stares. There were few who didn't recognize her with her uninhibited strut and fiery red hair. She was back and she would show this fool what real power was.

As she drew closer to her wing, the guards were fewer, until she was finally alone. It gave her a moment to relax, but not long. She'd need to stay vigilant. Stavin had been in her service long enough to know her ways. He would likely continue to bend as her body distracted him, but it wouldn't do to take any chances. He could easily kill her before she could convince him to withdraw his troops and bring the true threat home. Bormick. A shiver went through her. Stavin was child's play compared to what she'd heard of the man. He was unpredictable, and she prayed the rumors of his appetite for women were true, otherwise she might be dead the moment he returned.

"My queen, my queen!" she heard behind her. The interruption to her quiet annoyed her but she turned to the voice to determine the source.

Hentrom, her former advisor, came running up to her. "You're back! Talk is echoing through the castle. My lady, it is so good to see you."

She evaluated him. "To whom do your loyalties lie, Hentrom?"

He drew closer and whispered, "To you, my queen."

She turned his head, noting the scar that now lined his cheek.

"I had to prove myself worthy to keep my head."

She brushed her finger along the fresh bruises under his eyes. "And this?"

"Comes with Stavin's mood."

"Hmm." She despised abuse. She found pleasure a much easier method of getting what she wanted. Any deaths were swift and merciful. It irritated her that Stavin was abusing her servants and she clenched her fists in anger that she hadn't been here to stop it. She wondered how many women he'd raped, how many people he'd tortured and killed. If she didn't need to lure Bormick back, she'd kill Stavin now. The risk was too high, however, and patience was required. She'd make him pay when the time came.

"Come, you can talk to me as I see if anything still stands in my quarters."

"You won't be happy, my lady."

"I'm certain I won't. Tell me, Hentrom, are there any still loyal to me?"

"Yes," he responded in a hushed tone. "Many of us remain."

She opened the door to her quarters, finding it in disarray. Dried evidence that someone had satisfied himself in her bed was atop her sheets, and splattered bloodstains marred the floor. Dresses lay scattered from the bottom of her wardrobe, torn and crumpled. Toppled furniture accented the disrespect to her former status, and she saw no sign of the jewels that had once adorned her body. Clenching her hands, she held back the urge to turn back around and gut Stavin where he stood.

"We kept it for you, just as it had been the day you disappeared. The young king allowed it. He was good to us. It is a pity he went so quickly...and suspiciously."

She eyed him, raising a brow. So, she wasn't the only one suspicious of the boy's death.

"Stavin made his mark here right after he took the throne. He raped and killed two of the servant girls, favorites of your cousin. He refused to let anyone in here other than to remove the bodies."

She ran her fingers over the dried blood. "And Bormick?"

"Stays away mostly. He keeps to himself when he is here unless he's sharing a woman with Stavin or taking one of his own. He's a brute, but Stavin is far worse."

"I suspect Bormick saves his brutality for the battlefield," she mused. "Where are Stavin's quarters?"

"Your father's, my queen."

"Of course." She walked to the wardrobe, finding a few dresses that were still intact.

"Hentrom, I want you to have a bath drawn for me. Then I want you to be my eyes and ears. Find those loyal to me, weed out the bad seeds. Keep tally. When I take my kingdom back, they will all die."

"And Stavin and Bormick?"

She traced her fingers along his scar. "I think I'll keep them alive for you to have a bit of fun with before I kill the usurpers."

There was a glint in his eyes. "That would be most enjoyable, my queen."

She knew Hentrom preferred his own sex. It was one of the reasons she favored him. She'd known him since her earlier days, finding him fascinating, kind, but as deviant as she. He'd taught her his ways, and she'd found certain men enjoyed things out of the norm. She'd even shared a few men with him.

She'd let Stavin have a taste of his own medicine and maybe

she'd even watch. She took in the bed and the bloodstained floor again. Yes, he would pay for hurting her servants, her people, and for assuming he was worthy enough to sit on her throne.

A TUB WAS BROUGHT IN, and Crimson took the time to let her mind wander to Pete. She'd closed herself off from thoughts of him, knowing it hurt too much, knowing she wouldn't be able to seduce Stavin with Pete on her mind.

She suddenly missed everything about him—his touch, his body, his eyes, his lips. She ached for him like she never had for a man. Her mind drifted to their last night together, the way her body had responded to his. That sensation lingered in her stomach, then between her legs. She let her hand drape across her breasts, her nipples hardening. The tingle in her body grew. Reaching her other hand down, she touched her wetness, knowing she should wait, and save it to manipulate Stavin, but the need was too great.

She closed her eyes, imagining her hands were Pete's and let her fingers mimic his motion. With her other hand, she gently caressed her breasts until, in one overwhelming rush, her orgasm washed through her. She tightened her legs around her hand as the waves battered her, tears coming from her eyes.

The tears continued to flow as her heart rate calmed. Leaning her head back, she thought about the significance of the tears that now layered her face. She'd never cried over a man before, but here she was doing just that. Something about Pete caused her to be so unlike herself, so out of character that it left her confounded. No man had ever made her this out of sorts.

"Pull yourself together, Crimson," she told herself.

She had to put thoughts of him aside or she'd break. She wasn't like Skye. She couldn't think of Pete while Stavin was in her. It hurt too much. How did Skye do it? She thought about how she'd separated Skye and Mark. Guilt stabbed at her. Shaking her head, she stepped from the tub, closing her eyes and centering herself. There was no time for guilt, no time for melancholy. She had a small window to convince Stavin to pull his men back, then to convince Bormick to trust her. Otherwise, she would lose everything she was fighting for, including Pete.

PETE

Pete sat in the grove, flipping through the book Courtney had brought him. He'd gone through it repeatedly, searching for anything to help him out of this situation. She'd been unable to find anything and so had he. There was nothing. There was only mention of the word "Guardian" once or twice, but never with enough context. His family had lost the original stories of their past, and with them, the true reason for their existence here. The story behind the forest. There was more to it, more the Death God hadn't mentioned. Pete had a feeling that whatever knowledge his family had neglected to pass down, was his key to escaping this curse.

Cursed. That's what he was now. Cursed for falling in love with Crimson, given her punishment so that she could walk free. The thought made his situation seem better, knowing she was free, that she was safe. But there was no way to know if she really was safe. Pete didn't know what she'd returned to or where the Death God had sent her. He may have dropped her in the middle of the rebellion, a situation that would ensure her death. He had to think the Death God had been more strategic, and he prayed she'd been sent to Skye.

It had been Skye who had pleaded her case, after all. Even though that was the preferrable scenario, her safety wasn't guaranteed there either. She'd be in the presence of a man who held a grudge, one who wanted her dead. No matter which way he imagined, the lack of certainty was just as torturous as being trapped as Keeper.

Running his hands through his hair, he stared at the page before him, trying to push the thoughts from his mind. It did him no good to dwell on it. If he couldn't find a way out of his mess, it wouldn't matter what Crimson's fate had been. The thought only made the situation seem more dire. No longer able to focus on the page, his eyes drifted, the words simply a meaningless babble that provided no answers and, therefore, did little to take his mind from Crimson.

Closing the book, he stared at the tree across from him. The black of the trunk was stretching further, closer to overtaking the white. Its eventual fate was evident. The higher the ebony of a tree stretched, the louder the soul wailed. The cry of the trees was a constant murmur in his ears, never ceasing until he put them all to sleep. It was enough to drive him mad.

To calm his mind, he pictured Crimson. It wasn't the first time. He'd pictured her countless times. God, how he missed her. He didn't completely understand how that was possible when he'd only known her for a week or so, but he did, painfully. He wanted to hold her again, to touch her, to feel her below him. He craved her.

Standing, he stretched, his fresh erection reminding him that he couldn't think of her without a reaction. He leaned his forehead against the closest tree, this one gladly succumbing to the ebony of its trunk. He tried to clear his head, but each time, Crimson's body filled it, leaving his erection throbbing.

"Damn," he mumbled, gripping it.

With an eternity of loneliness facing him, Pete slipped his hand in and encased it, feeling the heat from it.

Guess I'd best get used to doing it myself again, he thought, stroking himself as he let his mind fill with Crimson.

He unzipped his pants and gripped his length, thinking of her mouth around him. With the thought, the need for release grew. He closed his eyes, letting his hand and imagination provide him satisfaction. As he was nearing his breaking point, he felt a sudden pressure accompany his hand. The sensation felt like another hand had joined his, and he noticed the same feeling drift across his chest. It wasn't a true touch, but something like one. It was enough to encourage his arousal even with his uncertainty about what was causing the sensations. He opened his eyes to see the mist of a female shaped soul before him. The sight would have freaked him out but for the stimulation she was giving his dick as her motion continued.

He removed his hand and leaned it against her tree, letting the mist-like hand assume his strokes from him. The pressure-like feel spread to the rest of his body, giving the impression that multiple women were touching him. He'd never felt anything so intense, and he dug his fingers into the bark. His climax was cresting so fast that it was all he could do to remain standing.

"Good God," he groaned.

His head fell back, and he arched further into the touch. The sensations continued until he was so turned on that the orgasm hit him hard, his seed spilling from him as he gripped the tree.

Catching his breath, he relaxed, the mist-like specter disappearing, the pressure of the hands fading.

"What the hell?" he muttered, pulling his zipper back up and backing away.

He ran his hand over his face. "I guess there are some perks to being stuck here. Wow, anytime you ladies feel the urge to do that, help yourself. Guys, hands off."

There was a strange cry like a laugh that filled the space, and he shook his head, not wanting to know the reason for it. The sound had been distinctly male, resting uncomfortably on his ears and in his mind. He shook it off, pulled himself together, and started his never-ending walk through the spirits.

Clearing his mind, he tried to focus on his duties. The release had been a nice distraction, but he needed to calm the trees, not fraternize with them.

Jesus, Pete. What is wrong with you? Letting a spirit jerk you off? That's a new low, he scolded himself half-heartedly, knowing he'd likely continue having lows with a lifetime of the grove in front of him.

He rolled his neck and turned back to his work. Being Keeper was a dull job, monotonous with no benefits unless he counted the spirit hands. He threw a look back at the tree and shook his head. Even if the occasional hand job were a benefit, he would have preferred scraping wallpaper to this. Anything would be preferable to walking a forest alone for eternity.

Only a few days had passed, but he already felt the weight of the emptiness, the loneliness that permeated the grove. He didn't know how Crimson had done this for a decade. When the Death God had made him Keeper, an awareness of the few others who had held this duty filled him. There had been others whose imprisonment here had been longer than he could fathom. Other sentences that made Crimson's time here seem like a small drop in an endless ocean of Keeper history.

There were two distinct connections. The first one had a sense of brutality to it, as if his death and even his time as Keeper had been fraught with violence. The next one's memories held a melancholy that was palpable even through the memory. The feeling was so permeating, Pete avoided touching his memories, but there was a sensation when he reached for them that was familiar. It was the same he'd had when he first saw Skye.

Crimson had told him how Skye's soul had been trapped here, and he thought it possible that this Keeper had been the one to free her. Pete couldn't access their thoughts, just the feelings that passed through them at certain times, like an emotional imprint.

This one's final moments had been peaceful, accepting. Pete paused, closing his eyes to see if he could feel more.

He touched the memory cautiously, feeling the warmth of the light, the knowledge of the moment the Keeper had been released from the grove. It had been a sacrifice and Pete knew from his Keeper knowledge that sacrificing for a soul's freedom was punished by an eternity of suffering in the Shadow Realm. He'd given himself to that retribution willingly. Suffering in exchange for something important. Possibly even someone important. Someone like Skye.

At the thought, the sensation grew, and he wondered at it. Perhaps it had been confirmation that he was right. He didn't know Skye, but he'd felt her power, seen her beauty, could tell without a doubt that she was special. Crimson had said Eliana, who Pete could only surmise was a goddess, had traveled with Skye's husband to free her soul. He couldn't fathom why she was special enough for a goddess to save or even a Keeper to sacrifice for. Then again, a god had coveted her so that he'd stolen her, and continued to steal her away for days every year to feast on her body. From the brief time he'd been in her presence, Pete could see why. She had a body to envy Crimson's. She wasn't as curvy, but her dress had highlighted the perfect curves she did own. The ones he would not have passed up if he'd come across her before he'd met Crimson.

He had a feeling Crimson was just as unique—the Death God had taken her as well. Both women had intimate dealings with a god. The thought was surreal and puzzling.

There were so many questions with answers that lie beyond the grove and in a world Pete didn't know. A world of gods and goddesses, of magic, of women whose beauty surpassed any he'd known. He wanted answers to those questions, wanted to know the history of their world, his world, to learn why Skye was favored by a god and goddess. He wasn't certain why he needed to know more about her, but after touching the Keeper's memory; he was certain he needed to.

First, he needed to find a way to free himself of this prison and find Crimson. Only when he had Crimson in his arms again, could he begin seeking answers.

CRIMSON

It had been six days, and, in that time, Crimson had given herself to Stavin and his greedy hands, convincing him that Bormick and his troops needed to return. It had taken some persuasion, but he'd finally decided to pull them home, claiming if she could seduce him, then seducing Theodore without a prolonged, bloody battle would be best.

"Save the troops for the Mage Warrior," he'd said and Crimson saw then that the greedy bastard was vying to rule every kingdom, a feat even she would never have dared on her own. He was clearly delusional.

While she'd forced herself to enjoy having sex with him, she'd found that he'd embraced the idea of her giving herself freely to him. Admitting to her that only whores had ever done so. She'd bit back the retort that they were paid and not freely giving their bodies but had refrained. He wasn't bad in bed, but he wasn't the best.

She sauntered through the halls, wearing a loose red dress that accentuated her breasts and hips. Her red hair had turned a richer shade during her time as Keeper and had remained that way upon her return. She missed the vibrant red but there was something empowering about the new shade, a visual symbol that she'd survived the Death God's punishment and she should be feared.

She pulled the dress down to enhance her cleavage, knowing it wouldn't be on long but still wanting the illusion of seduction present when she reached Stavin.

The door to the meeting room was cracked, and she heard voices. Curious, she drew closer and listened.

"You've pulled us back because some whore convinced you it made sense? Are you an idiot, Stavin?"

"She's quite convincing, Bormick, and her alternative makes sense."

"Convincing while your dick was in her ass?"

There was a loud bang, and she surmised that he'd pounded his hand against the table. This was the man in charge, the one she had her sights on.

"I didn't leave you to rule so you could fuck it up!"

"I think you need to get laid, Bormick. You're much too uptight."

"How about we change positions, and you can let me know how uptight you are after weeks of raiding villages and gaining land?"

Making sure both doors to the room flew open in a flourishing statement of her presence, she walked in, taking in the infamous thief. He was broader and taller than Stavin, and pure muscle. Physical power rolled from him in an aura that seemed to surround him.

He looked up from Stavin, his blue eyes narrowing as they perused her body. She saw the hunger there, but also the fight. This one would be harder to tame. His eyes lingered on her chest before meeting hers. Against the dirty blonde hair, they seemed almost the color of the sky on a sunny day.

"I prefer the term seductress over whore. It rolls off my tongue easier."

He smirked. "So, this is the infamous Crimson."

"And you are the notorious Bormick," she returned as she drew close, walking her fingers up his strong forearm, the one that currently sat upon the handle of his sword.

"I'm not a fool like my friend. Your temptations won't work on me."

"No? That's a shame," she whispered, letting her fingers drift across his chest. "Because you look like you'll be worth every moan that escapes my lips."

She saw the flicker of desire and knew it was only a matter of time, but it wouldn't be this easy. Her words held truth. He did have the appearance of someone who was well worth the time it would take to seduce him. She wondered at how many times he would bring her to ecstasy. After Mark and Pete, she'd found it was something that happened more frequently. Stavin wasn't up to par with either of them, but she'd still had her share of climaxes since she'd been here. Bormick looked like one who would send her toppling like Pete did.

"Why did you convince him to draw my troops back?"

"Your troops? Technically, they're my troops and I'm sharing them with him."

He grabbed her arm but instead of the fear and cry he expected, she licked her lips and let out a sigh, a reaction she hadn't feigned. "You like it rough."

"You have no idea how rough, woman. This kingdom is no longer yours. You lost it the day you disappeared. Taken by the Death God, they said. So why are you suddenly back and how?"

"The Death God favors me. I did my time. I gave him enough pleasure to satisfy him for eons and he returned me to my kingdom."

He pulled her closer, and she could smell the mix of sweat and cedar that lingered on him. "You fucked the Death God?"

"I've been in his bed for many years. It's amazing, the things you can learn to please a man when a god is teaching you."

The flame of need behind his eyes and the quick inhale of his breath, told her she'd hit her mark. No man could resist the temptation to perform better than a god. Their egos wouldn't allow it.

Letting go of her arm, he asked, "What do you want, Crimson?"

She turned from him and made her way to Stavin, letting her dress fall before she climbed atop the table where he sat, "Right now, I want to be pleasured." She sat on the edge and laid down before Stavin, making sure her hair spread behind her as part of her seduction. Resting her feet on the tabletop she widened her legs for him. Stavin grabbed them and yanked her forward. "Then I want to sit beside the man who can hand me the world."

Her eyes never left Bormick's and as Stavin's mouth met her skin, she saw him break.

"Everyone out!" he bellowed to the others in the room to which she'd paid no heed.

Stavin's tongue licked at her in a messy way. His talent did not lie with his mouth, but her goal had been to enrapture Bormick, and it had worked.

She brought her hands to her breasts, rubbing them as Stavin wrapped his hands around her thighs, digging further into her with his tongue. Bormick walked over to where she lay, close to the table's edge. She arched her back as Stavin sucked on her clit. Her fingers teased her nipples to hurry along her climax, and she let out a tantalizing moan. Heavy with lust, Bormick's eyes watched her. He pushed her hands away, and let his fingers graze her breasts before squeezing them tight. His hands were large and rough, and his touch elicited an uninhibited groan from her.

Lowering his face to hers, he whispered, "I know what you're doing."

She moved her head, meeting his lips. Slipping her tongue over them, she bit his lower lip. "And are you turning me down, or do you want to play?"

He squeezed her breast harder. Stavin pushed his fingers into her at the same time and both actions forced a cry from her. Her hand reached to Bormick's length and worked it free from his pants, her eyes never leaving his as she wrapped her hands around it. She gripped it tightly, knowing this man did not want gentle caresses.

"I take it you want to play," she answered for him.

He straightened his posture but didn't move away, so she turned her head, letting her tongue reach out to him until he brought himself close enough to fill her mouth. As Stavin continued to play, so did she. Bormick's hand painfully pinched her nipple, sending waves of arousal and erotic pain through her. He thrust into her mouth, holding her head and she took him, hearing his reaction as she reached his hilt soundlessly. As his fingers wrapped tighter around her hair, she let her tongue glide back up his shaft before he plunged her head back down. The aggression behind his moves was one that met her own and it sent her need for release cresting.

Focused solely on him, she forgot about Stavin. The intensity of Bormick's blue eyes was enough to bring her to climax. The sensation built, and as she felt him grow thicker, his body thrust deeper into her mouth. His hand pushed her head further into him, and she broke, her orgasm ripping through her, then drowning her. A cry escaped her as he spilled into her mouth. Through the tremors, he continued his release until after one final thrust, he pulled away, surprisingly still erect.

Bormick's eyes studied her, and she heard Stavin unbutton his pants.

"My turn," he growled.

"No," Bormick commanded.

"No? I'm about to come in my pants. I get her."

"Jerk yourself off. I want to bury myself inside of her."

"What the fuck, Bormick?"

But Bormick ignored him. He shoved Stavin out of the way

and yanked her closer, penetrating her with a loud grunt. Currents crashed through her at the connection, her body still quaking slightly from her last orgasm. He was powerful, thrusting with a force that sent the storm within her threatening to erupt. She sat up, pressing her breasts against him and relishing the way his strength felt against her chest. Wrapping her legs around him, she pulled him closer, sending him deeper. There was something about this man that called to that feral part of her, and she wanted more of him. She kissed him and his tongue forced its way into her mouth, demanding more from her, which she readily gave.

She heard Stavin pumping himself as Bormick steadily drove into her. A part of her wished he'd left the room, giving her Bormick to herself, and she wondered briefly about the feeling. But she needed to appease them both for her plan to work. Lying back, she reached to Stavin, her hand encasing his engorged length and taking over for him. He moaned as she worked him faster until finally, he released over her stomach. Bormick's hands tightened around her waist as he ignored Stavin, filling her with his final few pushes.

She let go of Stavin, then ran her fingers over her stomach. Bringing them to her mouth, she licked each one clean, making sure to keep her eyes on Bormick. She saw the excitement there, the curiosity he had about her. When he pulled free of her, she sat up quickly, going on all fours. She crawled to him, catlike, and took him in her mouth, licking him with every bit of seduction she could muster. She knew it was the final act to seal his addiction to her.

"Gods, woman."

"I told you," Stavin said.

Bormick pulled her head back to him as she went to move away. His fingers were wrapped tight in her hair, forcing her mouth to remain on him. He wanted more, and she'd give it to him.

"Leave us, Stavin."

"What? We're sharing."

"We were sharing. Go, you can share her later."

Stavin grumbled as Bormick removed his shirt, pulling himself from her mouth.

"Clean yourself," he said, throwing the shirt to her as Stavin closed the doors. She couldn't help but take in the defined chest, the large muscles that spoke of the warrior he was.

She started to sit, but he stopped her, his eyes still ravenous. Walking around her, he climbed the table, pulling her hips back roughly and slamming into her. She gasped at the force, then relaxed into his rhythm. He had an appetite she could appreciate, one that rivaled the Death God's. Something about him reminded her of Pete, and she let herself hold that thought as he leaned over and touched her breasts. Her desire rose again, and he pushed her shoulders down. Raising her hips further, he drove deeper into her. The further he went, the harder his thrusts, the more aroused she became until it consumed her. His fingers squeezed her ass, and she dug her nails into the table as the waves of pleasure crushed her.

Within the waves he came, his actions furious and hard, which only accentuated her own climax, taking it over the expanse and leaving her breathless.

Finally, he stilled, pumping into her one final time with a ferocious grunt before pulling away. His hands caressed her ass before he climbed from the table. As she turned over, still catching her breath, he ran his hand up her body, lingering on her breast before saying, "You are a dangerous woman."

She smiled and flipped to her stomach, drawing his hips closer and taking him into her mouth once more, slowly letting her tongue clean the taste of her from him.

"I know," she said when she was finished.

He glared at her, tucking his reawakening length back into his pants where it bulged.

"I like dangerous, but I don't trust it."

She rose from the table and pressed her body against his chest. He was strong and solid, once again reminding her of Pete. This man was dangerous to her. She'd never love him, but his very essence was power and that was something she craved. Yes, she craved this man, and that was very dangerous.

"You're the one who's really in charge, aren't you?"

There was a glint in his eyes.

"Stavin is just a figurehead with you dictating his moves."

"And now it would seem I have competition. And I don't like competition."

"Why do we have to compete? We both want the same thing."

He tipped her chin up. "Do we? Why do I feel like you're going to be my downfall?"

Because I will be, she thought, although she was wondering how she could turn on this man now that she'd had him.

"Maybe you're my downfall," she replied, catching his finger in her mouth and letting her tongue slide the length of it.

He gave her a crooked grin. "Perhaps we'll take each other down."

"At least we'll have fun doing it."

"Yes, we will." He backed away from her and sat, propping his feet on the table. "Get dressed. You're a distraction like that."

"That's the point," she replied teasingly as she bent down slowly to retrieve her dress, hearing the hitch of his breath.

"Dangerous," he muttered.

She turned. "Are you sure you don't want more?"

"Oh, I want more, but I'll have to wait. You'll be sleeping in my bed tonight, so I guarantee I'll have more."

"Your bed?" she asked, slipping her dress back on. "How will Stavin feel about that?"

"I don't give a shit how he feels. He can sleep there too, for all I care. I don't mind sharing."

"I can tell," she said, sitting at the head of the table. "Do you share often?"

"Depends on who we're taking."

"You mean raping?"

He let out a loud laugh that echoed through the room.

"It's my right to take whomever I please, and however."

She raised her feet to prop on the table, letting her dress fall to expose her legs and the curve of her hips. His eyes lingered, need filling them.

"How long has it been since you've had a willing woman?" she asked, draping her fingers along her bare skin.

"Too long."

"Pity. It's so much better when they're willing."

He eyed her. "Don't judge me for my cravings. You have quite a reputation, Crimson."

"I bring men pleasure. There's nothing wrong with that."

He let out another laugh. "Pleasure you force on them, manipulating them."

"Not every man. Some take a little persuasion, but others take the pleasure willingly."

"Before you execute them, taking what you can from them, just as I do with women. You and I are the same, Crimson."

"Every man I take comes for me. Do your women do that?"

He narrowed his eyes. "No man could resist that mouth of yours, even the strongest."

She rose from the table and straddled him. "Even you, the notorious Bormick?"

His erection pressed against her, and his hands reached to her hips, pulling her down further. He was as insatiable as she was, and she found it intoxicating that he matched her sexual drive. "Even me. You like playing with fire, Crimson."

"Don't you like the fire?"

That glint showed in his eyes again. "It's what I live for. Now tell me why you brought me back, other than to fulfill my needs, and how you intend to bring me Theodore's head."

She pressed against him, her lips finding his mouth, and let her tongue reach for his. His hands tightened on her hips, pushing her deeper against his length.

"With that dangerous mouth of mine," she replied, letting her tongue drag along his bottom lip. "Theodore is weak. He does anything I tell him for a taste of my body."

"So, you've had the king of Chenthom?"

"Many times. He's a puppet like Stavin."

"And do you like fucking him?"

"No, I prefer my men strong and forceful."

"Mmm, I bet you do."

His fingers moved along the material covering her breasts, toying with her nipples below, which hardened at his touch.

"And how will that solve my dilemma? I look weak pulling my men back." He pinched her nipple, her breath escaping. "I don't like looking weak. In fact, I had every intention of killing you when you walked into this room." He pushed the material down, kneading her breast and bringing it to his mouth where his tongue worked her nipple, biting and sucking. Currents ran in waves through her body, and she clutched his shoulders. He freed her other breast, wrapping his hand around it, tormenting the nipple so that the fire spread through her. She gripped his hair and tilted her head back, her body lurching. Every part of her was on fire and she pressed further into his arousal, rocking back and forth until his hand stopped her motion.

He sucked hard, eliciting a cry from her before his hand reached between her legs to her clit. He rubbed its swollenness with his thumb, two of his fingers reaching into her as she tried to catch her breath. Her body was screaming for release.

"You're so wet," he whispered against her breasts, his breath stimulating her even more.

Just as she thought she could take it no more, he removed his hand, and unbuttoned his pants. In one quick move, he picked her hips up and entered her with a thrust that sent her body into a frenzy. He gripped her hips, ramming himself deeper. His mouth sucked harder on her nipple until finally she broke. Her body shattered against him, and she released the loud moan imprisoned within her. She clung to him as it hit her over and over in waves that wouldn't stop. His hands still moved her pelvis, the feel of him inside of her threatening to tip her to madness.

He groaned as he continued to move inside her and the sound further tantalized her already sensitive body. His mouth brushed across her skin and sucked at her other nipple. Her body—still quivering from the last orgasm—was hit with a flood of overstimulation, but he didn't stop. As her climax built again, she took control of her hips, tilting and swinging them so his mouth pulled away with the force of the breath she'd loosened from him.

He tipped his head back as she turned the tables on him, her body still on fire. As if knowing, he brought both hands up, grasping her breasts and pinching at her nipples until they were so hard it ached. Her body lost control again, sending currents assailing her with the same force as he was now thrusting into her. He dropped his hands to squeeze her hips, their bodies banging together in a storm of need until she felt his release spill into her. He pulled her down hard, his final thrusts met with a grumble that reverberated through his chest.

Dropping her head against his chest, she was left wondering why this man had such an effect on her. The same effect Pete had. They sat there breathless for a moment until he pushed her away, wiping the sweat from his brow.

"Like I said, dangerous," he said, standing and fixing his pants. "When you seduce Theodore, how will you bring me his kingdom?" His demeanor had changed, the ruthless thief and killer returning.

"I'll slice his throat while he's in the throes of ecstasy."

He let out a wicked laugh. "Yes, you and I are very much the same." He ambled toward the doors. "Make sure you're in my bed tonight. Oh, and Crimson, do not leave this castle."

She raised an eyebrow at the command, but he'd walked through the doors before she could respond, leaving her to wonder how she had lost the upper hand and why she wanted this man so desperately.

PETE

So, these trees are filled with spirits?" Bo asked, looking around the grove.

He went to touch one, but Pete stopped him. "You don't want to do that. Trust me, they will bite."

Bo jerked his hand back as Pete grabbed one of the beers they'd brought him and half of the sandwich Courtney had made. He sat, and they joined him, their eyes still wide as they looked around. It had been another few days, and each night, Courtney had met him in the forest to visit. This wasn't the first time he'd brought her here. It was, however, the first time Bo had come to see him.

The trees had wailed incessantly as they'd approached, but he'd calmed them, assuring them that it would be all right. In the days of his imprisonment here, he'd come to understand them, reading the differences, noting which ones were kind, lost souls and which had been deserving of their fates. He steered clear of the latter but had made certain they understood he was the alpha.

Somehow, it had come naturally to him. There was some inherent knowledge that came as Keeper and another more primal knowledge that he couldn't place.

He took a swig of his beer. There was really no need for food or drink, something kept him fed and clean. He suspected it had something to do with his sleep, but had yet to figure it out.

"We found something," Courtney said, sitting across from him, her eyes still taking in the trees like she'd done each time she'd been here. Bo sat next to her, grabbing a beer and chugging quickly.

Pete leaned in. "What did you find?"

"Something big. We were going through Dad's stuff in the basement, not finding anything, when Bo noticed the stone in one of the walls wasn't even."

Pete glanced at Bo, who had finished his beer. "It wasn't flush in one spot," he said, wiping his hand across his mouth.

"What was it?"

"Another room," Courtney answered. "We made a bit of a mess down there, sorry. But there was a room hidden behind the wall." She leaned forward, excitement lighting her eyes. "That's where the good stuff was, Pete. Old writings, so old we were afraid to move them from the room."

Pete's head spun. The family had walled off a room of secrets.

"What did you find?"

"Who we are. What the Guardians are. Pete, we were royalty. There were three brothers, one remained king, the other two were punished by"—she dropped her voice to a whisper—"the Death God. One punished with death, the other with guarding the Forest of Souls until he could find his way home."

"Home? Where Crimson is?"

"I don't know. They just called it home. There was a kingdom mentioned. Bo, what was it again?"

Bo was quiet, his eyes looking far off for a moment. "Digremile. That's what it was."

"Yes, Digremile. The Death God sent our ancestor here to repay some debt and to remain here until one of us satisfied that debt."

"Debt? What debt?" he asked.

"I don't know. Nothing mentioned more than that, but it said something cool. We were warriors, Pete. Warriors. Fierce ones from what I could tell."

"Warriors?"

"Yeah, like with swords and brute force and all that. Some had magic even."

"So, the Death God sent us here to pay some debt and guard the forest. Why didn't anyone tell us this?"

"I don't know. That room had been closed off a long time. I doubt even Dad knew about it. Honestly, generations of our family may not have known about it."

"Your history lost as each generation passed," Bo added.

Pete sat back, contemplating all of it. Warriors? Magic? Royalty? Nothing about this seemed like anything more than a fantasy story, except he was living it.

"There was so much in there, Pete. About kingdoms, magic, gods. There were six kingdoms. Four held magic. Our kingdom formed an alliance with one of the four. We protected it against the two kingdoms who were powerless, the ones with no connection to the magic."

"This other kingdom was tied with ours?'

"Bonded to it. Some blood bonding that tied our royal line to their royal line but only in the second and third brother, not from our king."

"What?" Pete was confused.

"So, the king had three sons. The first was crowned, the second and third were bound to the royal family of the other kingdom and each generation after. Something must have gone wrong, and the Death God sent the second son here then murdered the third."

"Holy shit," Pete muttered. "What did our family do?"

"No idea, but whatever it was, it was bad."

Pete thought about what Courtney had told him. So, their

family had pissed the Death God off. It seemed an odd thing to say, but then again everything he'd just learned confounded him. The fact that his family had known and hidden the history from them was astonishing. He thought back to everything Crimson had told him about her world. "What was the name of the kingdom we were to protect?"

"Not sure if I'm saying it right but, Apendia," Bo answered.

It couldn't be. Pete's heart twisted as the name echoed through his mind.

"I need to see those pages—all of them," he demanded.

"They're old—"

"Now, Courtney!" he snapped, rising.

"Hey, don't be a dick." Bo stood and glared at Pete.

"I need those pages now."

"I'll get them, but you calm your ass down, Pete. If not, I won't let her return."

He didn't give Pete time for a reply. Instead, he turned his flashlight on and jogged away. Bo had always been a runner, long and lean in comparison to Pete's larger, muscular frame.

"Sit, Pete, please," Courtney said.

He sighed and sat, taking a long gulp of his beer.

"What's going through your mind?"

He took a moment to collect his thoughts, not sure if he wanted to say the words aloud. "That kingdom, Apendia...it's Crimson's kingdom."

She gaped at him.

"She told me... God, that's why I'm so drawn to her, why I can't get her out of my mind. We're tied by some ancient agreement."

"Holy shit, Pete, that's not possible. After all these centuries?"

"Likely more. They live a long time. There's so much about all this that seems impossible, yet here we are."

"Here we are."

They sat in silence, contemplating the chance meeting that no longer felt like chance until Bo returned. He tossed the pages at Pete. "There. I think it's best if we leave until you settle down."

"Bo, I'm sorry—"

"Just take the time. We'll be back tomorrow, but if you talk to her like that again, you're on your own."

"Bo—" Courtney started to object.

"No, Court. He's gone ten years, then gets his ass in this mess because he can't keep his dick in his pants and now he's taking it out on you."

"I wasn't—"

Bo raised his hand to silence him.

"Come on, Court."

He took her hand and pulled her up. Pete could have defended himself, could have knocked Bo on his ass, but he remained where he was, knowing Bo was right.

"We'll be back tomorrow," Courtney said, kissing his head.

Pete watched them leave, feeling the loneliness of the grove return. Bo was being overprotective, but Pete didn't mind. He was good for Courtney and Pete knew no matter what happened to him, Bo would keep her safe.

Turning his attention to the pages, he went through the same facts they'd told him, finding little more. There was nothing else about Crimson's kingdom other than what Courtney and Bo had mentioned. He stared at the words "repay the debt." Raking his hands through his hair, he tried to contemplate what that debt was and what the payment would have been. He knew guarding the Keeper of the Lost Souls was part of it, but he had a feeling there was more to it.

He stood, tucking the pages under a rock near one of the trees. Walking through the grove, he replayed the words in his mind. He was missing something, but there was too much to unravel.

He stopped at one of the trees, his fingers tracing the lines of black that stretched higher on her. This was the tree with the frisky spirit. The lines rose higher than they had that last night. As if she sensed his presence, the mist-like hands found his skin, sending chills through him. Maybe the Guardian wasn't just for the Keeper. The first pages he'd found had mentioned protecting the forest. It was what his family had always done, keeping the house and forest generation to generation, ensuring no one would harm or discover it. Maybe the Keeper and the Guardian both played central parts. If so, he had to figure out what those parts were and how they connected to the souls. It seemed like more than simply guarding and keeping them contained. There was something more that his ancestors hadn't seen.

The ghostlike hands stroked the outside of his pants, but his mind remained on the blackness. It climbed to overtake the ivory in the trees, something drawing it forth. But maybe there was a way to coax it further, to encourage it to climb faster. He knew the ebony was the Shadow Realm claiming its soul, keeping it from the Upper Realm. Not all the trees had ebony that stretched as far, the white seeping down in streaks rather than the black rising up. He thought about the tree that Crimson had sent back to the Shadow Realm. The Keeper could decide a soul's fate as punishment for escaping, but the trees decided their fates in all other instances, stretching high to the Upper Realm for redemption.

The pressure grew against him so that he could no longer ignore it.

"You want to play?" he asked it.

The soul seemed to shudder, the pressure like a squeeze on his growing erection. He wondered if he really could coax the ebony or the ivory the same way his length was currently being coaxed. It was worth a try, and there was no downside to it that he could find. He closed his eyes, thinking of Crimson, her body against his. His hands undid his pants as the spirit hands played over his hair and chest. He pulled out his throbbing length, grasping it as he imagined Crimson's body around it.

The mist hands lowered as he tugged on it, feeling the warmth fill his groin. He felt her on his balls, caressing them, before pushing against his moving hand, forcing him away. This time the feel was as if he'd slid into her. He could almost feel the tightness, the way it encased him like a real woman would. He groaned, resting his head on the tree as the phantom woman plunged against him.

"Jesus Christ," he grunted, the sensation sending him toward the edge. He wanted Crimson so badly that he ached for her, and it seemed this spirit knew it. Maybe that's why it felt so real. His mind wanted it to be. The sensation disappeared, replaced with a mix of mouth and hand motions that almost knocked him over. He pressed both hands against her bark, watching as the skin on his dick moved with the mist. The realistic sensation intensified his approaching climax which hit him with a force he couldn't stop. His essence spilled over her trunk as he came, leaving him breathless.

He rested against the trunk, catching his breath as his body calmed. His eyes followed the trace of his essence as it soaked into the bark, the black claws climbing further up the trunk.

"You are a naughty girl, aren't you?"

She shivered in response. But sex didn't make a person subject to the torment of hell. That seemed ridiculous.

As ridiculous as having a tree spirit jerk you off? he chastised himself.

He was still catching his breath, slight tremors still rocking him when a force pulled him to the next tree. His back slammed hard against its bark, a firm hand holding him back, another gripping his softened length tight, tugging in an upward jerk that sent tremors rocking through him. The misty hand wrapped firmly, its movements demanding, driving down to his hilt, then back in commanding moves that left him weak in his knees. This tree knew what a man needed, just the right amount of pressure, when to release it, when to constrict it, which direction sent the waves of his last climax building ferociously within him. In the back of his mind, he knew it wasn't a feminine hand, but his climbing orgasm left him too overcome to fight back. The force hit him so hard as he climaxed that he clung to the tree with a death grip until the hands released him and he stumbled forward. He dropped to his knees with a moan, his tremors slowing.

After catching his breath, he managed to stand. Stepping back, he tucked his aching member away and wiped the sweat from his brow..

"I said I was off limits to you guys," he complained, receiving only a howl-like laugh, the black on its trunk climbing.

"You're the first one I send back," he muttered, feeling slightly violated but wondering why he'd enjoyed it so much.

He looked at the two trees, the black that lined them. Punishment for sex made no sense. Sex wasn't a bad deed, even if the second tree had crossed the line. The act wasn't something that should have sent them to hell...unless the soul had taken more than his fair share in his last life. The thought worsened that feeling of violation.

The soul did its strange laugh again.

"I hope you have a raging hard-on you can't satisfy," he grumbled.

The thought left him questioning if trees even had hard-ons. That one clearly had enjoyed himself, as had the female.

The mist escaped his tree and Pete felt the stretch from its prison, the pressure against its bounds as its spirit hands reached into the female tree, yanking out its mist-like essence. She took the shape of a woman as the other filled out to an insanely large man. He forced her down and began taking her from behind.

"What the hell?"

She struggled and as he forced her down, the ebony on his tree climbed higher, reaching almost to the limbs.

"So, you are a bad one, huh?"

He looked at the female as she fought him. The ebony

climbed on her tree as well, but that didn't make sense. She was defending herself.

The acts weren't the reason. Crimson had told him that demons had killed most of the souls in the Shadow Realm. They had never had a proper burial, some dying so abruptly they'd lost their way so that the Death God never gave his judgement. They remained in a limbo of sorts. Only a few of the souls in these trees had actually been judged and sentenced to this harsh existence. Most had never been judged, all trying to find their way to peace or punishment.

"Shh," he said to the struggling one, using his Keeper's voice.

She calmed, the struggle stopping. A whimper-like wail escaped her as the male spirit continued his assault.

Pete stepped closer to the male tree, putting his hand against it and feeling a stir at the female's suffering. He muttered the words he said to them all each night, but this time there was an undercurrent of power that mingled with his Keeper magic. In that moment, he saw clearly the acts, the violations, the sins committed in this soul's prior life.

The male spirit shrieked with a sound that echoed through the forest, something forcing him back, locking him in the tree. He struggled and the more he did, the further the ebony climbed. Pete saw then that his role wasn't about sending them to the Shadow Realm like Crimson had done to the one that had come after Pete. That had been the power of the Keeper. This was different. This step was judgement and sentencing given by the Guardian.

He closed his eyes, pressing against the tree with his magic, which aggravated it. The more it struggled, the more Pete felt the Shadow Realm claiming it. He didn't know how he recognized its presence, but it was a distinct oppressive sensation that called to a part deep within him.

The tree struggled and screamed until it went silent. Opening his eyes, Pete saw the tree was now completely black. There was no longer a sense that a soul existed within it. He stepped back and watched as the bark peeled away, disintegrating until nothing remained where it had stood. A layer of black ash now covered the ground around his feet.

He let out the breath he'd been holding, understanding his role now. He was a Guardian. Not only to the Keeper, but to the souls. He was meant to guide them, the Keeper to silence them, maintaining the grove. The Death God had sent the first Guardian here on the premise that he was to guard the grove, but that first Guardian had never understood the way home. The duty had passed from generation to generation, each Guardian seeing only the punishment, not the key to redemption that the Death God had given them. But perhaps they hadn't been meant to. The Death god had made an error in making Pete Keeper. Or perhaps it had been a calculated error. Guardians were not to enter the forest yet here he was, cursed to it. Perhaps that steadfast rule been handed down from the Death God to trick them, manipulate them into thinking there was no way home, no way to break their curse.

Crimson had mentioned that the Death God's lover had returned, and since that time, the new souls had stopped coming. The Keeper in him could sense that, understanding that these souls had been here many years, likely centuries for some. He still felt like there was something more missing from the family knowledge his sister had found. More to his role in shepherding the souls home. But his family had hidden it for longer than he could determine and now he could only piece strings of that prior knowledge together.

There were too many unanswered questions, but one thing he did know was that he had found his way to Crimson, his way home. He looked around the large grove, knowing he had a lot of work ahead of him if he intended to clear this grove. For once he did, his family's debt would be satisfied.

CRIMSON

Pete's mouth was on Crimson's breast, sucking and pulling at her nipple until she was squirming uncontrollably. His fingers slid along her waist and down her stomach until they found her sweet spot, gently teasing it until she was a mess, her body a burning inferno. She opened her eyes, blinking from her dream to find the flames were real. Looking down, Bormick met her eyes, pulling her nipple up with his teeth. She let out a squeak of surprise, but he brought his hand to her mouth and gestured to Stavin, who was sleeping next to her, his naked body rising and falling with his breaths.

She'd been taking them both as they shared her each night. Every night and throughout each day was like a dream of erotic contentment. That contentment centered on her interactions with Bormick. Stavin had his strengths, but it was Bormick who sent her arousal to heights she couldn't descend until she was plummeting uncontrollably. The way her body responded to him left her feeling trapped. She didn't know how to escape or if she wanted to.

Bormick's mouth assailed her below, his tongue playing with her clit, before sucking it until she was so close to climax that her body was ablaze. Gods, this man and what he did to her. Only Pete had ever made her feel this good. He pushed three fingers forcefully into her, her back arching from the explosive feel.

"Gods, you're soaked," he whispered, his breath like fire against her already sensitive skin.

She brought her arm to her face, biting down to contain the scream building as her orgasm hit her, pounding upon her like his fingers were doing inside of her. She pushed at him to make him stop as the quivers soared through her, but he was relentless, raising her back up quickly with his tongue until she was on the cusp again.

He pulled his fingers out, licking them with a glint in his eye before he plunged his length into her. Grasping his shoulders, the waves crashed upon her with each thrust.

His lips met hers, his chest pressing against her as she rode out the ecstasy that was assailing her. Clinging to him, another wave overcame her. His motion grew fiercer, her climax rebuilding as he came until her body rebelled again, and she joined him. With her legs entwined around him, she urged him deeper until his body stilled with hers.

"Gods, what you do to me, woman," he whispered in her ear.

"My turn," Stavin said, ruining the moment.

Bormick drew back, looking into her eyes. If Pete hadn't already claimed her heart, she could have loved this man. The thought was one that tore at her heart, as if a piece of it was chipping away.

He pulled out of her with a grunt. "She's all yours. Well, maybe not all of her."

He rose above her, grabbing the head of the bed and bringing his moistened manhood toward her mouth. Stavin entered her, and she moaned, licking her tongue along Bormick. She could taste the mix of their sex, and her musk upon him. She licked the tip, then weaved her tongue around him as he gripped the bed tighter. In response, he shoved himself further into her mouth while Stavin penetrated deeper. A sense of contented fullness came over her. Taking them both at once was sending a force clawing through her core, one the burned so that she felt like her entire body was ablaze. Bormick, having grown to full length again, increased his rhythm, using her mouth as Stavin was using her body. She gasped for breath, meeting him each time he pulled out, then plunged back in.

A groan escaped them both. Stavin was getting closer, his morning hardness too easily satisfied. His hands surrounded her hips, holding them still as he drove harder, until she felt his body quiver with his climax. Her teeth barred against Bormick as he shoved inward again.

Bormick growled, but she knew it had been a pleasure filled pain.

"Leave us, Stavin," he commanded.

Stavin ran his hand down the inside of her thigh, finding her clit and rubbing his thumb against it, calling to the fire that was rising within her again. She released Bormick as she tipped her head back, his erection hitting the back of her throat as the moan poured from her.

"Can't I play a bit longer?" Stavin said.

"No, leave us."

His fingers pushed against her clit, stirring the fire, as she took Bormick's length and sucked with the intensity that burned through her.

Bormick's hands tightened.

"Go," he growled.

The pressure left and she let out a cry.

"Fine. I'll have a servant girl get me off again instead," he said, rising. "Looking at your ass is interfering with my focus, anyway."

He moved away from her and smacked Bormick's ass, causing him to plunge further. Her teeth gently bit down with the depth. He growled again, then moved from her mouth, pulling her on top of him.

"Ride me," he commanded.

"You two are too much," Stavin complained as she enveloped Bormick, stretching her back to lean her hands on his thighs. His large hands wrapped around her waist, holding her in place as he thrust below her.

"And too hot," Stavin said. "Fuck the servant girl."

He grabbed his dick and stroked it, watching the two of them.

"You don't listen to orders, Stavin."

"You made me king, Bormick. Let me at least watch the show in peace, since you won't let me fuck her again."

Crimson dropped forward, tired of their banter, and smashed her lips on Bormick's, opening her mouth to him. His tongue forced its way in, tantalizing hers as his hands moved from her hips and found their way to her breasts. Teasing and pulling at her nipples, he stopped moving his pelvis to let her take control. This was how she liked it, in control, commanding his body, his need, coaxing his climax from him. Her pelvis slowed to torment him with a long, exaggerated lift.

He grunted then pinched her nipple. Bending his head, he caught it with his mouth, sucking and grazing it with his teeth. His other hand reached down to her already swollen nub, his touch sending sparks through her. In one move, he'd stripped her of her control, and she melted to his touch, letting him take it. Her climax was cresting within her like a lightning storm that was building until it exploded. He moved his hand to her hips again, guiding them at a faster speed, the orgasm casting through every fiber of her. His climax joined hers, and she heard Stavin's release timing with theirs as his groan met her cries.

She fell upon Bormick, weakened to her core. She was breathless, her will gone, stolen by him as if he now owned her. His hands stayed clenched to her hips, his pelvis thrusting the remaining streams of him into her until he calmed.

"Damn, you two are intense. Not sure how my woman

became yours, Bormick," Stavin said, pulling his pants on after wiping himself clean.

"She never was yours. She's mine. I claimed her. You're lucky I share her." He paused. "Shared."

His hand brushed her hair back, her head still resting on his chest.

"Shared? What's that supposed to mean?" Stavin asked.

"It means she's off limits. Get your own woman to fuck. This one's mine."

"What the—"

"Leave, Stavin."

"I found her, Bormick."

Crimson stayed silent, seeing the first fractures between the two men, exactly what she'd waited for. But it was Bormick's words that echoed through her. He was claiming her and part of her wanted him to. She didn't know if it was possible to be claimed so differently by two men and want them both. She was in love with Pete. There was no doubt in her mind about that. Even the thought of him sent a flurry through her chest, but this man sent a fire through her lower half. It was as if her blood called to them both and she suddenly didn't want to give either of them up.

She closed her eyes as she heard the rumble in Bormick's chest.

"She found you and I'm taking her from you. Find a whore to warm your bed. This one is mine."

She bristled at the term but didn't move, waiting for Stavin to slam out of the room before she lifted her head.

"You're not happy with that term?" he asked, reading her expression.

"I am not a whore. I'm very particular about with whom and how I take pleasure."

"Like how you chose Stavin?"

"Yes."

"Whoring yourself to him, then drawing me in for what end?"

She tried to rise, but his arm was tight around her back.

"I am no whore. I am a queen."

"You were a queen who wants her crown back and now warms my bed, bowing to my needs."

"I bow to now one," she hissed.

He weaved his hand into her hair and jerked her head back. Drawing his tongue down her neck, he bit her shoulder.

"I claim you—"

"Who said I was yours to claim?" she retorted, biting at his lip.

He flipped her, pinning her down, although she didn't resist, enjoying the feel of his hard chest against her soft skin. He moved her wrists so that his one hand held both her wrists over her head. Cupping her breast, he slid his thumb across her nipple, which rebelled against her attempt to keep it tamed. It hardened with his touch, sending flutters through her abdomen.

"This tells me you're mine to claim," he said, his blue eyes holding hers, their blue so similar to Pete's that for a moment, she forgot it was Bormick. A quiet gasp slipped from her lips. Giving her a sly grin, he moved his hand along her curves, forcing her legs apart with his thigh. His fingers penetrated her, and another gasp escaped. His eyes glinted with humor.

"And that tells me you're mine to claim."

He worked his fingers in and out, slipping his thumb to drape across her clit with the touch of a man who owned each part of her. Then he brought his lips to her, his tongue gliding into her mouth to meet hers, skating across it before sliding along her lips. He grabbed her bottom lip with his teeth and tugged it as his fingers sank deeper. Her breath caught and every nerve in her body seemed alive, screaming for his touch as his fingers withdrew. A whimper escaped her, the ache for his touch screeching through her.

"Now, who owns you?" he asked, hovering above her body, which was arching to meet his.

She wouldn't give in, wanted control. She was always in control, but her body craved his touch again.

"Who owns you?" he demanded.

"Who owns you?" she whispered back, her voice heavy with need.

Her question flustered him, his expression unguarded for just that moment. She lifted her head, meeting his lips, slipping her tongue in. She caressed his mouth with it, then ran it along his bottom lip, turning the tables on him while his defenses were down.

He smashed his lips against hers with a passion that sent her body lurching. With the move, his grip relaxed but he still held her wrists captive. Her body clawed at her to finish its release, her hips picking up to press against his firm erection. He slipped his other hand under her ass to keep it raised as his hardness filled her. He was as insatiable as she was, and her body responded immediately. His hand squeezed her ass, pushing him further into her. She was on fire, his touch, his movement, his breath against her neck as he drew his lips from her, stirring her at a depth she'd never experienced. As she lost herself to him, her body exploded, every sensation a cacophony of stimulation. His body bucked against hers as his own climax joined hers, the intimacy of the moment something she could not take back, nor deny.

"Who owns you?" she panted against his ear.

"You do," he whispered.

He kissed the crook of her neck and picked his head up. It was the first time he looked vulnerable. Then his expression hardened.

"But you'll never hear me say those words again. Now, answer my question," he commanded.

She reached up and traced his face, knowing the answer, knowing she was his but afraid to say the words, to give herself to this man, just as she had to Pete. "You own my body, all of it. My blood calls to yours."

He studied her, likely noting how she'd specified her body and not all of her. He lifted himself and for a moment she worried he'd punish her, but he rose and picked up his pants. Her eyes took him in, his lips curving into a crooked grin as he caught her.

"Good," he said. "It's your body I crave, Crimson, and your body that I demand."

Pulling his pants on, he grabbed a shirt, then paused as she stood from the bed, sore from the countless rounds of lovemaking. Love? No, it hadn't been love for either of them, but they were bonded now, their need for each other on a primal level that went beyond her understanding.

He let his fingers drift up her body, caressing her breast. With his touch, the sparks within her lit again. Bringing his hand to her neck, he pulled her to him, his lips pressing against hers hungrily, leaving her breathless before he walked away from her and out of the room.

She sat back against the bed, staring at the closed door. There was no way she could turn on him now. She didn't care about Stavin. He was like any other man she'd seduced. But Bormick set her heart racing with just his presence. Her reaction to him was so similar to how she responded to Pete.

"Gods, what do I do?" she whispered.

Pete's life hung on her next move, yet she couldn't get past Bormick's bed. Both men had become a part of her, taken a piece of her so that she could no longer live without either of them.

The door opened, jarring her from her thoughts and causing her to jump.

Bormick's eyes perused her still naked body.

"Hungry again?" she teased seductively.

"Always for you," he replied, but he remained at the door. "Get yourself dressed. It's time you tell me how we take Theodore's crown. It was your lure, after all."

He closed the door before she could answer.

"Shit," she mumbled. She'd need to summon Skye if he demanded she make that move, then she would lose him. He'd know she'd tricked him. Although that trick was long gone with the last shred of her self. All of it was his now.

She'd need to delay him until she could figure out a solution. She twisted the ring, cursing her foolishness. Falling for the enemy was a novice move. She'd had one job—trick them, bring Skye and the others in, borrow the power, and take the usurpers down. Then she'd have Pete back.

Now it had all changed, and she needed to find a way to free Pete while keeping Bormick alive. There was a chance she could turn him on Stavin, but she wasn't certain it was possible. She'd wanted to turn them against each other, have them take each other down, but now she had a conundrum.

She walked to the balcony that overlooked her kingdom. Her kingdom, not Stavin's, not Bormick's. Hers. Hers to share with Pete, but now...now she was contemplating asking two men to share her. To rule her kingdom with them.

She laughed at her own audacity. Both were fiercely protective of their claim on her. Bormick had stated Stavin would not be touching her again. What would he think of sharing her body with Pete?

"Your delusional, Crimson," she muttered. That was the happy ending she wanted, and happy endings were not meant for her. The Death God was her ending—an eternity in the Shadow Realm as his possession. None of this mattered anyway, so she shouldn't even care. But she did care. So badly that it hurt and that was a situation for which she had not been prepared.

PETE

Pete stretched, glancing around the grove as the souls slowly woke. The last glimmer of sunset was caving to the night. Nights had passed and with each, he'd tempted the trees to decide their fates. The ones overcome with the ebony were the ones who struggled more. That ebony, he now realized, was the shadows stretching to cast them back to the Shadow Realm. The ones who calmed easily, who relaxed to his touch, were the ones destined for the Upper Realm. Pete imagined it must be that world's version of heaven. Their bark would grow completely white, disintegrating in a graceful shimmer of light as the white bark fell apart, spreading over the floor of the forest. He'd made some headway, the grove thinning each night, but it still seemed an endless task. He took breaks when he could, combing through the papers. Courtney and Bo had forgiven his outburst and brought him everything they found.

The papers had been a treasure of knowledge, explaining why the grove had been settled here, and about the rift between the brother gods—the Death God and his brother who ruled the Upper Realm. Their relationship had been so volatile that as the lost souls grew in number he had turned to his brother in this world. That brother, the devil, had granted him access to this land. Like the Death God, the devil had not cared what his brother in heaven thought. It seemed to Pete that both preferred to irritate their brothers. The thought of the devil irritating God was one that struck Pete as humorous in a confounding way.

Pete had stared at the writing in disbelief. He'd never been religious, his family having never attended church, and now he understood why. Why worship a god who wasn't really your god? But he knew of the Bible and the teachings, the beliefs of the different religions. He wondered what the people of this world would think if they knew there were more gods across the universe, all with their own worlds, all brothers, even sisters. It was a strange concept, one that seemed too surreal to even fathom.

He picked up the plastic folder Courtney had brought him to keep the papers safe and dry. He wanted to argue that it never seemed to rain in the grove but had refrained, knowing she was just doing what she could to be helpful. It was strange that weather never changed in the grove. There were nights he could tell it was storming, the rain making a distant patter sound. Sometimes streaks of lighting would light sections of the grove yet it remained free of its touch.

He walked around the grove, caressing his trees. The agitated ones he quieted, not ready to deal with coaxing them on quite yet. He let his fingers graze his female tree, feeling her purr, her mist-like hands coming to touch him. He'd decided to save her tree until last, her touch was too pleasurable to let her go. There was no question that he was using her, but she didn't seem to mind. Her hands stroked and caressed him each night until he came, sometimes multiple times a night. He was hungry for Crimson, to feel her body, to be inside of her instead of the ghostlike hands, but this would do for now and it kept him satisfied.

The prior night, his female soul had brought her form out. Each night, she seemed to become more solid, less ephemeral. He didn't know if it was his imagination, but he had felt her as if she'd almost been whole. He'd let himself imagine she was real, touching the breasts that had been there, the mouth that had found his firmness, bringing him to climax. That evening, he'd taken her again, her figure solidifying more so that he was able to slide into what felt like her body, more physical than mist-like this time, the mist slick against him as he'd moved within her. Her wails had filled the forest, peaking his arousal.

The sex had been the strangest he'd ever experienced, but he'd needed the release. His urge for Crimson was overwhelming, the blood that called to her unrelenting in his need to have her again. The spirit would have to do.

She stroked him over his pants, which filled out with his need.

"Not yet. Be patient and then we'll play."

She shook under his hand, and he wondered at her bark, the ebony still climbing. She didn't seem like a bad soul, a naughty one maybe, but not one deserving of an eternity in hell.

Rolling his neck, he adjusted his pants, hoping his bulge would fade before Courtney and Bo called for him to grant them access into the grove.

He moved from his tree to avoid her tempting hands and sat, pulling the papers out to study them again. Each time he hoped to discover another clue, but each time he only found the same things. He wiped his eyes, letting his mind drift to Crimson. His worry for her safety grew daily. There was no way to know if she'd taken back her kingdom...if she'd forgotten about him.

He prayed she hadn't, but part of him knew she had an appetite—one that demanded to be fed. She may have taken a lover to satisfy her needs. He couldn't judge her, he'd done the same in a way. The tree spirit wasn't real, solid flesh, but he was still reaping the benefits, enjoying her touch, already thinking of how he'd take her from behind tonight.

"Jesus, Pete," he said, rubbing his hand over his face.

He'd lost his mind. Sure, he'd been sexually active before

Crimson, but after taking her, sex was all he could think of. She was addictive, like a drug he couldn't get from his system, one he didn't want to. If he couldn't have her, he needed an alternative release. She was likely doing the same thing. And it wasn't as if they'd committed to each other. He'd claimed her as his, but that didn't really mean anything. They'd only known each other a week. If he found her again, then he would insist she be faithful to just him and he would do the same. The if was too great now, their lives separated by worlds and both of them too sexually needy to think of commitment right now.

"Pete?" he heard Courtney's voice from beyond the grove.

Quickly he rose, cursing the bulge that still filled his pants, and ran to meet them. The trees had grown accustomed to their presence, but they still couldn't enter the grove without him.

"Hey!" he said.

Bo gave a quick look at his crotch. "Did we interrupt something?" he asked with a raise of his brow.

Courtney followed his lead. "Ew." She smacked Bo on the back of the head. "That's my brother, asshole. I don't want to see that!"

"You two are asses. No, you didn't interrupt anything," he said, adjusting himself as Courtney rolled her eyes. "I was just thinking about Crimson, and it happens automatically."

"Gross," she said, walking past him.

"She that good in bed?" Bo asked.

"You have no idea."

"I guess I'd have a hard-on too then."

"Don't be a dick, Bo, and don't think those words won't cost you later!" she yelled back.

"Everything costs me with her," he replied with a wink.

Pete laughed, walking over to where Courtney was pulling beer out of her bag. Bo had a pizza in his hands and kissed her on the head as he sat next to her. She pretended to ignore him, but Pete caught the smile.

Bo was good for her. Like Pete, she'd been a bit wild in high school, falling in with a crowd that drank and smoked a lot of weed. The crowd was an eclectic artsy one that appealed to her free spirit, but it had buried her true self and Pete had been happy when she'd met Bo. He grounded her but understood that free spirit side of her at the same time. The days of pot and heavy drinking disappeared, the colored hair, the nose ring and the tattoos did not, but they were Courtney. Just as Pete had inked his body so had she. Her tattoos weren't so prominent as his, but he'd caught the glimpse of her tramp stamp when he'd been home from college one summer. And depending on what she wore, the ones on her ankle and shoulder were hard to miss.

The two of them were definitely cut from the same mold, but she had found her center in Bo where Pete had continued to search for his in various women until now. Crimson was his center; he had no doubt and he would get her back no matter the cost.

"Hey, deep thinker, come have a slice and see what I found," Courtney said, breaking him from his thoughts.

Sitting, he grabbed a slice of pizza and a beer, thankful his arousal had settled. "What's up?"

She reached into her bag and pulled out what looked like a dagger in a black leather sheath, and handed it to him.

He furrowed his brow, looking at it before glancing back at her. She gave him a shrug.

Turning it over in his hands, he studied it, running his finger over the gem lodged in the handle. It was a dark stone, smooth to the touch. Pulling it from its sheath, he tried to read the writing etched on the shiny silver blade.

"We have no idea what it says, but it was with this." She reached over and dropped something into his other hand. It was heavy. Opening his palm, he saw it was a ring. It had the same silver metal as the dagger, and an inscription spread from the ruby in its center.

"I think you're supposed to have them. You are the oldest and from what we found, the eldest holds the power, right?" she said.

He fingered the ring before letting it drop to his ring finger, where it landed perfectly. A strange jolt passed through him, calling to that part of him that had awakened the night he'd sent the first tree to the Shadow Realm. An understanding of what he was meant to do, why the Guardians were so important. He'd been right. The ruby glowed as if in confirmation.

"God, Pete, it's all true, isn't it?" she whispered.

"Did you think I was hanging out with trees because it's fun?"

"From that woody you were sporting earlier it sure seems so," Bo joked. He elbowed Courtney. "See what I did there? Woody? And we're in the woods?"

"If you have to explain it, it's not funny, Bo." She elbowed him back. "I meant the royalty part, Pete," she said, addressing Pete. "We really are from a royal family."

It was a strange thought, and he didn't quite know how to respond. He put the dagger back, studying the leather sheath. He ran his finger across it, watching as it glowed.

"It's not leather," he mused, bringing it closer to a stream of moonlight. "Bo, let me see your flashlight."

Bo handed it to him, and he shined it on the sheath. The sheath shimmered the way a snakeskin would, but with a strange quality he didn't recognize. Now that he could see it better, he noted its rich navy color. He traced it with his finger, watching as it shimmered.

"It's like snakeskin," he mumbled.

"What?"

"It's not leather. See how it shimmers?"

Bo took it back from him and studied it, running his finger over it. "That's not snakeskin. It's reptilian, but not like anything I've ever seen."

"Since when are you a reptile expert?" Courtney said, grabbing it from him and doing the same.

Pete continued to stare at it as she did, the strange consistency nagging at him. He thought back to what Crimson had told him about the Shadow Realm and the demons that resided there.

"Demon skin." A shiver went through him as he said the words, followed by a sense of confirmation.

"Why would you say that?" Courtney asked, her voice hushed as if she were afraid her words would draw the attention of one.

"I...I don't know. I just know it is. I'm just not sure how that connects to us."

They stared at him.

"And someone in our family killed one? We were demon hunters?" she asked.

He furrowed his brow, thinking about it as his finger touched the ruby. "No, I don't think so. How would that even be possible?"

"Don't ask me," she said. "It was your crazy suggestion, but I like that idea."

"No, but that's not it, Court. I'm certain of it," he said, furrowing his brows. "If the Death God cursed our family here, maybe there's more to it than we know."

"Like a connection to him? Demon tamers?" she suggested. "Oh, I like that better, even if it does scare the shit out of me."

"Whoa, that takes the two of you to a whole new level," Bo said. "My girl is a demon tamer. There's something really sexy about that!"

"Stop imagining me in leather pants with a whip."

Pete laughed. "I'm not sure that's it or that I ever want that image in my head again, but there's definitely a connection to them."

They sat quietly for a few minutes.

"You're going to that world when you finish freeing the souls, aren't you?" Courtney asked, finally breaking the silence, her eyes sad.

"Yes, I need to find her and...I think that's where I need to be. But it's your world, too. Aren't you curious?"

"I don't know. It doesn't seem like the nicest place."

"And this place is?" Bo said.

"Our town is quiet and safe."

"But the rest of the world is a mess," he returned.

"You've got time," Pete said to them.

Courtney nodded, but Pete could see the sadness that remained in her eyes.

They ate quietly and when Courtney and Bo left, Pete picked up the dagger, studying it before attaching it to his pants. He went to work, persuading more trees to find their way home until finally exhausted, his mind filled with visions of Crimson, he returned to his tree. She emerged from her prison, her womanly form waiting for him. His dick throbbed with yearning, the visions of Crimson's body he'd entertained on the walk to her ensuring he was ready.

He touched the more defined breasts, hearing her soft purr. Her mouth drifted along his neck, the sensation as if she were licking it as her hands pressed against his pants. He closed his eyes, imagining she was real, letting his hands peruse the body that had taken on more curves.

Invisible hands pulled his shirt from him, touching behind him. More than one tree was present. They reached for his pants, pulling them down. Her hands trailed his chest as he reached to spread her legs, feeling what shouldn't be there. Wetness. The strokes from her hand were too enticing for him to resist and need flooded him. The hands behind him pulled away as she pressed against him, her body firm, almost real.

She kissed him, a tongue slipping through his parted mouth. He could wait no longer, knowing he wanted her, wanted to be inside of her now. He turned her and pushed her against her tree. Gripping her solid hips, he heard the moan that escaped her lips. The ebony of her tree spread but not upwards. This time, it spread out to her misty skin. His hands caressed her breasts as he watched the ebony stretch to become long locks of hair. She felt too good to stop but he couldn't pull his eyes from the transformation even as he continued to push his erection against her. Pinching her hard nipples, his eyes followed the white of her tree as it streamed down her body, giving her a creamy hue to her skin. His moan escaped with the feel of her, and he dropped his hand to her hips, drawing her back and slipping his fingers into her folds. The dampness that greeted him layered his fingers and he released a deep groan at the sensation.

She was real, and he was bursting with need, too aroused to focus on her changing form any longer. He penetrated her, bringing his fingers to his mouth and tasting her. She felt like heaven. The cream of her skin accentuated the round shape of her ass, and he smoothed his hand over it. Her hands, now real, gripped the tree as he shoved against her. The need became too great, the sensation too overwhelming. He wanted to pull out, to spill over her back but his climax hit him fast. Gripping her waist, he let the tide drown him.

He pulled her to him, plunging deeper as the orgasm spread through him, until finally, he dropped his head to her back, trying to catch his breath. When he could breathe again, he released her, staring as she turned to face him. He hadn't imagined it. She was real. Stumbling back a step, he took her in, unsure how he felt. Her eyes, as brown as the bark, met his. He perused her body, taking in the long waves of ebony hair that fell to her full breasts. The pert breasts had nipples with the same dark hue as her eyes. Soft pale skin coated her body, and he followed it to the black patch of ebony between her legs where her curvy hips encompassed it.

She walked closer, her hips swaying. She brought her finger to his lips before kissing him. Her hands ran over the contour of his chest, sending a shiver of excitement through him. Terror would have been the appropriate reaction. He should have forced her back to the tree and never touched her again, but he didn't. Questions should have been running through his mind, concerns with the fact that a spirit had taken physical form, a fact that went against everything he understood. But his mind was silent save for the instinctual need to have her again. He let her find her way down to his reforming length and lost himself to her as her mouth took him to new levels of enjoyment. As he climaxed again, he knew he needed to walk away, but he couldn't. He pressed her against her tree and took her again until the sun finally rose, and she faded along with him. The wails of the forest filled the air, not silenced for the first time in centuries.

CRIMSON

Crimson let the hot tub water soak her aching thighs. She was used to pleasuring men multiple times, but with both Stavin and Bormick, it was more than she was accustomed to. She'd also been locked away for ten years with no man to satisfy her. Pete had been the first in that span and although he was her equal in sex drive, with Bormick and Stavin, it was like having two of him. Bormick himself was demanding and her body responded each time to him so that exhaustion overtook her after both men had had their fill of her. That tightness in her belly struck again when she thought of Bormick and what he did to her. Her other equal.

Gods, what was she to do?

"My lady?" Hentrom said, sneaking into the room.

"Yes, Hentrom." She didn't bother to cover herself. He'd been her servant for too many years, and she had never been one for modesty. "Have you brought me news?"

"Some good, some bad."

"You've uncovered loyalty?"

"Yes, the servants are all loyal. The women especially. Stavin has a penchant for the flesh, taking them at his will and frequently."

"Yes, I suppose he would. And I'd wager, he's not the gentlest with them."

"No, my queen."

"And the guards?"

"Well, that's where we have bad news. There are a handful who remain loyal, but many enjoy the freedoms Bormick gives them; particularly your troops."

She didn't have to ask what freedoms, knowing Bormick well enough to know they were doing more than seizing land. They were leaving a trail of violated women in their path of destruction.

"Damn them." She gritted her teeth. She'd noticed Bormick had stayed at the castle recently. The more entangled he'd become with her, the more satisfied he'd been. Finding pleasure in her willing flesh over the unwilling. It was a start, but she wondered if she could completely tame him. It was in his nature to take as he wanted. She wasn't certain she could keep him satisfied enough to keep his dick in his pants when he wasn't near her.

Whether she could tame him or not, didn't matter. It only mattered if she could keep him, and that was something she couldn't even fathom at this point.

"My lady?" Hentrom woke her from her thoughts.

"You've done well, Hentrom."

She reached her hand to his face and turned his cheek, seeing the fresh black eye. "Who?"

"Stavin, my queen."

She wondered at her relief that it hadn't been Bormick.

"He'll pay, I promise you. Now go before they catch you and be careful."

"Yes, my queen."

He left the room and after a few more moments, Crimson stepped from the tub, drying herself as she walked to the balcony. She was running out of time. She knew Skye and Mark were waiting for her move. She'd stalled them by removing the threat to Theodore, but they would still be waiting to hear from her. Mark was certain to be complaining by now. He hadn't trusted her in the first place.

Mark. She laughed at herself for her former naivety. He was Skye's—heart and soul. She understood that now. She'd tricked Mark, played on his jealousy, worn him down so that he'd taken her. His hunger had been there that day. The way he'd taken her that first time had been unique to all the future times that she now knew had only been his way of tricking her. For that one moment, she'd thought she had what Skye had. But she hadn't. It had been anger, and hunger driving him. Nothing comparable to what he had with Skye.

She recognized it now on two levels, with Pete and with Bormick. There was a difference in how she felt with them. She understood that each time she lost herself to Bormick's touch, she was risking what she had with Pete. Pete—she needed to get to him. He didn't deserve his punishment, sentenced to a lifetime in that blasted grove. The grove was a dull place with only the occasional satisfaction the trees provided. The thought of him seeking relief with the trees entered her mind. With the thought, a flare of jealousy ran through her. But then she reminded herself that she was willingly fucking two men, one of whom was breaking her the same way Pete had. No matter how much he indulged, what she was doing was worse.

Turning from the window, she took in the rumpled bedsheets, a wave of desire sweeping through her as she remembered what Bormick's tongue had done to her. The moment had held an intimacy they'd shared to the point where she'd known he was hers for the taking. Hers to destroy...if she wanted.

She pulled a dress on, struggling to bring the ties together in the back, then giving up and making her way to find the two men.

Stavin had a servant girl on his lap, his hand up her skirt, Bormick watching, expressionless from the corner.

"Do I not give you pleasure, Stavin?" she asked, entering the room.

"You're not allowed to give me anything anymore, Crimson, so now I have to take."

She walked over and yanked the girl from his lap.

"Leave my servants alone."

He gripped the bulge in his pants. "If you take my playthings away, Crimson, I'll just have to force you to satisfy me."

He grabbed her wrist and pulled her to his lap, putting her hand on his crotch.

She heard Bormick's growl from the corner.

"I don't think he likes that, Stavin," she whispered in his ear, squeezing his erection as his hand found her breast and fondled it.

"I said she's off limits," Bormick griped.

She undid his pants and stroked him, knowing it would only serve to anger Bormick. She would have preferred it be him, but the game needed to be played.

"Gods, Bormick. One more time at least," he complained, pulling her already-too-loosened dress down to expose her chest. "Once more, then I promise I'll just watch."

He drew her breast to his mouth, sucking on it, then circling her nipple with his tongue. She moaned in response to the tingles that fled through her belly. Bormick said nothing, only watched her intensely. His eyes never left hers as she bit her lip seductively, seeing the yearning in his eyes. Yearning that should have been fulfilled from their earlier activities but had risen once again.

"I'm going to take your silence as a yes," Stavin said. He pulled her skirts up and brought her to his lap, so she was straddling him. Squeezing both breasts, he brought them to his mouth while she pushed her wetness against his erection.

"You have the best tits," he mumbled between bites.

She gasped, arching her back. His mouth continued to torture her breasts while he drew a hand to her ass and urged her to move.

Rising, she enveloped him, bringing her eyes back to Bormick, whose hand was gripping his pants.

"Fuck me," she said to Bormick as she rose and fell on Stavin. He put his hand down his pants, bringing his length out, moving his hand to her rhythm. Her tongue licked sensually along her lip, and she saw him crumble.

The intensity threatened to bring her over the edge, and she increased her pace, pushing so aggressively that Stavin went deeper. The move elicited a heavy groan from him. His mouth lifted from her breast, and he encased his hands tight around her hips, driving her movement.

Bormick's hand quickened until—with a loud grunt—he released right as she did, her cries joining his, Stavin coming within moments of them. She continued moving as the waves of her climax receded. Stavin didn't let go, his hands digging into her hips as he pushed the remains of his orgasm into her.

Breathless, she continued to look at Bormick. His eyes were glinting, and he wore a crooked grin on his face. She lifted herself, hearing Stavin's complaint, and walked to Bormick. Moving his hand, she slid her thumb over the remains of his climax then brought it to her mouth.

"You are something," he said, his voice husky.

Pulling his head down to her, she kissed him. His tongue danced with hers in an aggressive manner before he brought her against him. Her chest pressed against his so that she could feel his heart racing. It was an intense moment, the desire he had for her spilling through, and she felt her knees weaken.

"If you're going to take her now, then I get to watch," Stavin said. "In fact, if I'm not allowed to take her again, I get to watch whenever I want."

"You won't be here to watch," she said.

Bormick drew away, his eyes questioning her.

She turned, lifting her hair. "Would you tie me up?" she said.

The groan that escaped confirmed he'd understood the sexual

inuendo she'd intended. He brought his lips to her ear, whispering, "Any time you want."

He liked it rough, and they had yet to fully explore that side of him. For a moment, she wondered if that was the key to keeping him from straying. She silently scolded herself for even worrying about that.

His hands caressed her back, and she felt his lips trace her bare neck. Stavin fixed his pants and waited for her explanation, crossing his arms like he was irritated, but she could see the truth in his growing length.

"Why won't I be here?"

"Because you're going to steal a mage for me."

Bormick let out a hearty laugh while Stavin stared at her, mouth agape.

"No one just steals a mage, my pet," Bormick said, finishing her ties.

She dropped her hair and went to walk away, but he brought his hand around her waist, pulling her against him. She could feel his firmness pressing against her back.

"I'm guessing my annoying cousin sent the remaining mages back to Kantenda, which leaves me empty-handed. That means I need a mage," she said.

"Something no one can get you," he replied.

"Stavin will get one for me, won't you?"

"She's joking, right?" Stavin said, his eyes wide.

"Crimson, no one just walks into the Mage Warrior's kingdom, let alone to steal a magic wielding mage," Bormick said.

"Have you two been playing king too long? Stavin, you were my best guard. You murdered the King of Eltander, with said Mage Warrior in the room, not to mention her two strongest Elite. I chose you for the job because you were stealthy and smart. Bormick, you are a renowned thief, one who never got caught—"

"Then why not send him?" Stavin asked.

"Because I need him here to please me."

"Did I not just please you?" he asked, appearing bitter at her response.

She gave him a sly smile. "Of course, you did."

Only she and Bormick knew the real reason she'd climaxed so intensely.

"Then send him. I'm not—"

"Yes, you will," Bormick commanded. "I've been out doing the dirty work for too long while you've been sitting pretty in this castle, getting laid. Get your feet wet again."

"I'd rather get my dick wet."

"You'll find a few unwilling women on the way. Besides, you're a king and women like power."

Crimson tried not to roll her eyes.

"Why do we even need a mage?"

Bormick's hand had strayed to her breast, momentarily distracting her.

"I need the magic."

He squeezed the traitorous nipple that had obeyed his command. "Explain."

It would be easier if you weren't turning me on again, she thought as a flush of arousal swept through her.

"I can't very well ride into Theodore's kingdom. Besides, it's a long ride." She leaned her head against his chest, slipping her hand back to feel his girth. "And I don't think you want me out of your bed for that long."

"What does that have to do with a mage?" Stavin asked, grabbing his growing erection. "Would you two stop that?"

The request only drove Bormick to slip his hand under the material of Crimson's dress and pull her breast out, continuing his play.

Gods, he was driving her mad.

"I can bleed magic from a wielder."

Bormick stopped his fingers, Stavin furrowing his brow.

"What did you say?" he said, speaking closer to her ear.

"I can bleed magic. How do you think I took down the Mage Queen that day, Stavin? You were there. She could have easily killed us all."

"That's how you did it? You stole her magic? All those years, you were stealing magic?"

She nodded, feeling Bormick grow harder. So, he liked a woman with power.

"It's my dirty little secret and one I never cared to share with anyone. Not even the mages knew I was doing it. I can make their magic mine, and it lasts a few hours. That gives me the ability to make a portal to Theodore's kingdom. Plenty of time for the few seconds it will take to seduce him, then take him out while he's otherwise occupied."

As she spoke, Bormick continued his assault on her chest, bringing her sleeves down so that her breasts fell out. The way his hands caressed them left her knees weak.

"Maybe I'll just follow you in and kill him before he pleasures himself with your body."

"No," she said, breathlessly, her body on fire with need. "He'll call his guards and they'll kill you. We do it my way."

"Fine, Stavin take Lentem and Fredek. They're my best men. If anyone can get you close to a mage, it's them."

"It needs to be a full mage." Her legs were quivering as his tongue ran down her neck and shoulder.

Stavin's hand was still clenching his pants.

"You'll find them—" She gasped as his hand, which had found its way up her dress, pushed through her dampness to find her sweet spot.

"You are so wet," he whispered.

"That's because I just came in her, asshole. Let her finish before I explode in my pants."

His fingers rubbed her clit, making her lose all train of thought, her body burning for release. What this man did to her over and over again was not natural. She clung to his length, unable to move her hand anymore.

"I think you can find them yourself," Bormick said to him. "Leave now and take the swiftest stallions."

She was reaching her summit, hovering right on the edge, his hands like ecstasy to her.

"Oh, no, I'm going to watch you fuck her first and then I'll leave."

He undid his pants, stroking himself as Bormick walked her to the table, his hands not stopping until he drew them away. Pushing her down on the table, he hiked up her dress. Her legs were quivering in anticipation, her climax hanging by a thread she knew he was about to unravel. He plunged into her with the force that sent her tumbling over the cliffs of ecstasy. Her body went weak as the waves crashed over her, then built again, the feel of him inside of her too great to ignore. The current swept her out again before washing over her a second time. Her climax was so powerful that she cried out in elation. Her reaction broke him, and his feral grunt timed with his release. She moaned as he filled her, feeling the spasms of her orgasm coax his essence from him. His hand was pressing so hard into her back that she could barely move, the table warm against her skin. She lay there, catching her breath until he collapsed against her.

"Well, that should tie me over until I'm back. Shit, you two are intense. I'm definitely getting to watch if I can't touch," Stavin said, the hoarse rasp of his voice a satisfied sound.

He tucked himself away, ignoring the mess he'd made on the floor, and walked out, shaking his head. Bormick stepped away from her, her dress falling with the movement.

He stood there as she turned and adjusted her dress to cover her breasts. She couldn't help but lean against the table to support her shaking legs.

"So you steal power from mages? Bleed their power from them."

"I do," she answered, nibbling on her lip. She was trying to hold her legs still and brought her hand back on the table for support.

"Do you bleed willpower like you bleed magic?" he asked her. She scrunched her brow, not understanding. He moved to her, brushing her hair back. "I'm lost with you. There's no control. I crave your body like I crave sustenance. Is that you enchanting me?"

"No," she replied, smiling. "That's you needing me as much as I need you."

"Hmm, I don't like weakness, Crimson, and you bring me to my knees."

She kissed him, grasping his shirt tightly in her hands.

"I don't do love, so don't get any expectations," he added.

She smiled coyly. "Good. I don't need your love. I need your body and what it does to mine. No more, no less."

He drew his thumb along her lips, then down her chin. "You're disruptive, Crimson."

"I know, that's how I like to be."

He squeezed her chin between his fingers, sending a flash of pain through her. "You betray me, and I won't hesitate to kill you."

She held back her reaction, the thought of keeping him slinking away with his words. He was as strong as she was, as deceptive, as ruthless. There had been no reason for her to expect any less.

He kissed her, bringing his hand down to pull her against him and squeeze her ass. When he released her, he walked away, picking his sword belt up from the table and donning it as he left the room, not looking back.

She leaned against the table, the need for him consuming her once again. Worry and confusion burying her.

PETE

His tree was still sleeping when Pete woke. He'd gone to her immediately, but there was no sign of her. His dick grew impatient at the thought of taking her again. Wiping his face, he walked away, over to his new cell phone. Courtney had brought it, along with a few portable chargers that she took home to charge every other day. He picked it up, wondering why the battery was dead. It usually lasted a while, and it had only been a day.

Strange, he thought.

He grabbed the portable charger and plugged it in, sitting while the phone charged and glancing back toward his tree. Still no sign of her. He rubbed his engorged erection as the phone came to life. As it loaded its home screen, he stared at the missed messages and calls from Courtney that layered the screen.

Pete, where are you?
Looked today but can't find the grove without you. Pete?
Are you okay?
The trees are loud, Pete. I can hear them all the way to the road. What's happened?

Pete, we looked again but can't find you. Please tell me you're just getting it on with a tree or ewww an animal, and that's why you're ignoring us.
Pete, the trees won't stop.
Where are you? We can hear the trees all the way into town. It's freaking people out.
Pete?
Peter!
Where are you?

What the hell? he thought, looking at the days of texts..

He dropped the phone and looked around, his ears just starting to tune into the cacophony of sounds all around him. All the trees were wailing, their cries earsplitting, their souls struggling in their prisons.

"How? It's only been one night."

But it hadn't, not according to the phone, which read almost a week of texts from Courtney.

"Shit." He rubbed his hand over his face, seeing the shimmer of movement in the distance from his tree.

He'd only thought it was one night but that one night of sex had somehow turned to several. Night after night lost from his recollection with only memories of the woman from the tree to fill the space.

He walked to the tree, his mind clearing through the cobwebs. The nights of euphoria she'd brought him were coming back to him. Her body had pushed even Crimson from his mind. The thought angered him, and he gripped his hands wanting to do nothing more than strangle the woman for seducing him. But he knew he was to blame as well, he'd started it, returning to that tree each night until she'd taken form.

"Idiot," he grumbled at himself.

She was waiting for him, her brown eyes enticing, her nipples taut and ready to be licked. His body's response was immediate, and his pants were suddenly tighter. Maybe he was being too hard on himself. He was stuck here, Crimson lost to him. It wouldn't do any harm to entertain himself until he was free. He was a man with needs, after all. Every step closer to her brought more silence to the trees until he no longer heard them. His lips met hers, and her body pressed against his bare chest.

For a moment, he didn't remember how he'd lost his shirt in those few steps. But then he recalled removing it as her eyes had drawn him in.

He couldn't resist her touch, which was demanding tonight. It didn't feel like he'd just taken her the previous night. He was suddenly desperate for her, like he hadn't had her in years. She tore at his pants, backing him against her tree and wrapping a leg around him. He was aching with how hard he was. Scooping her up by her ass, he tilted her so he could enter her, sliding into her moisture. Losing himself, he let all thoughts of texts, screaming trees, and missing days drift away to her spell. He turned her and slammed her against her tree, pounding into her until he came with a force that stole his breath. As his climax rippled through him, he pushed his release as deep as he could. Her back arched with her cries, further intensifying the sensations that were barraging him. His climax should have left him satisfied, and there was a thought in the back of his mind that he had something else to do, but her body continued to writhe against him, and he wanted more of her. Once was never enough.

He walked them forward, bringing her to the ground, so that she was over him. Dropping his mouth to suck on her perfect breasts, he cupped them. He took her nipples between his fingers, rolling them gently as she arched her chest closer to him. Flicking his tongue over her nipple, he realized that each time she pleased him, she never had her own release. It was always him.

"We're going to change that," he mumbled, forcing her over and rising above her. She reached to draw him back into her, but he resisted. Filling his mouth with her breasts, he slid his hand between her legs. She tried to block him, but he moved his thigh between her legs.

"I want to hear you scream," he said, pulling her nipple between his teeth and feeling her heart race.

He made his way down, ignoring her hands as they kept trying to pull him back, and spread her legs to bring his mouth to her.

She tasted of heat and spice, the taste of him mixed within, and it was like an aphrodisiac. He sent his tongue flicking over her clit and heard her moan, loud and feral.

He sucked it until she was squirming. Leaving his tongue to tantalize her, he reach his fingers deep inside of her. With his other hand he caressed her breast, her nipple pert and waiting to be touched. She moved below him as her climax built until, with a scream, she came, her body lurching with the force. As her legs tightened around him, her scream echoed through the grove. When the tremors of her orgasm had stopped, she lay breathless. Giving her clit one last suck that made her squirm again, he draped his tongue up her stomach. The further he rose, the more he noticed how her skin was shimmering.

That was new.

When he reached her breast again, the cream of her skin faded, overtaken by a strange reddish green snakelike texture. He jumped back, his eyes taking in the thing that no longer looked human.

"Holy shit!" he yelled, stumbling away.

His ears filled with the wails again, the lost days coming back to him. Wiping his mouth with his hand, he stared at her. There was something strangely beautiful and seductive about her, but terrifying at the same time.

She had the shape of a woman but with a reptile hide, her eyes slits of yellow. Small curled horns protruded from her head. Her shape seemed to flicker from that to a human shape, like it was having trouble deciding what she was.

"What the hell are you?"

She gave a mischievous grin, then a frown. It occurred to him that he'd never heard her talk. There had never been a need.

"You are not meant to please a sex demon. We feed from pleasing you, not the other way around. Now you've gone and broken my spell. The master will not be pleased. Damn you." She ran her hand up her body. "Only other demons get to please me, but that was by far the best orgasm I've ever had, so I won't eat you as punishment."

He backed further away. "Eat me?"

"Don't worry, the master said to play only. No eating this prey. Although you are much too tasty alive."

"Prey?" His stomach churned thinking of his dick and his tongue being inside of this thing.

"Now, why don't you come back and let my mouth make it up to you? I promise you'll be in the throes of rapture when I suck the seed from you."

He was uncomfortably turned on by the thought of her mouth around him again, until her forked tongue slid across her lips.

"Nah, I'm good." He looked for his pants, but they were too far.

She stepped closer, and he moved back a few steps.

"Who's your master, and why did he send you to seduce me? Because I really want to repay the favor with a few punches," he said, trying to keep away from her.

"The Death God is master to all."

Pete's mouth dropped open. He looked around the grove, suddenly cognizant of the cries.

"He sent you to distract me. Damn, that's why I've lost days. Days no closer to getting Crimson. To breaking free from this place."

He'd been right. Freeing the souls would free him and repay a debt the Death God clearly didn't want paid unless...

"Does he have Crimson?"

Her eyes shone. "Mmm, the redhead. I've played with her and the master before. She is yummy. The Death God said you would like curves like hers. Did you like my curves?" She asked, morphing to the human shape again, her hands moving over her breasts.

His body reacted, against his will. "Does he have Crimson?"

"I haven't played with her in a very long time and not many get to play with the Death God now, not since Death's Mistress has returned. She keeps him too satisfied. No one but the Mage Warrior. She gets to feel him inside of her, but only while his mistress is gone."

Skye.

So Crimson wasn't with him, which meant he was trying to keep Pete from his task and not necessarily from finding her.

"Go back to your master..." He thought about it. As pissed as he was that a demon had tricked him into screwing her, it wasn't her fault and as gross as the thought was, he'd enjoyed himself far too much. He didn't want the Death God to punish her for failing.

"I don't want to go back," she said, her body suddenly against him. Her full breasts pressed against his chest. "You're my favorite pet." Her hand surrounded him, and as per its usual singlemindedness, his dick rose to her touch.

"You're a demon," he said, trying to push her hand away. "And you are not sucking me into your trap again. I have work to do."

"How about I just suck you without the trap?"

She dropped to her knees and had him in her mouth before he could react. It felt too incredible to make her stop.

But she's a demon, Pete! his mind screamed. *A scaly demon with horns.*

Shut up, his dick yelled back. *She'll please us until we get Crimson back.*

Damn...Crimson. With the thought of her, his mind imagined it was her mouth. All thoughts of the demon erased, his hands gripped her head, pushing himself deeper into her mouth. She took him all the way to the hilt, then pulled back to his tip, licking it with a sensuality that quickly had him close to breaking again. Her hands held his thighs as she enveloped him again. Her moves brought his arousal to a crest, the thoughts of Crimson pushing it over the edge. She sucked him through his orgasm, which took his release over the top, his legs shaking from it.

Removing her mouth, her tongue traced its way up his body.

"You brought me pleasure. I'll let the spell go." Her fingers danced along his chest, playing with his nipple, which he knew was hard with the waves of his orgasm still soaring through him.

"I will tell the Death God that you outsmarted me and maybe, as a reward, he'll let me come back and play." She leaned closer and whispered, "I can be your Crimson until you find her. She likes to share. Maybe I can play with both of you one day."

The thought left him entirely too aroused again.

She's a demon, he yelled at himself as he fought to make his erection obey his command. He was nauseous from what she was but turned on at the same time by her body and her words.

"I'm a sex demon. No one can resist me and once you've had me, you want more." She patted his chest. "I promise I won't enrapture you again if you promise to use your tongue like that again."

"I'm not promising anything."

She brought her hand to his dick, squeezing his reforming erection. "We'll see."

She leaned up and kissed him, then turned and walked back to her tree, her hips swaying hypnotically until the black of the tree took her away.

Pete wiped his face, cursing himself.

"Jesus, Pete."

What the hell had he gotten mixed into? Death Gods,

demons, demons that gave head better than most women. He shook his head, pulling his pants on before rushing for his phone, and texting Courtney.

I'm okay. Still alive just got distracted.

Dots, then nothing, then dots again then, ***Asshole, were you fucking someone again? A tree? Get your dick stuck in its bark?***

She was pissed, and he couldn't help but laugh.

Just be here in 30 and I'll explain.

Fine, but shut those damned trees up!

He dropped the phone and turned to the trees, their cries hitting him. Something in the demon's spell must have dimmed his senses to them, but they were screaming now.

He walked around, chanting the words he knew as a Keeper. The ones that had come to him the moment he'd been imprisoned here. The trees calmed, their cries simmering to a dull wail until they were only a whisper. He felt the peace return to the forest beyond just before he heard Courtney yelling his name.

The fact that he'd been able to find the grove on his own, but she couldn't, still puzzled him. Maybe he really was the Guardian, and that was part of being one. His father had found it. He'd been an only child. Birth order may have come into play.

He didn't have time to ponder it more as he stepped from the grove and greeted them. Courtney shoved him back, slamming him into a tree.

"Oof, nice to see you, too, Court."

"You asshole! Couldn't bother to text me back?"

"I can explain," he said, backing up and leading them into the grove.

He wasn't certain he could explain without massively embarrassing himself, but he knew his sister wouldn't let up if he didn't.

"Better make it good," Bo said, "otherwise she's disowning you."

Courtney put her hand on her hips, waiting for him to talk.

He reached his hand around his neck and rubbed it. There was no way to avoid her expectant stare, so he opted for the truth.

"The Death God sent a demon disguised as a very naked, very voluptuous woman who put me under her spell."

The words sounded as idiotic out loud as they had in his head.

Courtney's mouth dropped open, then closed with a smirk. "And you couldn't keep it in your pants?"

"Well, it's hard to do that when she's tempting you with... Well, you can imagine."

"Holy shit," Bo mumbled.

"What happened to the new love in your life, Crimson?" She smacked him in the chest. "I should have known that was bullshit, just another piece of ass, like everyone else you fucked through high school and college. Who the hell knows how many heartbroken women you've left since you moved to New York? Forty-freaking-years-old and you still can't keep it in your pants."

Pete stood there, his arms crossed, taking it. "Are you done?"

"No—"

"Too bad. I still love Crimson. I can't explain it, but I do. But Jesus, I knew her for a week, neither of us committed to each other and if I know her as I think I do, I can assure you she's spending every night with some guy who can fill my place until I get to her."

"Wow, that's just...how do you get a woman like that?" Bo said, whistling.

Courtney smacked his chest this time.

"Of course, I would totally hate that. I'd never want to see someone else going at it with Courtney."

"Gross, Bo. That's my sister," he said.

"And you just traumatized me with the news that you've been fucking a demon for the past seven days," Courtney said.

"Well, more than fucking—Wait, seven days?"

"More than that?" Bo asked, then pointed to his mouth.

"Holy hell, yes," he answered.

"Calm your hard-on, Bo," Courtney grumped. "Yes, seven days and ew again. There's nothing that will get that image out of my head."

"Seven days? I had no idea." The thought was terrifying. He'd lost an entire week ."Wait, your texts were only a few days."

"I gave up on you after day five," she said, walking away.

Bo came closer. "You mean to tell me you were getting laid and getting blow jobs for the past seven nights?"

He nodded.

"All night?"

"Oh, yeah."

"Shit, you have the stamina of a bull, man."

"You two need to stop," Courtney snapped. "That is so beyond gross."

"Every night?"

"Yeah."

"Was she at least hot?" he whispered.

"Seriously hot, almost as hot as Crimson."

Bo gestured in front of his chest to guess the size of her breasts and Pete nodded then added an hourglass figure.

"Crimson's that hot?"

"No comparison to anyone here."

"You just had your dick inside of a demon, jackass, for seven nights. I don't care what cavity you were in, it's gross," Courtney said, shooting an irritated look at Bo.

"Only when she went all snakeskin and horns, Court, and even then she was pretty hot."

"Did you—"

"No, I do have some standards."

"Not many," Courtney yelled as she sat down.

Pete sat under the weight of Courtney's glare.

"No beer?" he asked.

"Nope, she cut you off as punishment," said Bo.

"You clearly don't need it, nor do you need food," she spat, still pouting.

He and Bo talked, Bo catching him up on the latest news until Courtney decided to move on from his transgressions.

"We're coming with you," she said out of nowhere.

"Coming with me, where?"

"When you finish with the souls, we're going to the other world."

He stared at her before responding to her unexpected statement. "I don't think—"

"It's not a debate, the decision has been made," Bo said. "And there's no swaying her."

"You'll lose everything you built here, Court."

"That land is our homeland, Pete, and I want to see it. Dad died trying to figure all this out. I owe it to him to go and see it. I didn't get to say goodbye to him. I owe him this much."

Sighing, Pete ran a hand over his face, the musk of the demon still strong on his fingers. He dropped his hand quickly. "You'll be stuck there. Come on, Bo, reason with her."

"Eh, tried that. It's not gonna work."

"And you're willing to leave everything behind?" Pete asked him.

"Where she goes, I go. You know that."

Pete developed a new sense of admiration for the man and his love for Courtney.

"We may not be stuck there anyway," she said.

"Pretty sure that's a one-way ticket."

"I don't know. You said that magic person came here right before the god sent Crimson back. Maybe she can take us back if we change our minds."

"Skye? I don't even know her and I'm pretty sure I'm an automatic enemy to her husband, since I'm involved with Crimson."

"Involved is a bit of a stretch, considering your recent activity," she bit out, her tone snarky.

"Are you pissed because I worried you, or are you pissed because I had sex with someone other than Crimson?"

"You cheated on her, Pete. You can't claim to love someone and then do that."

"So, you're pissed off for her?"

"She's not here to yell at you, so someone needs to."

"I have a feeling you'll find Crimson is not your typical woman, Courtney. She likes sex entirely too much to remain celibate."

He should have been annoyed or jealous at the thought, but he wasn't. He'd done the same thing. If she fell in love with someone else after what they'd shared, or chose someone over him, that would hurt. The thought was like a punch to his gut.

"Besides, we're not officially a couple." He gestured to his surroundings.

"Keep telling yourself that, Pete, but when she goes all vindictive, jealous woman on you, you might want to have a backup plan," Bo joked.

"Can we leave my sex life out of the conversation?"

"Kind of hard when we're in your sex den," Courtney answered, but he caught the curve of her lip.

"Funny."

"All right, I'll lay off. It's your sex life and Lord knows I want no part of it."

He rolled his eyes. "Are you sure you want to go with me?"

"Yes. When you get to your final tree, you wait for us, and we go together. I'm not letting you run off again. This week was hard enough. Your leaving last time was hard enough."

So that's what this was about. He had no doubt she'd meant what she'd said about their dad, but there had been more to it. He couldn't argue with her. She was as stubborn as he was.

"Fine. I'll text you when I get to the last one."

"How long do you need?" Bo asked.

"A few nights at the most. It's tedious, but it goes quickly, and

I think they realize what I'm doing. The Death God certainly does."

"He really sent that thing here to keep you from finishing?"

"Yeah."

"Pete, this is dangerous," Courtney said. "He doesn't want you doing this."

"I know, he could kill me for it, but I don't think he will. Otherwise, why not just do that? He came here and took Crimson. Why not come here and kill me?"

"He was testing you," Bo said.

"I think so. We'll see if she comes back."

"You gonna—"

"Of course he's not!" Courtney yelled. "Right?"

He didn't know if he really would, but that body reminded him so much of Crimson's. Unless, of course, she was in demon form.

"Sure," he replied, trying to get his mind from her.

"You disappear for days again. You're on your own, Pete."

"I'm not going to disappear again, Court."

She'd stood to brush her pants off. "Good. Now get to work. I want a text from you every night when you wake, understand?"

"That would require a phone with a battery that doesn't die."

She handed him a small bag he hadn't noticed. Peeking inside, he saw a new pile of portable battery chargers.

"Should be enough to make it to the end. They're all fully charged. No excuses, Pete."

"I see that. Fine, I'll text every night. I'm assuming no more beer runs?"

"No. You have work to do."

Courtney kissed him on the cheek before grabbing Bo's hand. Bo gave a wink, then followed her out of the grove. He stared at the space where they'd been and, taking a long breath, turned back to the grove, ready to go back to work. He had a kingdom to claim and a woman to find.

PETE

Pete worked tirelessly that night, coaxing the souls to their final resting place. No distractions presented themselves aside from a few stubborn trees who fought their destiny with the Death God. His tree did not come to life and part of him had been disappointed when he woke the next night to find no sign of her.

He texted Courtney as promised and kept his mind from thoughts of Crimson and the demon, knowing it was his dirty mind and his hand job that had caused the trouble in the first place.

He'd successfully settled many of the trees, but he'd underestimated the sheer size of the grove. He would need more than a few nights. Needing a break, he headed to his phone, his eyes lingering on his tree. A sex break would have been nice.

"Jesus, Pete, you've become an addict," he mumbled to himself, passing the tree.

As if it had heard him, its branches shook. He turned back to it. Maybe he shouldn't have left it until last. He hadn't been certain what to do with it since no soul resided in it. That fact worried him. If no soul lived within it, there might be a chance that he'd be stuck here.

As the thoughts swirled, he watched her long leg emerge followed by the rest of her beautiful naked body, designed to ensnare him, and to mimic Crimson's.

"Oh, no, you don't," he said, backing away.

"I've come with a message," she said. Still, he kept his distance. She gave him a seductive smile. "I told you no more spells, my pet. The Death God has granted you your freedom once you have paid the debt. He admires your skill—how you broke my spell. After all, I am his most powerful enchantress. You may proceed with no obstacles. When you reach my tree, your touch will call you home."

He was at a loss for words. He had a chance to see Crimson again and excitement burst through him at the prospect.

"As reward, you will have me until the time you are ready to return home."

A different excitement shivered through him, his pants rising. He shook his head. She was a demon, albeit a very hot demon.

He backed away. "I'm good."

She cast her eyes down, raising her prefect brow. "I see otherwise."

His mind slipped back to something she'd said. She was the Death God's most powerful enchantress, but he'd broken her spell somehow.

"So, besting you is breaking you with an orgasm?"

"Only a rare few can seduce a seductress. I should have known. No one has ever captured Crimson's heart," she said, her body suddenly against his.

"You're doing it again," he complained.

"You're too hard to resist. Can I keep you?" Her hand encompassed him, and he felt his willpower sliding with each stroke of her fingers.

"No, you can't keep me." His voice sounded hoarse when he spoke.

She brought his hand to her breast, and he felt the reaction in her nipple as it pressed against his palm.

"Take me, make me come again. No spells, I promise just amazing sex."

She kissed him before he could respond. No matter how he wanted, he couldn't resist the strokes of her hand that had found its way into his pants.

His hands slid down her curves, pulling her closer. The feel of her body against his was enough to make him disregard what lay below her beautiful façade.

"No spells," he mumbled between kisses.

"No spells, you have my word."

He drew back. "And the word of a demon is..."

She laughed, tilting her neck back. "You have his word, and I must obey."

"Yours alone would be untrustworthy?"

"Definitely," she said with a twinkle in her eye.

"Good to know." He pushed her away gently, her lips pouting in a way that called for him to kiss her.

"Okay, I'll play along. I'll fuck you, but not with Crimson's curves. I want to see what you really look like." She looked questionably at him, then shimmered to the green demon form. "Yeah, not that. Sorry, I just can't, even with those magnificent curves."

She flicked her forked tongue, and he held back the gag, chastising himself for even thinking of having sex with her again.

"Then how? I can become anything you desire."

I only desire Crimson, he thought. He was torn for a moment, knowing he was using the demon to ease his need for Crimson but, then again, she was thoroughly willing.

"No, you. What you looked like when you were alive. I see it flickering."

"That was a very long time ago."

"How long?"

"Before Eliana fled. Eons ago. Things were different then. We kept our shape most times. Since her return, we flicker in and out, but I have not held that form since before then."

"Show me who you were."

She furrowed her brow. "You are a strange one, pet."

Her skin transformed to a light bronze, her height lowering a few inches, her hair turning a golden blonde that stood prominent against her soft brown eyes.

"Hmmm." His eyes pursued her body. She couldn't have been much more than twenty when she'd died. Her small breasts were perky, with large nipples waiting to be sucked. A patch of golden hair hid the place his length was itching to enter. For a moment, she seemed small and shy, her tiny nose holding a drizzle of freckles.

"That's better," he said, moving to her.

He bent over and kissed her, feeling her small mouth with his tongue, her own greeting his. He touched her breasts, finding they were the perfect size for his hands. Rubbing his thumbs against her nipples, he felt them rise in reaction. She moaned, and he sensed her give control over to him.

He considered that this might be dangerous. That he risked this demon falling for him or that he would fall for her. He was certain the latter wouldn't happen, though. Her hands brushed along his chest, and down to his pants. No, this wasn't dangerous. There was no risk he'd fall for her, even though a part of him had grown addicted to the pleasure she gave him. She understood that Crimson owned his heart, that he wouldn't love another. She worked him free of his pants, her hand grasping him so that he lost all focus. But he wanted to break her again, wanted to continue hearing her moans.

Pushing her hand away, he settled her to the ground, enjoying the dominance she was giving him. He spread her legs with his thigh and sank his fingers into the wetness that awaited him. Taking her nipple in his mouth, he sucked and kissed, his hand stimulating her below and rubbing her clit until she was clinging to him. The throes of her climax drove him close to the edge and, unable to take the throb of his dick any longer, he penetrated her. An ecstasy filled cry slipped from her lips but he stopped it with his kiss. He brought her to climax again as his orgasm hit him hard, a certain intimacy to the moment that shouldn't have been.

As if knowing, she flipped him before he could catch his breath. Her cheeks were flush still from her release, adding a beautiful shade of pink to her skin.

"That was naughty," she said. "Now it's my turn."

The sex demon was back, the innocence and vulnerability gone. She devoured him, her mouth irresistible as she stoked a fire in him that he couldn't calm. With a burst, it raged through him in one exhausting flame. For the remains of the night until dawn, they explored each other. There were no spells, no magic, only their bodies and what they did to each other. As the effects of his final orgasm hammered through his body, she rose and returned to her tree. He laid there, knowing he'd chosen his path, that he would continue to take pleasure from her until he had Crimson in his arms again. A moment of guilt surfaced, but it faded as the first rays of dawn took him away.

EACH NIGHT PETE'S demon would appear but now she waited for him, sometimes accompanying him as he freed the souls. She would talk to him as he worked, answering his questions. Her true mortal form was ever present now, although she remained naked, something that made focusing extremely difficult. Needing to call her something other than his demon, he'd nicknamed her his tree nymph, a term with which she seemed particularly pleased.

He would take her whenever the impulse overcame his concentration, pushing her up against a random tree or bending her over in the grass. Sometimes she'd simply sneak below him as he stood, working him into a frenzy with her mouth until he could do nothing but clench his hands against the tree and wait for her to finish him.

Each night, he texted Courtney, assuring her that he was working.

This eve, he'd taken his tree nymph when he'd reached the final patch of trees, knowing there wasn't enough time to finish his work. There was a part of him that wanted to delay finishing another day. There were many unknowns awaiting him, including Crimson. What he'd had with her here in the grove may have been lost the day she left. She may have let another man claim her heart and forgotten about him. Allowing one more night in the grove delayed that possible reality. Taking one more night of pleasure seemed a good alternative.

As Pete lay there, letting her blonde hair drift between his fingers, he asked, "What was your name? I don't think it was tree nymph, although I have taken a liking to that nickname."

She traced his chest with her nails. "I don't have a name."

"Well, what were you called before you died?"

She thought for a few moments. "I don't remember."

"How do you not remember your name?"

"It was many thousands of years ago, my pet. No one uses their real names but the living and the gods."

"Huh. Well, you need a name."

She lifted herself so that her soft brown eyes locked with his. There was a flicker of that vulnerability again and he caressed her cheek with his thumb, her mouth catching it as he traced her lips. Her tongue slipped over it stirring his arousal.

He could think of a few dirty names to call her, but he passed them by.

He released a moan as she moved her thigh over his rising erection. *Traitor,* he thought.

"Ash," he said, thinking of the way the trees turned to ash as they moved on, knowing hers would do the same when the time came to part from her.

He didn't love her. There was nothing but physical need on both their sides, an understanding that their bodies went well together. His heart was Crimson's, always. It didn't matter what lay in wait for him when he finally stepped from the grove.

"I like it," she said with a purr. "Although I do like when you call me your tree nymph. I like being yours."

He moved her head so that he could look at her. "You're not mine."

"I am. But you know we can't love, right? Your love for Crimson is safe. I'll never want more than this."

"You can't love?"

"No, silly. I'm a demon. I have no heart, just desire, lust, hunger, thirst. But not love."

"Wow."

"So, your heart is safe with me. I can never steal it."

"But I could have fallen for you."

"No," she said, putting a finger to his lips. "I can feel the pull you have to her. It's right here." She placed her hand on his heart. "And here," she continued, nipping his chest and drawing blood.

"Ouch."

"She's in you. Your blood bound to her as yours is to her. That cannot be severed."

"You can sense all of that?"

"Mmhmm."

He watched as she studied the blood on her finger before licking it from the bite. Her eyes glanced curiously at him.

"There is something that sleeps below it, however. Far below your blood."

"What does that mean?"

Her fingers drifted over his chest, her eyes following their motion. "Your bond with Crimson is unbreakable but...something lingers. Something not ready to be revealed, but it's there. You have a fate that has yet to be shown. In time, my pet."

She flicked her eyes to his, a seriousness in them that had him concerned until it faded, her features relaxing. He let it go, not certain he wanted to know more about his fate. There'd been enough revelations.

Instead, he asked, "What did you do to end up with this curse?"

"Running from your destiny will not help you escape it."

"I don't have a destiny. There's nothing more than me freeing myself and finding Crimson."

She gave him a doubtful look that told him how wrong he really was before saying, "I stabbed my husband to death, then murdered my parents before I drowned myself."

A flicker of fear shivering through him.

"I won't hurt you. I made an oath to the Death God when he sent me here. I would shred anyone who dared harm you."

"That's reassuring. Why did you murder your husband?"

He was still trying to figure out why the Death God hadn't had her murder him but was curious about her story.

"He was a prick. My parents married me off to him, and he was old and horny. I was a virgin. I didn't understand the enjoyment of sex. He was cruel, demanding, and impatient. He degraded me, abused me. He took me in the ass on our dining table and as he was recovering, I brought the kitchen knife to his heart, then his dick, then his... Well, let's just say he was full of holes when I was through. I went to my parents' home and slit their necks before I drowned myself in the river."

He'd pulled his hands from her, his eyes wide with disbelief.

"The Death God punished me, saying since I had murdered

because of sex, I would spend the rest of my days craving it. As further punishment, he tied the soul of that asshole to me. He'd been naughty as well, and the Death God made him a demon at judgement. Both of us were stuck with each other until I fed him to a hunter."

"A hunter?"

"They are great big beasts that roam the Shadow Realm. The Death God uses them to hunt down demons who cross him or souls he needs to destroy. But they will feed on anything that crosses their paths."

"And you fed him to this beast?"

"Right as he was ready to climax, I pulled my mouth back and pushed. Sneaky, I know. I saw it behind him, stalking as I was sucking him."

"Good God, you're something."

"It broke the tie. They're soul eaters. They get you and poof, no more anything."

"Remind me not to visit the Shadow Realm."

She traced her fingers up his chest, slipping herself above him. There was no delay in his reaction to her body, and his length rose to the moisture it met.

"Is there anything that doesn't turn you on?"

"No," she replied with a laugh. "I'm a sex demon. I live for pleasure and feed on death. There are others who are worse. Demons who feed on pain, who torture their victims and climax to their screams of agony. I torture through sex."

He thought of Crimson and what she'd told him about her past.

"Why is that so bad?" he asked her as she tipped her pelvis back and took him into her. Warmth surrounded him, distracting him from the conversation. Longing for the softness of her breasts, he reached up and caressed them. She sighed, melting into his touch.

"You really want to know?" She gave him a long kiss that caused his dick to jerk inside of her.

"Yes," he muttered against her lips.

His arousal climbed quickly, and he dropped his hands to her hips, urging her movement. He didn't care what she told him, as long as she continued to satisfy him. She dragged her lips down his neck.

"First, we seduce our victims, we shift to whatever their fantasy is. Yours was Crimson. I could have appeared to you as her, but the Death God had warned me that you would see through that façade. Your body would know the difference. So instead, I made myself as close to her as I could, to remind you of her and pull you into my spell."

"So, you give them a fantasy and the kind of sex they dream of? Still not seeing a downside to you." He couldn't help the grunt that followed when she gyrated her hips with his thrust. His hands tightened on her hips as she drove him closer to the peak of exultation.

"Shh. I'm not done," she said against his lips. "Once we have them enthralled, we pleasure them."

She stopped her kisses and lifted her chest from his. Her body moved faster, driving his dick further into her. The motion stole his breath from him. Just as he was ready to climax, she stopped, leaving him aching for more. Her body slowly lifted from him, falling again in an amazingly erotic way, his climax heightening so that it was pulsing to be freed.

She leaned over, bringing herself up so that his tip teetered just inside of her. "Then as he's at the height of his orgasm..."

She dropped back down, enveloping his shaft, his orgasm breaking. It crashed through him with the intensity of her movement so that all he could do was hold her hips down as he filled her with thrust after thrust of his pent-up essence.

"We slice him open right down the middle." She shivered,

moving again as the last shudders of his climax were still pummeling him. Her orgasm was powerful. The thought of her action stunted his but urged hers forth. She cried out as she grasped his shoulders. Her body arched forward, a move that caused her breast to hit his mouth. Even with that image in his mind, he couldn't help taking it and sucking on the supple skin and taut nipple. His response to her story was a combination of horror and erotica. With her hips thrusting again, her second climax building, he grabbed her ass and flipped her to her back. Pinning her arms, he let his semi-hardness slip from her. Her cry of agony echoed through the grove.

"I don't want to know anymore," he mumbled, taking her breast in his mouth again. Her body pushed against his in response. He took her other breast in his hand, roughly tugging at her nipple until her groans had him firm again. He drove back into her, feeling the need to take her with the aggression her story had spurred in him.

His hands released hers and pulled her leg up, squeezing her waist as she brought her arms around him. She urged him deeper until her legs were shaking with the need to come. But he wanted to torment her for turning him on with the brutality of her demon ways. Forcing himself to stop, he dropped to her waist, his finger brushing her clit before his tongue followed. Her moan filled the silence. Every time she drew closer, he'd pause, letting her hover just at the precipice, his own desire flaring at her response so that he too was dying to join her.

"Stop, please," she cried out, her voice husky.

He thrust his tongue into her, tasting the mix of their juices. Her legs clenched around him while her body erupted, her cry one of ecstasy that clawed at his need for her. He plunged into her, unable to resist any longer, her wetness enveloping him as she convulsed around him. As his climax crested, he exploded inside her, the force taking him to a place he didn't think he'd ever return from.

"If I'd known telling you about my demon ways would turn

you on that much, I would have done it days ago," she said after some time, breathless still.

He lifted himself, tracing the curve of her breast.

"Not sure why hearing about you gutting a man while he comes would be a turn on but please don't tell me what you do next."

"We join his orgasm. The mix of pain and rapture makes for quite a turn on. Then we make sure our partner comes and we feast on our victims."

"I said not to tell me."

"We're not that bad. At least we bring pleasure in death. The succubus is truly evil. They have this nectar that drips from their breasts and keeps their prisoners wanting more. It also keeps them from climaxing. They fuck and fuck until they're bleeding from their dicks and orifices, but they don't know it, they just want release. Now that's a demon you don't want to meet."

"Good to know," he said, intensely disturbed and irritated that her words had stripped the high of his climax from him, "and thank you for not gutting me."

WHEN ONLY HER TREE REMAINED, they stood before it. Pete had taken Ash as he always did, making time for breaks to feast on her until there was no more need for breaks. As they'd reached the last tree, he'd taken her again, memorizing her curves, her taste, her sighs, knowing he'd miss her. She'd left a mark on him—one he'd have to explain to Crimson, one that to any other woman would mean the end of any further talk. He wasn't worried, though. His heart still belonged to Crimson. There was only room for her. But he was fond of Ash, and he would miss his tree nymph.

"Well, this is our parting," she said, a hint of sadness to her voice.

He took her hand but remained quiet, knowing all the consequences that came with the last tree. This moment meant losing her, leaving this world, hunting Crimson in a world he didn't know, facing a myriad of unknowns. And then there was the destiny comment Ash had made the prior night, the suggestion that something lingered below his connection to Crimson.

As if sensing his apprehension, she pulled him closer to the tree.

"It's time Pete." She turned to him, bringing her hand to touch his cheek tenderly. "Another time, another place, I could have loved you and you me, but we are past that time. Find Crimson, do all the things you do to me to her, and love her."

She kissed him, then drew back. "You are a king, Peter. Your destiny awaits and I'm glad I got to know the man who will change the course of our world. Goodbye, my pet."

He should have asked her what she meant—what his presence had to do with the course of their world. But he let it pass, grabbing her instead, and pushing her against her tree. He kissed her greedily, his hands touching everywhere for one last feel of her.

She reached for him, bringing him as close to her as she could, pulling at his pants with the same desperation to have him one last time that he was experiencing.

"I want to be inside of you once more," he whispered before penetrating her, lifting her body and guiding her legs around him. Her breath caught with the motion. In a frenzy, he rode the tides of his need until he came once more, breathless and shaking with her as the night sky faded.

"I'm glad I can't love," she said as he withdrew from inside of her.

"Why is that?"

She gave him the beautiful smile of the innocent girl she'd once been. "Because you would surely break my heart."

Stunned by her words, he stared at her, unsure what to say

and knowing if it had been another time and other circumstances, he could have loved her, too.

The innocent look faded, her eyes twinkling as the sun peeked above the horizon.

"Tell Crimson if she ever wants to play, to find me. I will always answer your call, my pet."

She kissed him again as the morning took them both, stealing her from him forever.

CRIMSON

With the details settled, Crimson's tension only worsened. Stavin was preparing to leave for Kantenda with Bormick's men where he would kidnap a mage for Crimson's use. It bought her some time, but it didn't bring her any comfort. She would still need to go to Theodore and beg for his help. Not to mention, she'd need to convince Stavin and Bormick that she had killed Theodore or risk them discovering that she'd been plotting against them. And she would lose Bormick. No matter how she played the scenarios, she lost Bormick. The thought was enough to make her knees buckle.

The morning Stavin was to leave, he grabbed her as she was walking toward the great hall, shoving her against the wall. Lost in thought, she hadn't seen him approaching her. His move caught her off guard, sending her heard racing in momentary fear. "There's something I don't like about this plan, Crimson. Something I don't trust."

"I thought Bormick was the distrustful one."

"He was until you controlled his dick. Now that I can no longer touch you, I'm seeing clearer."

"And what do you see, Stavin?"

"Trickery. You're turning him against me with your curves and your mouth."

"I'm doing no such thing. Now let me go."

"I know who you are better than you think I do, Crimson. I was in your service far too long to not know that everything you do and every man you touch serves a purpose."

He traced a finger down her neck to the swell of her breasts.

"Do you want to fuck me, Stavin? Is that what this is about?"

He grabbed her hips. "I'm definitely going to fuck you. He's cut me off from touching, so I'm going to take."

"I thought you didn't trust me?"

He undid his pants, pulling out his growing length to stroke his hands along it before pulling her skirts up. She didn't fight him, she didn't care. This was what she'd wanted—a divide between the two men.

He shoved his hand between her legs. "I don't trust you, but that doesn't mean I don't want to feel you again."

She grew weak at his words as his fingers filled her. She let a sigh escape.

"Come for me, baby," he whispered against her ear.

"Seems an odd thing to ask of someone you just insulted."

He shoved his mouth against hers, pulling her dress down to expose her breasts. Drawing his finger over her nipple, she lurched into him as it rose to his command. She wrapped her hand around his shaft while his fingers continued their assault below her dress. She knew Bormick didn't want him touching her, but it felt good, and if Bormick found out, it would further divide the two. Her body wasn't protesting, and she shuddered against him at his touch.

"You're going to scream in ecstasy for me, then I'm going to fuck you before I'm sent away. If Bormick gets this every night, I want a piece to hold me over."

His mouth dropped to her breast, and she threw her head back, his tongue stimulating shockwaves through her.

Wrapping her fingers in his hair, she bucked as his fingers dug into her. His mouth never left her breast, taunting her arousal, and when he rubbed her clit the flames that he'd been stoking flared through her lower body.

She was gasping, her climax building, and he knew it. He didn't have the same effect on her as Bormick, but he was still good at what he did. She'd ensured he knew how to treat her in the days she'd first taken him. Making certain he'd changed his taking ways and started giving. Pete had spoiled her and now she needed release as often as she could get it.

Lifting his head, he kissed her. "I will find out what you're up to," he said against her lips before removing his hand and replacing it with his hardened length. She let out a cry as he entered her, her orgasm right on the edge, the feel of him bringing it crashing down around her. He grunted as she shook from the force of it, continuing his thrusts until he too came, his arms tight around her with his final shudders.

"Gods, you are a temptress," he said. "If he'd kept me in your bed, I'd still be under your spell."

"You just spilled your seed in me, Stavin. You are under my spell."

He slammed his mouth against hers, his kiss rough and force-ful. Within seconds he was torn from her. Bormick shoved him against the other wall as her skirts were still falling.

"I said no touching, and you put your dick into her against my command?"

Stavin glared at him. "She's ours, Bormick, and I wanted to fuck her before you send me on this fool's errand."

Bormick punched him. "I find your dick in her again and I'll rip it from your body."

Stavin rubbed his jaw. "She's enchanted you, Bormick. Wake up. We've been friends for a long time, shared many women, but this one we can't share? What has she done to you?"

"You touch her again and we're no longer friends. She's mine."

Stavin jerked away from him and pulled himself together. "I know who you are, Crimson. I watched you manipulate men for years, even breaking the Mage Warrior's husband. Don't think I don't see what you're doing. You're a great fuck and an even greater deceiver."

He stormed off.

Shit. Her mind raced with worry. His words insinuated that he knew something and that was a problem. But only Hentrom knew the truth. It was possible that his inquiries had gotten back to Stavin, and that's why he'd become suspicious.

Bormick grabbed her face, his eyes boring into hers. He said nothing for a long while, and the intensity of his stare had her heart in tremors.

"Are you enchanting me?"

"No."

"Is that why my blood calls to you? Why I can't stop wanting you?"

"No."

He stepped closer. "You deceive me, I will not hesitate to kill you."

She heard the threat but read the need in his eyes. The need for Stavin to be wrong. In that moment, she didn't want to hurt him.

She gripped her hands, her breaths short.

"Did he make you come?" he asked, throwing her off.

"Yes." He was causing her to be flustered, and she couldn't seem to give him more than one-word answers.

"And you let him?"

"Yes."

"Hmm, then I believe punishment is due."

"What?"

He picked her up and tossed her over his shoulder.

"Bormick, what are you doing?" Fear reared its head and for a moment she worried what he would do to her.

"Making sure you know to not fuck with me and to keep your legs closed for other men."

A flutter of anticipation danced with the fear.

He took her to his room, tossing her on the bed in an undignified manner. Before she could react, he ripped her dress from her.

"I liked that dress."

"Too bad. I like your body without Stavin's cum inside of it."

He dragged her to the top of the bed, tearing a strip of her dress and tying her hands to the post. She drew in a breath, her arousal rising.

"You are mine, Crimson. Not Stavin's, not anyone else's."

But she was someone else's and her eyes must have reflected the truth. He grabbed her face roughly, searching her eyes. "Who?"

She remained silent, her vulnerable position giving her sudden worry.

"Your body. You gave me claim to your body." She saw the sudden understanding in his expression.

"That's all you asked for."

He gave a menacing laugh and positioned himself over her. "I claimed you. All of you. What part of you is not mine?" He was growling, which both stoked her arousal and her fear.

He put his face to hers, his lips so close she could have kissed him. "What part do I not own?"

"My heart."

He moved back, his eyes intense. "If someone owns your heart, they own all of you."

"My body is—"

"Another man's. Whose?"

She swallowed. "It's complicated."

"Complicated, Crimson?"

"No one can own all of me, Bormick. I've never been whole. The Death God owns my soul."

His brows furrowed as her words sank in, his face softening slightly.

"My father traded it before I was born to secure my throne. I told you I have favor with the Death God. I never lied about that."

"And who owns your heart?"

"Peter," she murmured, his name painful to say.

He sat back on his knees.

"You love another man, yet you..."

"Want you with the same need I have for him. My blood calls to you just as it does to him. I need you, Bormick."

He hovered over her again. "And this Peter, where is he while you've been fucking me?"

"Lost to me. The Death God sentenced him to take my punishment. He is beyond my reach for eternity."

He studied her, looking for any sign of doubt.

"You said you don't do love, Bormick."

"I don't."

"Then you don't need my heart."

"If he's claimed your heart, he's claimed your body, the same one I claimed."

"The same one I let you claim because..." She paused, unsure if she wanted to be vulnerable, to say the words aloud. "Because I need you, like I've only ever needed him. I don't think I can live without you, Bormick."

"And if he were free?"

"Then I would claim you both. There is no life without you now. You...you do something to me. There's some hold you have on me that's too strong to resist."

He wiped his hand over his face. "Do you love me, Crimson?"

"I don't know if that's what it is. It's different from what I feel for him."

He rose from her. "Dammit. You're asking me to share you, to share your body, to not touch your heart." He stopped, his eyes meeting hers, the vulnerability in them crushing her. "What if I can't do that?"

"Then I suppose you'll have to kill me."

His expression hardened. "Damn you, Crimson," he muttered as he paced the room.

Her wrists were growing sore from the tight bind that held them, and she momentarily wondered if he would leave her this way.

"You love another man. Your soul belongs to a god. What do I do with that?"

"You take my body."

He stopped pacing to look at her.

"You don't love me, Bormick. You told me that. We're about fucking, not love."

"And if I find him and kill him?"

"You would kill a piece of me in the process."

He sighed, coming back to her, and running his hand over her leg. "He's trapped?"

"Yes."

His hand climbed to her thigh. "Tell me about him."

She creased her brow, unsure of what he was asking.

"Don't give me that look. Tell me about him."

He climbed over her again, hovering above her. "What does he look like?"

She thought about it before saying. "A lot like you—the same bright blue eyes, same build, but his hair is black. He has all these ink markings on his chest and arms, and they climb to his back, covering his muscles."

"Ink? Strange."

"He's from another world, belonging to the gods' brothers. That's where he's trapped."

"Hmm." His fingers came closer to where her warmth lie, teasing the edge of her entrance. "Does he make you come?"

She drew in a sharp breath, arousal soaring through her as his fingers sank into her. "Yes."

"Like I do?"

Her eyes rolled back with the slow cadence of his fingers that were moving slowly in and out of her. "Yes."

"Wrong answer," he said, pinching her clit.

She drew her leg up and let out a cry in response.

"Let's try again," he said, pushing her thighs further apart, his fingers slowly stroking her so that her breath caught. He licked her nipple, pulling it into his mouth, and scraping his teeth against it. Her body was an electric current that sparked at his touch.

"Does he make you come like I do?" he asked, drawing up to look at her, his fingers teasing her so that her entire lower body yearned for more.

"No," she gasped.

He sank his fingers into her, her stomach knotting and twisting in pleasure.

"Better answer. Nobody makes you come like I do," he stated, his tongue circling her nipple before sucking it back in. She shivered in expectation as he dug his fingers deeper, but he drew them out, lifting his mouth from her breast.

A cry escaped her before she could catch it, the desperation laden in its tone. He moved back and removed his shirt. She watched him intently, her legs tremoring in anticipation. Lowering himself so that his chest touched only her nipples, he slid toward her mouth. The move tantalized her so that she couldn't help but arch into him. He dropped his mouth to hers, kissing her with a ferocity like he'd never done before. The power of it left her breathless, the demand of it melting her.

"First you let Stavin fuck you," he said, licking her lower lip before biting it gently, "then you climax for him." He pressed his engorged bulge against her, her legs so spread she could feel him straining to enter her. "Then you tell me you're in love with someone else, that what I claimed is his."

His hand traced her curves up to her breast, where his fingers circled the skin of it, lingering softly over her nipple.

"What am I supposed to do with that, Crimson?"

He pulled her nipple, a shudder of pain flickering through her as his mouth dropped to the other, biting at it. His erection pushed harder against her. Her body was screaming for him. She wanted release worse than she ever had, so badly it was burning through her. All the times she'd ever tormented men, teased them like this until they'd broken and now the torture had been turned on her.

"What do you want me to do, Crimson?"

"Give me release, please," she begged.

"I should leave you like this, leave you to suffer as punishment."

A whimper escaped at the thought. His body lifted and the area between her legs was suddenly cold without him. He rose, then jerked her body to the side of the bed. The ties around her wrist dug uncomfortably as he forced her legs wider and went down on her. Her building climax rose again with his touch.

"Fuck, you taste like Stavin," he spat, nipping at her clit so that she yelped before his tongue soothed it. She arched her back, waves of need gripping her from the inside out. Her climax climbed with each lick, sending her fighting the restraints, her legs wrapping around him to stay him.

Laughing, he pushed them away, their strength no match to his. His tongue traced the inside of her leg, his fingers stroking her again. Her body was an inferno of unmet need.

"Beg me," he commanded, biting the inside of her thigh and lifting his fingers from her.

"I-I don't beg," she stammered.

He swiped his tongue across her, then moved from her.

"Beg me," he said again, rising above her, his breath hot

against her ear. "I want to hear that I'm the one you want, the one who owns you."

"Please."

"Please what?" He spread her legs open again, undoing his pants and pressing himself against her. His mouth took her breast while his tip rubbed through her moisture sending currents pouring through her.

"You know I'm yours."

"Do I? When part of you is owned by the Death God, the other by another man? What does that leave me, Crimson?"

"It leaves you the rest of me, every inch of my body."

"The body previously claimed." His hand slid under her ass, the head of his hardness sinking into her. Her cry shook with her body. "This body is mine. I own you. Say it, Crimson, and beg for me."

"It's yours. You own me. Please, Bormick. I want you inside of me. Please give me release."

He traced his finger down her neck. "Because no one makes you as hungry as I do. No one makes you come like I do."

"No one," she replied hoarsely.

His mouth covered hers and he pushed into her with a force that sent her over the edge, her body convulsing as release swept through her. Her head fell back with her cry. Still, he continued his thrusts, going deeper with each one. His mouth stifled her cry as another orgasm broke her. The ecstasy of it sent her spiraling so that all she could do was hold onto him with her legs. While she was still in the throes of her release, he joined her, his own anguished grunt meeting hers.

He dropped his head to the crook of her neck. "I want all of you, Crimson, and I will not share you."

He released her wrists, bringing her hands around his neck. She held him while the blood flowed back into her hands. This time, when his mouth met hers again, it was softer, more sensual. He made love to her, the closest thing to making love that either could do, both knowing to go past that line would crush them both. But as she climaxed with him again, she wondered if she'd grown too close, too hungry for him. He was the perfect mate for her, as was Pete, both calling to her in different ways and like no man had ever done before.

"Dangerous," he whispered before lifting himself from her, his blue eyes twinkling as his hand drifted down her leg.

She watched him dress, taking in the muscles that lined his back, the tightness of his ass atop his thick muscular legs. He was a warrior. Every inch of him was trained to kill, his reputation known for having no mercy. No one crossed him. But with her, he showed a soft side she'd never attributed to the rumors of Bormick the thief, the brutal man who had raged his way into her kingdom.

As his eyes met hers, devouring her with their glide across her body, she realized she'd broken him, just as he had broken her, as Pete had first shattered the facade she'd spent her life building.

Pete was a good man, naughty but good. She and Bormick, however, were wicked. They had pasts that were rife with the deeds they'd done. Those pasts were their battle armor. Neither could ever have hoped for redemption, but perhaps that's what made them perfect for each other.

He shook his head, muttering, "Dangerous," before he walked out the door, leaving her to her thoughts whether she wanted them or not.

PETE

W hat happens now?" Courtney asked. She, Bo, and Pete were standing before the lone tree.

"I'm not really sure," Pete admitted.

He'd texted them when he'd woken, meandering the empty grove until they arrived. Ash hadn't returned. They'd said their goodbyes, and they had been final. A part of him missed her and he wondered at the attachment he'd formed to her—a sex demon, a demon who gutted men in the throes of orgasm, and whom he'd grown to adore. His attachment to her was warped, he knew, but she'd shared her true self with him, been his companion in a void of solitude, and something told him if he were to ever find himself in the Shadow Realm, she'd protect him.

The thought of taking her and Crimson together, his tongue tasting her as Crimson tasted him, crossed his mind, but he brushed it away quickly. Not quick enough, however.

"Can you get your mind out of the gutter for two seconds?" Courtney complained.

"How do you know my mind was in the gutter?"

"Besides the sheepish grin and the hard-on you're sporting?"

"Is it appropriate for my sister to be looking at my dick?"

"It's hard not to notice when it's sticking out so far."

"That's gross, Court."

"You're gross, Pete."

"You two done?" Bo asked. "I don't know what's worse, her bitching about you being gone all those years or her bitching at you for everything else."

She elbowed Bo, who grunted in pain.

"Just do what you need to do, Pete," she griped.

He wasn't really sure what he needed to do. Ash's tree was soulless. She had told him how the Death God had taken the soul. Eliana, whose place he still didn't completely understand, had crossed her over to the Upper Realm.

He had no idea how to return a soulless tree.

Wiping his face, he drew closer to her tree, placing his hand on it and trying not to think of his tree nymph. He sifted through the pages of notes he'd read, the things he'd learned, but none of it tackled an empty tree.

As he stood there thinking, the black of the tree began to move, the ebony following, both gliding over his hand and wrapping up his arm like ivy.

"Pete? Is that supposed to happen?" Courtney asked.

"I don't know."

The ebony continued to spread across his body in long tendrils, inching up his face. He could feel the two sides of it—the good and bad, Shadow Realm and Upper Realm, the call to both. The tree had emptied its essence upon him. It swirled, stirring his blood, before seeping into his skin with a tingle that coursed through him like electricity. Power. But he didn't know what to do with it or what it meant.

The tree disintegrated, a strange weight upon his head as it did. He heard Courtney inhale sharply, but he couldn't draw his eyes from the woman who now stood where the tree had been.

She was glorious. Power shimmered around her form. Her long auburn hair cascaded down her back in thick locks, her blue eyes reminding him of ones he'd seen before...ones he'd seen on Skye. He did a double-take, thinking it was her for a moment, but this woman had an ancient knowledge to her eyes that Skye hadn't held.

"Child of Digremile, you have done well." Her eyes glanced around the empty grove. "You have done what no other before you has done. Keeper and Guardian now as one, previously forced to work together and failing."

"Who are you?" he asked.

"You know the answer to that question."

"Eliana."

She laughed. "Only a few are permitted to use my name. To all others, I am Queen of the Shadow Realm, Ferrier of Souls, Death's Mistress. But perhaps I will make an exception for you."

She looked at his head, and he brought a hand up to feel the thick metal. Bringing it down, he studied it. A crown—black as the ebony of the trees, its diamonds white as its ivory—glinted in the moonlight.

"When your family betrayed my brother, he punished the two offenders, leaving their brother as king and imprisoning the soul of the third, whom he murdered. My brother sentenced him in the afterlife as Keeper to the lost souls. The second brother, he let live, banishing him to this world as Guardian to the forest. His curse was to free himself and his brother's soul, but his pride failed him. With every passing generation, the story morphed until, in time, your family lost the original knowledge and with it the true test. The Keeper fared only slightly better, replaced with my lover before my brother cursed Crimson to that duty. His soul was ravaged by the demons lurking in my brother's kingdom. The Guardian's son continued to carry the punishment until today when you broke the curse."

There were so many questions tumbling through Pete's mind, but he didn't have time to ask them before she continued.

"The Kingdom of Digremile is yours. The eldest brother's

line now gone by Crimson's doing. Wear your crown proudly, for it will cost you. Are you ready to return home, Guardian?"

He thought of Crimson. She would be worth all of it, everything he was leaving behind. "Yes."

Her eyes softened. "Crimson is not my favored child, but be gentle on her. I believe there is more to her than she sees, and perhaps you will be the one to lead her to discover that. But be ready. You will need to truly love her for what awaits. The call of blood is irresistible and cannot be avoided."

A portal, like the one he'd seen Skye emerge from, appeared. Eliana glanced over at Courtney and Bo.

"I expected one, but I see there is more than one limb to this tree. Are you certain you want to follow him? Our world is wrought with danger, especially now."

"Yes, he's my brother. I lost him once; I won't lose him again." Pete met her eyes, and she gave him a proud smile. "You have a destiny to claim, Pete, and I owe it to Dad to see you claim it."

He only nodded, unable to form the words, and turned back to the goddess.

"And you?" she asked Bo. "This is not your path."

"She is my path. Where she goes, I go."

"So be it."

She came close to Pete, laying her hands on his, and a sense of her endless power engulfed him. For a moment, the reality that a goddess—a being with the power to create worlds, to easily take his life—was standing before him, touching him, speaking with him, was overwhelming. Her blue eyes shimmered, as if she'd known his thoughts, and perhaps she had. She was a goddess, after all.

"I can see why she loves you. Keep your mind and your heart open. She loves you, but the call of blood is strong, just as it was to you," she whispered.

She faded, leaving him to wonder at her words. The portal stood before them, awaiting their move.

"Wow, that was intense," Courtney said.

"Yeah. You guys ready?" he asked, grazing his crown with his one hand and feeling the small hilt of the knife with his other.

"Yes, let's go claim your destiny, King Peter," she teased.

"That sounds even stranger out loud than it does in my head."

Taking a deep breath, he stepped through the portal. The air was forced from his lungs for just a moment before the grove disappeared and he found himself in a room filled with guarded faces. Courtney and Bo bumped into him, almost knocking him over, but his eyes never left the angry hazel eyes of the man holding the largest weapon he'd ever seen.

"What the hell?" the man said, taking a defensive stance and aiming the strangely glowing weapon directly at Pete.

PETE

Pete?" Pete heard a familiar voice, then saw Skye put her hand on the man's arm. Pete remained tense, but the man raised his brow and lowered his weapon.

"This is Crimson's latest victim?" he said gruffly.

"I don't think he's a victim, Mark," Skye said.

So, this was Skye's husband.

"Pete, how are you here?" Her blue eyes were the most beautiful navy color. They mesmerized him. It was hard not to look at her when she was so breathtaking.

"I broke the curse. Where's Crimson?" he asked, finally pulling his eyes from her and looking around.

"Wouldn't we all love to know," Mark muttered, lowering his weapon the remainder of the way, the glow of magic fading from it. Pete pondered his comment as the weapon transformed to a small obelisk and Mark sheathed it.

"What curse?" Skye asked, as if that astonishing sight hadn't just occurred.

Pete was still staring at the weapon when Courtney said, "Our family curse." She raised Pete's hand as he still gripped the crown.

Skye furrowed her lovely brow. Jesus, she was striking. *Focus, Pete,* he chastised himself.

"Who are you?" she asked, taking the crown from him and looking back at Mark, who moved next to her. The two shared a concerned look.

"I'm Pete's sister, Courtney, and this is Bo."

"Interesting." She turned back to Mark, not bothering to introduce herself, her eyes inquisitive.

"Don't give me that look. He's got the answers. How did you get here Pete, and what curse?" Mark asked.

"Where's here?" he finally forced himself to ask.

"About time you wake up," Courtney muttered.

"You're in the Kingdom of Kantenda. My kingdom," Skye answered.

"Not earth?" Courtney asked.

"Different realm, one world lower through the interlaced worlds."

"Wow, that was a *Dr. Strange* moment that has my mind blown now," Bo said.

Pete shot him a look.

"So we're home." The word seemed odd to say, and Pete wasn't certain he'd ever adjust to calling another world his home.

"Home?" Mark scrunched his brow, and Pete could read his confusion.

"It's a long story, one I think we need to talk about." He looked around the room. It was a sitting room of sorts. There were several men and women with similar weapons to Mark's, standing in protective stances. All wore what looked like a uniform, as if they were some sort of guard.

"Can we sit? It's been a long few nights."

He caught Courtney's snort and elbowed her.

"Yes, please sit," Skye said. "Noah, I think we're fine. Can one of you get some drinks for our guests?"

"I think drinks can wait, Skye," Mark said. "Noah, you stay. Camin, summon Elspeth and Trent. This sounds serious."

A man in the far corner emerged from the shadows, his dress different from the guards. He eyed Pete but remained silent. The colors of the room shifted, and a portal appeared, distinctly different than the one he'd seen Skye create. However, he'd conjured it the same way. He walked through, and the portal dissipated. Pete couldn't help his shock. There was no doubt it would take him time to grow accustomed to magic.

"Does everyone have magic in this place?"

Skye smiled, and it about knocked him from his feet. He was tempted to ask if they made all the women in this world so beautiful, but thought better of it, not knowing how Mark would react. Both she and Crimson were stunning. At the thought of Crimson, his focus shifted, and he remembered his purpose.

"Where's Crimson?" he asked again. "The Death God pulled her away—"

"He pulled her here," Skye answered.

"Much to my annoyance," Mark grumbled, standing behind Skye as she gracefully sat. Her dress billowed perfectly around her legs before she gestured for them to sit. The one named Noah remained in the corner, his hand on the hilt of his weapon. These people were not ones to mess with. Pete caught Bo's eyes, his expression carrying the same tension Pete was feeling.

"Tell us everything," Skye said, her voice entrancing.

He began to speak, but another portal formed and the one named Camin stepped through, followed by two people in long robes of royal blue matching their queen's eyes.

"Elspeth, Trent, this is Peter, his sister Courtney, and Bo."

"The Keeper Crimson told us of?" Trent asked as Elspeth evaluated them silently.

"Who are the other two?" Courtney asked.

"Who?" Skye asked, looking around.

"I mean, I know who you are based on what Pete told us, but

who's the intense guy behind you and that brooding guy in the corner?"

Skye laughed as Mark muttered, "Brooding. I'll have to remember that one."

"The one behind her is Skye's husband, Mark, right?" Pete asked.

Mark crossed his arms. He was an imposing presence, very soldier like, his muscles bulging under his shirt. Pete had no doubt this man was trained to kill.

"You seem to know a lot about us," Mark said.

"More than you probably want me to know."

Mark grimaced.

"The brooding one is Noah," Skye said. "He's Mark's second in command."

"Second in command? Kings have a second in command?" Bo asked.

"No, the commander of the Elite has a second in command," he said. "Now talk. I want to know why you're here and how you came to be here."

It was clear there would be no more talk of their kingdom or what an Elite was.

"Then you'll tell me where Crimson is?" Pete asked.

"As much as we can," Skye answered.

"Fine," he said, then proceeded to tell them everything they knew, bringing out the pages from his family's basement, the knife, and ring. He opted to leave out the details involving Ash, offering an abbreviated version.

"There was a legend about the Kingdom of Digremile, three brothers, two of which deceived the Death God, avoiding the blood pact that had been sworn to him," Trent said. "The story never said what happened or gave details about the blood pact, but the legend stuck. The remaining brother went on to rule the kingdom, his family continuing until the Mage Wars when Crimson's Mage Warriors killed the last remaining heir."

"It sounds like one of the lines continued," Skye observed, her blue eyes rich with color.

"The second brother was my ancestor."

"Which makes you King of Digremile by default," she said. Her eyes had grown wide with understanding.

"And undermines Crimson's claim to it," Mark added.

"Shit," she muttered, sitting back in her seat. Mark's hands went to her shoulders, but he remained tense.

"Where is she?" Pete asked.

Skye sighed, and for a brief moment, he wondered what that sound would be like in bed. He shook the thought from his mind, wondering if his time with Ash had corrupted him.

"We think she's still in her kingdom. When Derrant sent her back, he sent her here, but she went to Apendia right away."

"Derrant?"

"The Death God."

"You're on a first name basis with the god of death?" Courtney asked.

Pete noticed the clench in Mark's jaw.

"It's complicated," she said, and Pete could see her discomfort.

"Why do you *think* she's there? You sound uncertain," Pete asked, changing the subject.

"Because she went to do what she does best, determined to take her kingdom back," Mark said with an obvious irritation to his voice.

"And what's that?" Pete understood the insinuation and challenged the man to say it. He wasn't sure why he felt the need to defend Crimson, to excuse whatever it was she'd done or everything she'd done before she'd met him, but he did.

"What she does best, manipulate men with sex."

"Wow, Pete, you were right," Courtney taunted. "You two are like two peas in a pod."

"Enough, Court," he said, staring Mark down.

"What is this?" Skye asked. "Do I need to let you two fight it out?"

"I'd win," Mark said through gritted teeth, crossing his arms over his chest again.

"Maybe not," the woman in the robe said. Pete had forgotten her name. Whoever she was, she seemed important. She had an authoritative air to her, one that her piercing blue eyes accentuated. They weren't the entrancing shade of Skye's. They were a light blue, framed by a head of mousy brown hair. But they held power to them. This woman wasn't someone to mess with either. Pete started to wonder what kind of world he'd walked into.

The woman had been studying the pages intently while they'd been talking.

"No one bests an Elite, Elspeth," he growled.

"He's not just anyone. He's a warrior, and if I'm right, he's a Shadow Warrior. The fiercest, deadliest magic wielders in our history. They ruled Digremile. The firstborn always took the throne, the second and after fought. They were sworn to protect the crown. They were terrifying. I remember my grandmother telling me the legends. His line—if he indeed comes from the second brother—always bore Shadow Magic, a gift from the Death God. The third brother was also a warrior, but his power was in his brute strength. The two warriors were the sword and shield of the kingdom." She looked up at Pete's surprised eyes. "I had no idea the two legends were the same. This is ancient, ancient history that goes back thousands of years."

"You're saying these Shadow Warriors can defeat an Elite? With Mage Warrior magic powering us?"

"They have the magic of the gods, just as Skye does."

Pete drew in a breath, all eyes on him now. He didn't like the scrutinizing looks, the suspicion they held. He ran his hand through his hair, remembering the current that had gone through him when the last tree had faded. It had been magic. That's why he hadn't recognized it.

She picked up the dagger. "The weapon was only given to a warrior when he passed his trials. I remember now, the gem glows, like yours does from your bond with Skye, but this weapon is directly tied to him, no matter who in his line wields it."

"It's never glowed," Bo said, staring at the weapon.

"I was never free of the curse." Pete took the weapon and rolled it back and forth in his hands. "There was this strange feeling when the last tree faded. Remember how the black seemed to take over me?"

"Yeah."

He thought about what he'd felt and about the black aura as he gripped the knife. His skin began to tingle, the stone to glow a deep onyx. The weapon hummed in his hand.

"Holy shit," Courtney muttered.

"That's Shadow Magic," Mark said.

"Derrant's magic," Skye whispered. She reached a hand out, her eyes glowing a richer shade of blue. Her fingers began moving like they were pulling at something. He could see a thin stream of the ebony drifting toward her and watched as it danced along her fingers. Her move entranced him so that it was hard to draw his eyes from her. He stared at her in wonder, feeling his eyes widen. "It's rich with it."

Pete watched as the strand thickened, feeling a pull in his gut as she continued to study it.

"Skye" Mark's voice held worry in it.

More of the color flowed from Pete, and he gripped the dagger. The sensation was unsettling in a way he couldn't quite pinpoint.

"I can feel Crimson—his connection to her. It's old, power-ful, and woven through his magic and...this might hurt, Pete, but please trust me."

"Not the most comfortable currently," he muttered, not mentioning the undercurrent of seduction that layered the discomfort.

Her other hand rose, and he felt a deeper draw, a light red stream of color coming from him and intertwining with the ebony strand. She let it drift through her fingers, his eyes watching with awe.

"It's in his blood. Powerful blood magic. And it ties them in a way that cannot be broken."

"The two brothers from the pages made a blood pact with the gods," Courtney said. "So, it's all true."

"Yes. That's why the two of you found each other. Once you were in the same realm, within proximity to one another, it was inevitable."

"She's why you stayed away all those years, isn't she, Pete?" Courtney asked, her voice sad.

The strands of color made their way back to him and he relaxed, the feeling of Skye's hold over him releasing. The fleeing of her magic left him with a strange, empty feeling he wished he understood. Skye looked at him curiously, then down at her hands, as if seeing something she wasn't sharing, and his mind went back to Ash's words. Had Skye sensed what Ash had?

He let the thought go, knowing they were all waiting for his answer.

"Yeah, I heard her voice. That night I left ten years ago."

"Ten years?" Mark asked, his eyes narrowed as if he hadn't appreciated how Pete's eyes had lingered on Skye.

Pete shrugged it off, thinking back to Crimson again, everything else falling away. "Yes, the night the Death God cursed her there. It was a scream that haunted me, I realize now it called to me, but back then I ran. I didn't understand what it was, but it stayed with me, calling me back and I ignored it."

"Until now," Trent said. "Because you can't ignore fate, and fate ties you and Crimson to each other. The blood pact ensured it through the binding of your two lines. Blood pacts are dark magic and vowed to the Death God or even one of his shadow gods. Whatever the two brothers did to avoid it, they paid heavily for it and the Death God insured it was honored in you and Crimson."

"Maybe he had other reasons to curse her there," Skye said.

"Then why didn't I go to her that night and why would the Death God care if some ancient blood pact was honored if he'd already had his vengeance?"

Skye sat back, looking up at Mark.

"Damn," Mark muttered. "Because Derrant favors Crimson, whether or not he admits it. Her father sold her soul to him. He owns her, so he has stake in seeing her succeed. That's why he didn't kill her that day. Why he sentenced her to the Forest of Lost Souls."

"And why he sent her back," Skye added. "He made it seem like he wanted to halt the flow of souls flooding the Shadow Realm, but he wanted her here."

"And me," Pete said. "He tested me—tried to stop me from releasing the souls, but it was only a test of my willpower and since I passed, he stood aside."

"How did he test you?" Mark asked.

"Oh, this should be interesting," Courtney said, her voice smug.

He shot her a look, then leaned forward on his knees, rolling the dagger between his hands.

No sense in holding back now, Pete thought. "He sent a demon to occupy me."

"What kind of demon?" Mark pressed. "Did she take human form or have a tail?"

Skye visibly shivered at his last word.

"Human form," he answered.

"A sex demon. And you survived?"

"Yes, he told her to occupy me but not gut me, thankfully."

"Gut?" Courtney asked. "I didn't think that could get any worse, but somehow you made it worse."

"How did you break her spell? If they don't want to be seen, they won't break their façade," Skye said.

"Let's just say I turned the tables on her, and she dropped her glamour unintentionally."

"You made her come," the man in the corner said, the one who'd formed the portal.

"Really Camin? That's a bit crass," Skye said, but Pete could see the hint of a smile below her frown.

"As often as you and Mark fuck around this castle, I don't think that was crass, Skye." The man ignored her glower and Mark's snicker, continuing, "A sex demon is only weak when she's in the throes of climax. Is that better, Skye?"

"Yes, thank you."

Pete was still wondering at the man's first comment. He glanced between Skye and Mark, curious if Skye was as insatiable as Crimson. There was a twinkle in her eye that led him to believe so. No wonder Mark hovered over her protectively, as if she was something he coveted. If she was anything like Crimson, then she should be coveted.

"Nobody seduces a seducer. Those demons are precise and deadly."

"Who are you and how do you know this?" Pete asked.

"I am Camin. Call me their advisor if you'd like—"

"That's a strong title," Elspeth said.

"One that still irritates you, Elspeth. That's why I like saying it," he replied with a wink. "And I'm very familiar with demons."

"Camin spent a fair amount of time in the Shadow Realm. As did I, and Skye still does, thanks to Crimson. We're very familiar with demons."

"But you tamed one, didn't you?" Camin asked, moving closer, his brown eyes excited. He was a tall man, lean but muscular, his dirty blonde hair messy as if he'd just woken. "Did she show you her true form?"

"Her demon form?"

"No, her original form. I tamed two myself. They are very loyal once you do and, if asked, they will reveal themselves to you."

"Yes, and she remained in that form."

"She returned to you?'

"Yes."

"I'll be damned. Only the blood of Derrant would allow you that control. You tamed a sex demon, and she traded favor with Derrant to return to you. Impressive."

Pete could feel Mark's eyes on him, evaluating him, and he looked back to meet Skye's, which were also studying him. He wasn't certain what to make of the flicker he saw in them. Couldn't tell if it had been fear, curiosity, or something else he didn't think she'd want him seeing. She looked away quickly.

"You tamed two," Pete said, turning back to Camin.

"Ah, but I had Derrant's help with that, a bit of his Shadow Magic to help me. Otherwise, I would have died like any other man they feast upon. They're particularly fond of living souls."

"So Derrant considered whatever debt your family owed him paid and sent you here?" Mark asked, thankfully moving the conversation forward.

"No, it was a woman. Beautiful and powerful," Courtney said. "In fact, she looked a lot like you."

"Eliana," Skye said.

"Skye comes from Eliana's line," Mark said. "She's Derrant's lover, the goddess who ferries the souls deemed worthy to the Upper Realm."

"The resemblance is uncanny," Pete noted, remembering how he'd thought the same when the goddess had appeared to them. No wonder Mark was so protective.

"He sent her because he didn't want to look weak. What is he up to? He only does things that serve his interest," Skye continued.

There was no question about the intimacy to which she knew the Death God, and Pete saw the irritation on Mark's face.

"There's something greater going on. Something we can't see yet," Camin said. "All of you are somehow tied to the Shadow Realm, either by the Death God or his queen."

"Crimson the most," Skye said. "On multiple layers. Her soul belongs to him. She is from Eliana's line, branched off from my ancestor, and she's in the middle of a blood pact to Derrant. I think Crimson might be more important than any of us realized."

"Shit," Mark mumbled, wiping his hands over his face.

"Wait, you're related to Crimson?" Pete asked.

"In a very distant way, but yes."

"So, what do we do now?" Camin asked.

"We wait for her move," Pete answered, his mind still reeling that Crimson and Skye were related. "Tell me where she is and what the intention was."

"She's in her kingdom, Apendia. Stavin and his troops took the throne before she returned. He's lethal and experienced. He was her commander. He murdered the king of Eltander for her, and we believe he was at her whim, doing much of her dirty work."

"And sleeping with her," Pete muttered.

"Well, now that's the funny thing about Crimson," the broody guard, Noah, said. "She loves using men, but her guards were off limits."

"How do you know that?" Skye asked.

"When you spend a month locked in her prison as her sex toy, you learn things from the jealous guards who like to watch."

"Wow, she sounds like a winner, Pete. I'm so glad Mom and Dad are dead, so you don't have to bring her home to meet them," Courtney said in a snarky tone.

He noticed Mark hide his chuckle and shot Courtney a look. "I told you she had a past, Court."

"One you clearly don't mind."

"He doesn't have a choice. Blood magic will do that," Camin said. "She could slit his throat and he'd love her with his dying breath, not that she could because she loves him just as much. And this blood magic is ancient. There is no resisting their call to one another, only the Death God himself could break it. If the other brother had lived to have an heir, the blood tie would have connected all three of them. That spell would draw her to them both with a force she could never deny without shattering her from the inside out. The pain of loss would be so heavy that it would literally drown her, the two of them suffering the same fate."

The words hung heavy in the air.

"Well, thank God there's no other line, Pete, or you'd have to share her," Bo said.

"Wait, does that mean I'll have the same reaction to her?" Courtney asked.

"No, my guess is that night Pete heard her triggered the connection. The tie would have only been with one from each line, the eldest most likely, so it landed with Pete. If you had been the eldest, which I'm guessing you aren't, it would have been you tied to her."

Courtney's mouth hung open.

"Is it wrong that I find that really hot?" Bo asked before she glared him.

"Thank you, I guess, for taking that burden, Pete," she mumbled, the shock still evident on her face.

"Yeah, no problem. I'm not sure how I'd feel about the other option."

Courtney shot him a look.

"Not you and another girl, just you and Crimson."

"Can't say I would either if I had a sibling. Crimson's relentless, like an animal with that sex drive of hers," Noah mumbled.

Skye's face soured, and Pete was certain she was thinking

about what Crimson had done to Mark, who shifted behind her uncomfortably.

"Not much different from the Death God," Mark muttered under his breath. Skye's mouth tightened.

"Wow, there is seriously some angst in the room about the two of them," Courtney observed.

"It's complicated," they both snapped.

"So Crimson went to *convince* Stavin to give up the crown?" Pete asked, hoping he could change the subject.

Mark and Skye both looked relieved.

"Yes, but he's not the only concern. Stavin's right hand is Bormick, just as lethal and brutal with a reputation for thievery, murder—you name it, his name has been attached to it," Mark said.

"Crimson was supposed to weaken them, then send us a signal," Skye said. "She wanted to do it all on her own, which is fine by me because it helps keep us out of a war we didn't want part of. When she sends us the signal, we'll provide mage power for her to bleed so she can take them both out with the magic and reassert her dominance as queen. Although, if I know Crimson, she might just murder them while they sleep."

"Bleed magic?" Bo asked.

"Crimson has the ability to steal magic from other mages. It lasts only a few hours, but it would give her enough time to dispose of them and take command of her army without our involvement."

"But she hasn't signaled, has she?" Pete asked.

"No, it's been weeks. The only movement we've seen is the pullback of Bormick and his troops, who had been closing in on another kingdom. It was a good sign and placed Bormick back in Apendia, but since then, it's been silent."

"So, either she's in trouble or..." He didn't want to say the words, but Mark finished for him.

"Or she's enjoying her two new bedmates too much and has crossed us."

Pete sat back.

"Which I don't believe," Skye said.

"Because you have some warped faith in someone you should hate, Skye."

"I did hate her, Mark, but she's complicated."

"Like everything with Crimson," he spat.

"Wow, you do not like her, do you?" Courtney asked.

"Courtney," Pete scolded.

"No, you seem to know what she's done, Pete. Why not fill your sister in? Go ahead."

"Mark," Skye cautioned.

"Skye," he growled back. "Go on, Pete, tell them."

There was an uncomfortable silence before Pete finally spoke, unsure if he really wanted to say the words aloud and see the hurt in Skye's eyes or feel the wrath of Mark's anger.

"She kidnapped Mark, took advantage of him, and sent Skye to the Death God. Sound about right?"

"No," Mark snapped.

Skye rose, and Pete could feel her power brush against his skin. It was an oddly comforting feeling that tingled, touching his own new power in a way he didn't understand. Her eyes had grown a shade darker, like a starless night sky.

"I think that's our cue, we'll do some research and...yeah," Noah said, the others all leaving the room as streams of color drifted through the space.

"Courtney," Pete hissed under his breath.

She gave him a confused look. Her comment had been innocent. She had no idea what the connection was between Crimson, Skye, and Mark. Pete had a feeling she was about to find out the severity of the truth and knew it would shade her opinion of Crimson even more. There was no escaping Crimson's past. It would always be a part of who she was, and others would always judge her for it.

"Why don't you tell them, Skye?"

"It's been ten years, Mark, and I'm not the one who—"

"Who what?"

"Don't make me say it. We put this behind us."

"Did we? Because every year I relive it for five days and now she's back!"

"I'm feeling like we should leave and let you two work this out," Bo said.

"No, you want to know the truth about us and Crimson? We have an extremely complicated past that neither of us can seem to move from. Crimson leaves a path of chaos in her wake, Pete. Do you love her enough for it? Because she almost crushed us and fate binds our love as strongly as it does the two of you," Mark said.

"Tell me what she hasn't told me."

"Crimson leaves a heavy toll on everything she touches, including us. She murdered our friend, granted it was done by Stavin's hand, but by her instruction after she lured us all in on the false pretense of peace. She bled my power, severing Mark's tie to it and rendering him powerless. As her final act, she handed me to the Death God who..." Skye searched for the words. Pete knew what came next and didn't want to hear them from her mouth, feeling slightly protective of her even though he'd just met her. Something about the idea of the Death God forcing her into his bed rubbed him the wrong way, and not simply in a chivalrous way.

Mark finished her thought. "Fucked her. Put her under a spell, and fucked my wife, repeatedly."

"And you were having such a hard time as Crimson's prisoner," she spat. "Did she mention how she kept my husband and Noah prisoner? How she fucked him every day with her mouth or her body?"

"Against my will, Skye."

She glared at him, unspoken words passing between them. Pete knew his suspicion had been right and Mark had slipped. Crimson had worn him down and he'd caved to her.

"Ouch," Bo whispered.

The colors around the room began to stream faster from the objects. Even the colors in his clothes were fading. Skye's power was astounding, and he couldn't draw his eyes from the hues that seemed to lick against her skin.

"Skye," Mark said, his tone softer now.

The streams thickened and Pete felt his power react in defense as the color fled from Courtney's eyes.

"Skye," Mark said again, moving closer to her and bringing a hand to her cheek. The stream stalled before it began reversing. The breath flooded back to Pete's chest. "Crimson has done her damage, and it continues to this day." Skye dropped her head, and he kissed her forehead. "To this day, I give her up for five days each year, forced to hand her over to share Derrant's bed as payment. Five long painful days while another man touches my wife." She looked up at him and a tender moment passed between them— one Pete felt he shouldn't be privy to, but he couldn't turn his eyes from. The intensity of their love was tangible.

"Crimson has left her scars on us in unimaginable ways. My wife has chosen to forgive, but I can't."

"I didn't like her before, but now I really don't like her," Courtney muttered.

"There's good in her," Skye said in her defense. "The same blood that runs through me, runs through her, but it's warped and scarred, morphing her to become what she is—*was*. I think she deserves a chance, one that wasn't given to her before and the fact that you have stolen her heart, Pete, and she yours reassures my faith."

"You won't have my backing on any of that," Mark said.

Skye glanced at him, giving him a breathtaking smile. "Yes, he will."

Mark shook his head, the tension in the air fading. As fast as the storm had come, it was gone. Pete now understood the two of them, the intense love they had for one another, the storm that ran through them both, and he had no doubt that intensity carried to their bedroom. The thought strangely turned him on.

Mark met his eyes as if he'd read his mind. His eyes narrowed until the curve of his lip let Pete know his thoughts had been right. Mark pulled Skye to him, his arm around her in a protective grip. He was letting his claim be known, but Pete had no intention of disrupting that claim, just a strange compulsion to think about it. He had his own claim on Crimson to protect.

"So, we don't know if she's safe or if she's changed her mind?" Pete said, trying to turn the tide. He was glad that what Skye and Mark had shared was nothing more than what Crimson had already confessed to him. It confirmed his belief in her, reassuring him that she had changed from the Crimson they had known.

"I don't think she's changed her mind. I promised her I would help free you of the forest if she kept her word. After seeing her the day she was torn from you and hearing what Camin said, I have faith that she will call us."

"Then we wait for her call, and I go to her when she does."

They looked at each other again, and Mark said, "Well, then we'd better find out what you're made of before then and get you a proper weapon. Both Stavin and Bormick would take you down in seconds with that tiny thing."

"I'm not sure he'll need a weapon, Mark," Skye said.

Pete flexed his hands.

"That power is calling to be used," she commented. "I felt it when mine was out of control."

Mark studied him, the weight of his stare heavy before he said, "Hmm, then we train on both fronts."

"Sounds about right," she said. "Courtney, Bo, you come with me. We'll find you some quarters and some proper clothing for our world while Mark works with Pete until he's warmed up. Then I'll test him."

They all rose as Skye led Courtney and Bo out.

"Do I want to know how she'll test me? That power of hers is insane."

"Don't worry, she'll go gentle on you...at first." Mark then called after Skye, "Meet us on the training grounds, Skye. If he's got Shadow Magic, you'll want to bring Camin along, too."

She nodded, and they were gone, leaving Pete alone with a man whose discontentment with Crimson made him beyond uncomfortable.

PETE

Morning sun rays poured through the open balcony to Pete's room, and he knew Mark would be impatiently waiting for him. Pete wondered if the man ever slept but after seeing him with Skye, he had a feeling there wasn't much sleep that occurred in their room. Something about that thought stimulated him as he fought to tuck the white tunic into his pants. Days had passed, but he still hadn't adjusted to this world or its queen. She was still difficult to look at. Her beauty was captivating, but it was the eyes that drew him in. Looking into them was like falling into an endless well of a serene star-filled night.

A knock startled him from his thoughts, and he ran his hand over his face, turning his thoughts to Crimson to sweep Skye from his mind. As with each time he thought of her, everything else slipped away and she was the only woman he wanted.

The door slowly opened, and he half expected to see Mark on the other side, ready to grill him about his lateness. Instead, Courtney's happy face peeked around at him.

"Oh, good! You're dressed. I did not want to walk in on you any other way," she said, her eyes taking him in.

"How else would I be?"

"Given your track record—"

"My track record? What's that supposed to mean?"

"If you can't keep it in your pants in a creepy forest, I can only imagine what will happen here. There are boobs everywhere with these dresses. Even I have cleavage in these things."

He laughed and shook his head. "I'm not sleeping with the staff."

"Not that beautiful queen, either?"

His body had a strange reaction to the idea, but he ignored it, scowling at her. "No, Court. Besides, she's married."

"So, you have thought about it," she teased, humor lighting her eyes.

"Why are you here?"

She came over and adjusted his shirt for him, making him feel like he was her little brother for a moment.

"Just checking on you. You've been non-stop out there, all that magic flying around and playing with swords." She met his eyes, evaluating him. "You okay?"

Giving her a warm smile, he nodded. "Fine, just wish I knew what was going on with Crimson."

Sadness filled her eyes. "What if she's not going through with it, if she's content where she is with those other men?"

It hurt to think about, not the physical so much. Although that did stir his jealousy, but the thought of her falling in love with another man—of forgetting about him—was like a knife to his heart.

"I don't know to be honest."

"Huh. You would still love her, wouldn't you? Just like they said you would."

"I think so."

She patted his chest. "I worry about you, Pete."

"You don't have to worry about me, Court. I'm the big brother here, remember? It's me who should worry."

"I've always worried about you. Never settling down, always moving, always searching for happiness." She sat on the bed, her hands smoothing out the bottom of her heavy dress. "I think you belong here. I think this is the reason you've never found whatever it is you've been seeking the reason you've always looked. And maybe Crimson really is the one for you. That is, if she's not off sleeping with those other men."

"I guarantee she's sleeping with them," he said, giving her a grin. "Just like I was sleeping with the—"

She put her hand up. "Don't even say it. It's so gross."

She flopped back on the bed, and he flopped next to her.

"Remember how we used to lie together when we were little?" she asked.

"You mean when you annoyingly crawled into my bed anytime it even threatened to thunder?"

"Maybe," she replied with a laugh.

"Yeah, I remember."

"You used to tell me stories, like Dad would. Made up stories about dragons and castles. Who would have thought they were real?"

"I haven't seen any dragons, so I'm pretty sure they're not real."

"Well, the castles and magic are," she corrected.

"Yeah, they really are, huh? Maybe those stories were our heritage, the only thing any of them knew to pass down to the next generation. I remember Dad telling me grandma told him the same stories when he was little."

He brought his arm around her, and she snuggled against him.

"Bo and I are going home once you're settled." He peeked down at her, narrowing his gaze. "This is such an unbelievable place, but it's not ours. It's yours. Your destiny, not mine. Bo and I are just side characters to your story and, as much as I want to be there to witness it, I miss home, too."

He kissed the top of her head. "Whatever you want, Court."

"That's what I want. I'm not one for fancy dresses and castles. I want my little café and our small cottage house. You can keep all this fancy kingdom stuff. The queen said she can take us back whenever we're ready. That still boggles my mind. She has magic that can cross her to other worlds."

"I suppose she does." He hadn't thought about it, but Skye had visited Crimson there, so she had the ability.

"And she says she can teach you how to come visit me. Which better not be another ten years," she said, elbowing him.

"I promise to make it shorter this time. Maybe nine years?" he joked, finding it unbelievable that he'd have that ability. There was no way he had that kind of power. Her laugh flittered through the air. "Are you sure you want to miss out on a life with no indoor plumbing and no caffeine?"

"Good God, yes. I think I've gone through withdrawal repeatedly. I want a hot cup of coffee and a chocolate chip muffin so bad right now that I'd kill someone for it."

"No murdering for chocolate or coffee, Court."

"If she hurts you, I'll murder her," she said, her voice serious.

"Who? Skye? Because I don't think she'll hurt me. Although it doesn't feel good when she wallops me with her magic during training."

"Crimson, dummy."

"Ah. No, you won't. Because I won't let you. Blood, remember?"

"Stupid blood. Well, I'll still beat the shit out of her."

"I'd like to see you try."

He pulled her close and held her like he had when she was little, missing the innocence their childhood had held for that moment.

"Is this something normal in your world?" he heard Noah ask. "Because here it is absolutely frowned upon."

"What? Ew!" Courtney said, sitting up quickly.

Pete sat, shooting the man a nasty look, only then noticing the grin on his face.

"I mean, Crimson's pretty kinky," Noah went on. "She might be into that stuff, but it's not something we do here in our kingdom."

"Are you always such an annoying prick?" Pete asked. He'd grown comfortable enough around Mark's second in command to say such a thing. Noah had a unique sense of humor that offset the fierce seriousness of his commander.

"Always. Now if you two are done with that weird incestual stuff, you need to get your ass on that training ground. And I'd be prepared. Mark's pissed he missed another round of sex with Skye to be out there early. You're in for quite the workout."

Pete tried to hide the fact that his comment had placed an image Mark wouldn't want him having in his mind. It hadn't taken him long to discover that Skye was as insatiable, if not more so than Crimson. Yet another stimulating fact that he had trouble ignoring. And the two were not subtle about it, something Noah had shared as soon as he'd gotten to know Pete. A warning that he should avoid following if Skye dragged Mark away or vice versa and that he was to never go back into the meeting room once the two were alone. Noah had shared quite the tale of walking in to find the two were doing more on that table than discussing kingdom business. That image had yet to leave Pete's mind.

"We were not doing anything incestual, and that's gross," Courtney said, storming past Noah.

"She's easy to rile up, isn't she?"

"Too easy, but be warned, she has quite the temper, and a good left hook."

Noah glanced back into the hall. "That tiny thing?"

"Yup. She may be dainty-looking, but she's like ten of your Elite if you get on her bad side."

"You may want to take her with you. She can defend you from Mark's wrath when you get out there."

"Great. Something to look forward to."

"Oh, you're in for a treat. No one makes the commander wait, and no one takes him from between Skye's legs unless they want a fight."

"That's your queen you're talking about," Pete said, unable to stop the picture of those long legs wrapped around his waist. He rubbed his face. He really needed to find Crimson. He'd gone too long without her touch, or even Ash's for that matter. That had to be the reason he couldn't get his mind focused recently, or out of the gutter.

"My queen and my king are like rabbits, Pete. There's no avoiding talking about Skye or Mark like that. It was worse when they were first together. Couldn't keep their clothes on long enough to even make it to their bedroom. I remember this one time..."

Pete let him go on, rambling about how he had to pick clothes up in some tower, tuning him out for fear he'd have an obvious tent in his pants when he saw Mark, or even worse, Skye. He would have thought about Crimson, but then it was a sure bet he'd have a ridiculously large lump that he couldn't hide. He ran his hand through his hair, wondering how he would survive this world if he couldn't even control his dirty thoughts about the insanely attractive women in it.

MARK WAS A GRUELING TRAINER. The only time he allowed Pete a break was when Skye and Camin joined them. The man was relentless. Camin wasn't much better, but at least Skye let him catch his breath.

Her magic was fascinating the way it worked, and he had a hard time not staring in awe when she used it. Where his magic seemed to come from within him, hers came from everything around her. It was jaw-dropping to watch and intimidating, not to mention quite a turn on. This woman had the power to literally suck the life out of not only a person but the entire world. She was a weapon of unimaginable capability. The outfit she trained in didn't help his concentration any. It emphasized her delicate curves in such a way that he couldn't avoid lingering on them. The cream of her stomach was revealed above the perfect waistline as her pants settled on the cusp of her hips, dipping just below her belly button. He couldn't help but think of licking it as he imagined his hands touching the supple breasts that swelled above the shirt she wore. Those thoughts were difficult to keep from his mind. She was hot in a fantasy movie kind of way that left it hard to concentrate. He absently wondered how Mark, who was clearly possessive and overprotective of her, let her wear something that revealing. But then, Skye didn't seem the submissive type, so he had no doubt she'd wear what she wanted.

When he'd first seen her like that, he'd asked if it was a distraction technique, but Mark had shot him a look as Skye had teased that it was her distraction for Mark, so he'd go easier on Pete. The way Mark had worked him, it hadn't been enough of a distraction.

As they trained, he asked questions, learning about their world, his world, the different races, the different magic classes. Learning that Mark and Skye had spent most of their lives in what they called the human realm, made him feel less out of sorts. That history also explained why Mark tended to use expressions like Pete did. He knew some of the words he said seemed out of place here, but hearing Mark say them made him less conscious about it. Learning that there were countless worlds all connected to one another, all created and ruled by gods who were somehow related, did not make him feel any better, however. That blew his mind, and he thought how shocking that would be for people to learn back home, that they weren't the only ones, that there really was a heaven and hell.

He was becoming more comfortable with his magic. Skye's

training had helped him get a better feel for how it worked, and how to embrace it.

They'd been practicing for half the day, yet he still hadn't bested Skye. Of course, he hadn't been able to conquer her any of the times he'd faced her, so another day of finding his ass on the ground after one of her strikes was not a surprise. She was standing across from him, her blue eyes sparkling in the sun. Her expression was confident, her stance sexy enough to derail his concentration. As he called his magic forth, feeling the familiar strands of it encase him, he struck back at her. The streams of red she'd sent toward him distracted him momentarily with their brightness, but he knew not to be fooled: they were beautiful, but they were also lethal. They ripped through his shadows as he began calling his magic. He stepped back, hearing Camin instruct him to keep his defensive state. Defense seemed the only thing he could do against these two. He stopped and backed away, reinforcing his shield while he thought through the situation.

He was a king. They'd said his magic came from the Death God. If that were the case, he should be able to do more than just defend himself. He took a moment to look deeper at Skye's streams of magic, questioning if he could do something similar without risking harm to himself. He'd learned her brighter colors stung the worse, but her darker hues were welcoming against his skin, seductive even. This gave him pause to think there might be a connection between his magic and Skye's that involved the darker shades.

"Growing bored!" Camin yelled.

"Give him a chance," Skye defended back.

"He's had days!"

"You had a lifetime and I've had over a decade. He needs time."

As they argued, he studied his magic, the way it settled in stream-like ribbons around him. He focused on one, moving his fingers through it and watching as it danced around them. With his other hand, he continued to hold his shield in place. He looked back at Skye's magic. She'd pulled it from a patch of flowers behind her, their now muted tones disturbing to his eyes.

Studying the strand, he loosened his hold on the stream in his fingers, aiming it for Skye's streams. His magic hesitated for just a moment, a strange sensation tingling through him as it touched her magic. Her eyes met his with a flicker of curiosity, her brow narrowing briefly. He shook the feeling off, then pushed his power forward, his magic fleeing as he thought of snuffing out the hues. Striking quickly, his stream laced around hers and transformed it.

He felt her pull on it as her eyes grew large, startled by the swift change. The streams turned black, their strength empowering him. A wave of green lashed at him. In defense, he sent another strand at it, engulfing the hue quickly and pushing it toward her. Dropping his shield, he continued to send his power in her direction.

"What the hell?" he heard Mark mutter as his power pushed Skye back a step. Her eyes grew a deeper shade of navy, and he felt her change tactic. Something pulled at him—a command of sorts that wrapped around his magic. She was bleeding the hues from his magic. He watched, stunned, as the shadows drew around her, fading from his hold and leaving the stream that flowed from him a foggy color.

"Seriously?" he asked, shooting her a look that matched the irritation in his voice.

"That was a good try, but nobody steals my hues," she said with a smile, a glint of humor within her dark eyes.

"I didn't steal them. That's what you're doing. I simply snuffed them out."

Her smile dropped slightly.

Something about her invasion of his magic bothered him at a deeper level. He studied how the essence of it bled away. Finding another ribbon of her magic, he let his stream out toward her, snakelike, slithering closer to her. Her brows creased and a questioning expression overtook her features. He watched as her lips pursed and felt her begin to bleed his stream of shadow magic. Staying focused, he took the moment to strike at her. With the attack, he felt the power rising in him. There was a moment where her hues and his shadows danced around her as her magic fought his invasion. He could feel the way the two connected, the give and take of control right before his shadows overtook her magic. The hues shattered, his stream sweeping to encircle her and reclaim his magic before tightening around her.

"Holy shit," he heard Noah, but he couldn't look away. The magic was like an electric current through his body that hummed. Skye was fighting the cocoon of his magic. He could feel her struggling to bleed it, but it was too strong for her.

"That's enough!" Mark yelled.

"No, let her find her way out," Camin instructed.

"He's suffocating her!"

"She's the most powerful Mage Warrior we've ever had, Mark. Give her time to fight without you stepping in."

Their words irked him, and he rolled his neck as he tried to ignore them. They expected him to fail, but then again he was new at this. She was searching for hues, reaching out below his power for them, so he commanded the stream to lower. It ran through the grass below her feet to overtake the green, his shadows filling the space with an ebony hue she couldn't claim.

"That's why they were so feared," he heard Camin say. "That's not an enemy you want."

Skye glared at him as she reached upward. He glanced at the sky, giving her a grin. Pushing his hands forward, he sent a burst of his shadows out, letting them run free. They spread across the sky, shifting the blue to gray. The clouds turned thunderous, covering the sun, and encasing it in shadows, his shadows.

"Well, that's not fair," she pouted.

He shrugged, trying to hide the smile at how cute the pout

was. There was something about their banter, about the back and forth of their magic that reminded him of foreplay, and the thought made him wonder if she released her magic during sex. It gave him pause to think maybe he could do the same. He could only imagine what it would feel like in the height of the moment, his mind envisioning Skye with his power wrapped around her as he climaxed. The thought nearly broke his concentration, so he pushed it away.

Shit, Pete, he scolded himself, not sure why his mind had gone to that extreme or why it hadn't been Crimson in the image.

He brought his focus back to caging her within his power, ignoring the dirty thoughts and praying his magic didn't carry them to her. Magic was so new to him that he didn't know if that was a possibility, but he didn't want to take a chance.

He finally felt at one with his magic, understanding his connection to it better. Confidence emboldened him and for a moment he thought he may have bested her. Then he saw the sliver of blue as it broke from the cocoon around her. It struck as quick as a viper, knocking him to the ground. His hold on her broke, and the shadows dissipated.

He looked up at her, noting the blue of her shirt, the entirely too revealing one.

"The clothing, damn! How did I miss that?"

She offered him a hand, and he found his footing again. A crowd had drawn, all of them wide eyed as Camin and Mark approached. Mark glowered at him, but he knew it was just in defense of Skye, so he let it go.

"So that's a warrior and why they were such a force," Camin said.

"Shadow Warrior," a woman with a long blonde braid and purple cloak said as she studied Pete.

"Pete, this is Bridget, she's one of our advisors and oversees the wizards."

Wizards. Camin had briefly explained the difference between mages and wizards, but he still wasn't sure he understood.

"Shadow Warrior?" Mark asked. "Elspeth mentioned the same thing."

"Yes, Shadow Warriors were the strongest, most feared line at one time. So, it's true. A son of Digremile has returned."

"Explain, Bridget."

"You know the history of the brothers, Elspeth said she explained it."

"Yes, and I know I come from a line of warriors," said Pete.

"Not just any warrior. Your people were warriors, fighters, but your royal line held the Shadow Warrior. In each generation only one Shadow Warrior was born. Direct descendants from the Death God."

"I thought the Shadow Magic was only a gift from the Death God?" he asked, trying to remember what Elspeth had said the day he'd arrived.

"It was but through his blood. The royal line of Digremile descends from the Death God. About the same time the first Mage Warriors emerged, so did the first Shadow Warrior."

Skye and Mark shared a look.

"What?" he asked.

"The Mage Warriors came from Eliana's turn from Derrant. She and Derrant are lovers, but there was a time when he pushed her away and she fell in love with the King of Kantenda, Skye's ancestor."

"He must have struck out and taken the Queen of Digremile as payback. Damn, he's vengeful," Skye muttered.

"That's why he favored you, tested you, and let you free yourself."

"The power of the Shadow Warrior was feared as greatly as that of the Mage Warrior. There was no defense against them.. The Kingdom of Apendia befriended them. Other kingdoms built walls and made allegiances with our kingdom. This was long before the three brothers. When the brothers fell, the power disappeared. The kingdom was said to be cursed," Elspeth continued.

"That must have been the punishment for the first brother. Derrant left him as king, but without the protection of the Shadow Warrior." Skye's eyes sparkled as her mind worked through it. Pete could see a small crease forming between her eyes.

"We think so. Their kingdom was never the same after the Death God's punishment. They became as susceptible as Chenthom."

"Theodore's kingdom?"

"Yes."

"So, you're telling me that the Death God's magic runs through him?" Mark asked.

"As much as his sister's magic runs through Skye. They are equals and you'd best keep an allegiance with him, or this world will be back in chaos once more. We had enough of that with the Mage Wars."

Mark appraised Pete before turning his eyes to the sky. "Any way you can fix that?"

Pete looked up, seeing the overcast appearance.

"Shadow Warriors control the shadows. They prefer the darker side of magic while Mage Warriors prefer the brighter side of it," Bridget said, following his gaze.

"Except for Skye," Mark said, his tone serious. Pete thought he could detect a sense of worry in it, but he didn't know the man well enough to be certain of it.

"What does that mean?" he asked.

"Because I am the first Mage Warrior to command the dark hues, the shadow hues. Only the wizards wield the darker hues and they do not hold sway over the colors. I am an anomaly."

"Perhaps," Camin said. "Or perhaps not."

"Why do you say that?" Mark asked.

"Because like Pete's sudden appearance and his tie to Crimson, there may be more to her abilities than we thought, something we didn't see."

"And what would that be?"

"Whatever it is that we're not seeing about Pete."

Pete wasn't certain what to say. As the silence ensued, he put his hand up and called the magic to him, unsure if it would answer. The gray of the clouds drew to him, streaming around him as the sky lightened, the sun returning. They all took a step back. The darkness swirled into his skin, a warmth spreading through him as his body hummed. He rolled his neck and flexed his hands.

"I really don't know what to make of you right now," Mark said. He moved closer to Skye, putting a protective arm around her waist. "I think that's enough training for today."

"Fascinating," Camin muttered as the others dispersed.

"Impressive," Skye added, her eyes bright with curiosity.

Bridget was standing close to her, eyeing Pete suspiciously. "Concerning," she said. "Skye, Mark, I'd like to speak with you for a short time before I head back to the village. I think I've seen enough here."

"I could use a bath," Pete said, getting the hint.

It had taken him a few days to adjust to the lack of necessities this world offered. Baths were certainly not comparable to showers and without Ash to fill his need for Crimson, his sex drive was unsatisfied. A good hot shower would have provided better relief. Maybe that explained the way his body reacted to seeing Skye in her training garb or the feel of her magic against his earlier. God, he needed to get laid, or he'd risk Mark's wrath if his eyes lingered too long, which they were apt to do when her navy eyes held his.

Walking back to his room, he felt as much an outsider now as he had his first day here. He didn't belong here, with these people, and from their reaction to his magic, it was apparent they were weary of him, especially Mark. Although Bridget's expression didn't make him feel too welcome.

Courtney and Bo, on the other hand, were fitting right in. They'd befriended Camin's wife, Jane, who strangely enough was human as well, and they were running around learning the ways of the society. Touring the kingdom as if he weren't dealing with strange magic, an overbearing Elite commander, an entirely too tempting Mage Queen, and a lover who was currently MIA with two other men.

He rubbed his face in frustration, deciding he didn't care much to chase down a servant to heat the water for a bath. Instead, he lay down, placing his arm over his eyes to block out the sun, his mind wandering to Crimson. His body reacted with just the thought of her. He imagined her curves, the ample breasts that softly pressed against him when they'd made love, the feel of her mouth on him. He hadn't had sex in days and between her and Ash, they'd left him spoiled. Add in Skye with her navy eyes and killer body, and he knew he needed release, or he'd make enemies with Mark and lose any chance of finding Crimson.

Humoring himself, he grabbed his hardness, thinking of both Ash and Crimson, their touches on his skin. Ash had said she'd been with Crimson before and the thought alone sent his blood rushing, his dick throbbing as he undid his pants. He needed release and he let himself go, his imagination driving his hand as he stroked himself. His mind filled with thoughts of their tongues against his shaft, their hands on each other's breasts, Crimson enveloping him as Ash played with her. With her fantasized movements, his hand sped until, with a furry, he came. His muscles tensed until the last of him splayed across his stomach, the orgasm fading as he lay there catching his breath and cursing all that had happened.

∾

AFTER HE'D CLEANED himself and rested, Pete wandered the castle, fascinated by the idea that he was in a real castle. It still seemed surreal. Stepping out to the front, he took a seat on the long expanse of stairs that ran to the courtyard, looking out at the gardens beyond. He tried to keep Crimson from his thoughts, knowing he'd only get himself aroused again. Relieving himself again was something he didn't want to contemplate, not when showers and sinks were not an option for a quick cleanup.

Sighing, he stretched his feet out and rested on his elbows, watching the setting sun. He heard footsteps but chose to remain as is, not caring to look back.

"Quite a view, isn't it?" Mark said, sitting beside him.

"Something out of a movie."

Mark laughed. "You know, only a few of us would have any idea what a movie is."

"So I've gathered. How do you stand it? Everything is so..."

"Backward?"

"Yeah."

"It takes some adjustment, but I had an advantage. I spent the first ten years of my life here before we left to live in the other world."

"You and Skye lived here first?"

"No, Skye was a baby. She doesn't remember any of this. It was all brand new to her, just like it is to you. Even now, after ten years, she still complains about the lack of coffee."

Pete laughed. "Yeah, that will take some getting used to."

"As will most things here. It seems backward, but there's a lot of beauty to the simplicity."

Pete thought about the comment. He had yet to go beyond the castle, but even within it there was an ease to life, no rush to get places, no pollution. The air was fresh and clean.

Mark remained silent, leaving Pete to his thoughts until he clasped his hands and asked, "Do you really love her?"

"Do you really love Skye?"

Mark furrowed his brow and shot him a look. "Don't compare what Skye and I have to you and Crimson."

"Why not? You love her, I love Crimson."

"Because we're different. The situation is different."

"Is it really? Did you love her the moment you saw her?"

Mark stayed quiet for a moment, looking at his hands. "Yes, I've loved her since she was a baby. I loved her the entire time it was inappropriate to love her because she was ten years my junior. I loved her when I had to push her into another man's arms for twenty years, all to protect her. Fifty years where we should have been with each other, but destiny forced us apart. You can't compare what you have to us."

Pete didn't know their past and didn't want to pry, but he couldn't imagine being separated from Crimson for that long. The torment it must have caused.

"I'm sorry you went through that."

"It's over now. The decisions that were made for us then left their mark, but that seems to be our way of life now. Events, people—they leave their imprint on us, like Crimson."

"I can't excuse her behavior before I knew her, but that's not the Crimson I know. She's changed."

"I find that hard to believe."

Pete didn't know how to convince him otherwise, and perhaps it wasn't his place to.

"The first time I saw her, I knew," he said instead, "it was in a sketch my father had made of her. He'd spotted her in the grove. That sketch haunted me just as her scream did that first night. I couldn't forget it, even when I tried to run. For ten years, I ran from that scream, but her voice stayed with me, no matter how far I went. The first time my eyes fell upon her, she owned me. I don't know how to explain it, but I knew she was mine, and I was hers. I'd been hers since that first connection. Maybe it is the blood pact of my line that's done it because I feel her as if she is in my blood. She calls to me, even though she's nowhere near. And I know I would die to protect her."

Mark sighed.

"Look, I can't make excuses for what she did in her past—what she did to you and Skye. All I can do is tell you how I feel."

"And if you find her and she's still that woman? What will you do?"

He thought about what she'd done, the men she'd had, those she'd forced, the lives she'd taken. She'd been honest with him, held nothing back.

"I love her, Mark. No matter who she is, but it doesn't mean I won't convince her to change her ways. I'm not keen on having her give other men what she should be giving me."

"Oh, you're in for a treat then. I hope you have some stamina. She's relentless."

"You enjoyed it, didn't you?"

"Does your dick always listen to your brain, Pete?"

Pete laughed. "No."

"My dick enjoyed it, but I was pissed the entire time."

"Except the one time she broke your resolve," he said, knowing it was the truth.

Mark stared at him sharply and, for a moment, Pete thought he might walk away. "Except the one time, which will forever haunt me. I fell for her trick, fell for it when she told me Skye was enjoying the Death God, and that she'd been with them, confirming it with intimate details. I let my anger, my jealousy get to me, and I broke before I realized Skye was under his spell. That one slip nearly broke us, and I will hate her forever for it."

"It seems to me it's you who you hate and she's the easy target. Maybe it's time you forgive yourself for something most men would have done, and I suspect much earlier than you did."

Mark eyed him, then let out a small chuckle. "Maybe you will be good for her after all."

He stood and reached a hand down. "Come on, we may not have coffee here, but we do have some strong ale."

Pete took his hand before following him into the castle, where they drank and talked until Skye rushed in. Mark stood quickly, his hand falling to the weapon he never seemed to be without.

"What's happened?" he asked, his expression reflecting his heavy concern.

"Someone has stolen a mage." Pete stood as she continued to talk, knowing from their faces and her hurried tone that this was serious. "They took him from his home. He's one of the professors at the magic school. They tied his wife up and gagged her so she couldn't draw on her magic. He didn't show up for classes today and when neither arrived for a dinner they were to attend, someone found her."

"But not him," Mark finished.

"Why would someone abduct a mage?"

"How is that even possible?" Pete asked.

"Crimson," Mark said through gritted teeth as Noah and two more Elite hurried in.

"Full mages require a conduit. If they knocked him unconscious and made it so he couldn't move his hands or mouth, they would have rendered him useless with no ability to channel his magic," Skye said. "His wife was a novice mage; her magic defenseless to help."

"Shit, what the hell is she up to?"

"Mark, why would she kidnap a mage? She has the ring. All she needs to do is break it and we'll give her mage power. It makes no sense."

"Something's changed," Pete said. He'd had a nagging suspicion since he'd arrived. There had been plenty of time for her to take her throne back. Either she was in trouble, or she was in too deep with the men. Possibly falling for one or both. He gripped his hands at the thought.

"What would have changed to have her send men into my realm to abduct one of my subjects?" Skye asked.

"I don't know. Maybe she's stalling?" he suggested.

Skye chewed her fingernail, a move that seemed a dichotomy to the powerful woman she was.

"They came into our realm. That's enough for us to stop this nonsense and attack," Mark said.

"He's right, Skye," Noah confirmed. "Our forces are strong. Hers aren't good enough to defeat the Elite."

She looked at Pete, that tiny crease between her eyes again. He had the urge to reach out and smooth his finger along it and take the stress from her. "Why one?"

"When she had two or even you at her disposal," Pete added, restraining himself.

"Something has changed her plan. If she were crossing us, she could easily have done it. She could have taken the ring, met me and the others, and stolen my power again," she said.

"Not on my watch," Mark said.

"She could have then knocked all of you out and let Stavin's forces through the portal. It was a risk we discussed, remember?"

"Yes."

"But this...it gives her time and mage power."

"Not enough to take both of them and an army."

"But enough to send a sign," Pete said.

Skye brought her hand down. "Or a message. One mage lets her travel."

"To us? Then why not use the ring?" Mark asked.

"No, it's too risky to go directly to us, but not to Theodore. Stavin and Bormick both want his kingdom. They'd be willing to let her go to him on the pretense that she'll kill him," she surmised.

Understanding reflected on Mark's face. "But instead, she'll give him a message to tell us what's changed. She returns to them with evidence of his death or an excuse about failing, and Theodore delivers her message to us."

"So, what's changed?" Noah asked.

Pete knew the answer, felt it in his heart. She'd grown attached, or maybe she enjoyed the sex too much. Maybe Mark was right. Maybe she had reverted to her old ways. As much as it hurt, he still loved her, which made the pain that much worse.

"I don't know, but I think we wait for her next move," Skye said, her eyes studying Pete in a way that made him think she could sense his thoughts.

"They can't be far. We could catch up with them," Noah said.

"No, Skye's right. We wait," Mark said, surprising Pete. "Go, but make sure the men are on high alert. I want no other instances of outsiders in this kingdom."

Noah nodded, then left the room.

"She loves you, Pete," Skye said. "I know that look, and she had it. Trust her."

The words of the goddess came back to him. *You will need to truly love her for what awaits.*

"Do you trust her?" he asked.

She took a moment before answering, "Yes."

"Why?"

"Because someone has to."

Mark led her from the room, and once again, he felt like an outsider as they discussed going to warn Theodore, someone Pete knew Crimson had been intimate with in her past as well. He ran his hands through his hair, pondering the world and situation in which he found himself. Knowing there was no more for him to do, he made his way back to his room, finally drifting off to visions of Crimson.

CRIMSON

Eleven days had passed since Stavin had left for Kantenda. Bormick filled each day so that they passed quickly. Crimson couldn't get enough of him, and it seemed he felt the same. The way he touched her brought her to her knees, and he touched her often, no matter where they were. He was insatiable, just as she was.

Her mind wandered to Pete often. Anytime Bormick wasn't preoccupying her. The more he took her, the further she fell, and the more she worried about what she would do. She didn't want to give either man up. Both were a part of her, and the thought was like someone taking a limb from her. At one point, she even thought she'd give up her kingdom to have them both. They had such a strong hold on her.

"Where are your thoughts, Crimson?" Bormick asked, pulling her to him. As always, need swept through her. There wasn't a moment when that need didn't rise. Brushing her hand through his hair, she kissed him.

"I just made you come. Are you hungry again?" he asked, his hand skimming her breasts.

"I'm always hungry."

"I can put the horses back and fuck you in the stables."

"That's romantic," she teased.

"I don't do romance, sweetheart, just you."

She rested her hands on his chest, feeling the strength beneath. "It's tempting." Her eyes settled on the ring, her connection back to Skye and to Pete. "No, you promised me a day of riding—"

"I didn't specify the type of riding," he said with a cocky grin.

She couldn't help but laugh. "Aren't you satisfied? How many times did you get relief this morning?"

He brought his fingers up to count. "Let's see...two times in bed, and then there was the time with your mouth. Hmm, then I can't forget the time on the table while we broke fast. Only four this morning."

"You are relentless."

"Only for you," he replied, kissing her again.

Her horse bumped against her, growing impatient for his ride.

"I think he's trying to get my attention. You're going to have to share me."

"I don't share you."

"I don't think he's happy with that response," she replied, petting the horse.

"Fucking horse," he mumbled. "All right, riding the horse first and when we return, you ride me with that mouth of yours again before I take you from behind. I want to see that ass bent over and those nice hips in my hands as I squeeze the shit out of them."

"You keep talking dirty like that and you're going to get the horse excited."

He let out a hearty chuckle and was moving to help her up when three riders approached quickly.

"Looks like Stavin's back," he said, dropping her foot and grabbing her ass.

"Time to share again," she playfully said.

Bormick's response was anything but playful. "Time to kill a king."

His words sent a chill through her. This was the moment. Her hand was now forced, and she'd need to make a decision. They would want her to kill Theodore. In another lifetime, she would have happily obliged. But now, there was too much at stake to turn on Skye's trust. She prayed her plan would work. Convincing Theodore to play along would be challenging. It was a risk to rely on him to send word to Skye that she was still on their side. That had been her plan when she'd sent Stavin to retrieve the mage, but things had grown complicated.

Complicated wasn't a strong enough word to describe what this was. And the further she fell for Bormick, the more she felt herself tangled in a web she could not escape. There was no happy ending, no matter what way she looked at it. She glanced up at Bormick, seeing the excitement in his eyes. He was ready for action, ready to claim another kingdom. He wanted to be on the battlefield, in the fray again, the one from which she'd taken him. She'd tamed him as much as she'd been able, but she wasn't positive a man of his nature could be tamed.

Stavin drew his horse close as the other riders headed to the stables. He sprung from the horse dragging the unconscious mage down and tossing him on the ground. Something about the way he glared at her caused Crimson to hesitate. Her fingers turned the enchanted ring nervously.

"Welcome home. Took you long enough. Take the mage to the dungeons," Bormick commanded.

Crimson noted how Stavin's hand had fallen to his sword.

"What is it, Stavin?" Bormick asked.

"I took some time to wander the castle grounds before we left."

"You what? I told you to stay away from the Mage Warrior and her Elite."

"Don't worry. I stayed hidden, but I gained some interesting insight." He stared at Crimson, his eyes narrowing. "Do you want me to tell him, Crimson, or do you want to break it to him?"

Bormick turned to her, his brows furrowing. "Tell me what?"

She loosened the ring, Bormick's expression terrifying her. "I don't know what he's talking about."

"No? They seem quite concerned about you, Crimson. Something about you not communicating with them."

"Why would you communicate with the Mage Warrior?" Bormick growled.

For once, she was at a loss. Too content from her time with him, she'd let her defenses down, the manipulation, the scheming ways left behind.

"I wouldn't."

Stavin backhanded her, and she fell against the horse, the ring falling from her fingers. It rolled away, coming to a stop under the second horse and out of her reach.

"What the fuck, Stavin?" Bormick pushed him away.

Crimson stared at the ring as the horse pranced around it. It sat too far from her reach.

"She deceived us, Bormick," he said, grabbing Bormick's shirt.

They moved further back as they'd argued, but she couldn't figure out a safe way to retrieve the ring. Coming back to her, Stavin grabbed her and threw her at Bormick, who caught her. Fear pummeled her as he walked away from the horse and toward them. The ring remained precariously positioned under the horse, which was still prancing around it, the tension from the two men stirring its nerves.

Pull yourself together, Crimson. You're not weak, she told herself, but Stavin's eyes were deadly and Bormick's grip tight.

"What does he mean, Crimson?" he asked, squeezing her arm. His grip was painful. Uncertainty paralyzed her. She was unable to think of what to say, how to alleviate the situation, or erase the anger from his voice.

"I don't know," she replied, hearing the shake in her voice.

Stavin yanked her from his grip.

"You don't know?" he asked, pushing her so that her feet slid under her, tangling in her skirts and sending her to the ground.

"Stavin, let her talk!" Bormick yelled.

"No! The bitch came here to trick us and kill us."

Bormick turned his head sharply, the look in his eyes like a dagger to her chest.

"I should have known she was up to something," Stavin continued. "That body, and those tempting ways. For all those years, I watched you pleasure those other men while I craved your touch and you finally spread your legs for me. Whore, I should have known you were just up to your normal ways. Fucking us to get your crown back."

"Is it true?" Bormick asked, a flicker of hurt in his eyes.

She couldn't speak, afraid to hurt him, and lose him, even with death staring her in the face.

"Is it true?" he screamed, and she flinched at the pain within the words.

"Yes, but..." Stavin drew his sword as Bormick's expression hardened. "But I fell for you. I couldn't do it," she said with a desperation to both save her life and ease his pain.

"Lies!" Stavin shouted, raising his sword.

"You claimed me, Bormick. Everything we have is real."

"Shame to lose a good whore, but I'll be glad to send your bloodied body to the Mage Warrior before I take her kingdom," Stavin said.

She didn't take her eyes off Bormick. The myriad of emotions going through his eyes was death enough.

Stavin swung his blade down, but Bormick drew his sword and blocked him just before the blade met her body. The clang of it echoed through her ears as her breath escaped in relief.

"What are you doing?" Stavin growled.

"You won't kill her," he growled back.

"Are you bewitched? She deceived us."

They glared at each other, swords pushing against one another. Crimson held her breath. Her plan had worked too well. She didn't want Bormick hurt. Stavin was a well-trained soldier, no matter how he claimed to be king. He'd commanded her forces through the Mage Wars. She'd chosen him to lead her guard because of his brute strength. Bormick was strong, lethal in his own right, but he was a rogue, nonconforming, and never properly trained for battle, no matter how he preferred to be on a battlefield. Against a common man he was deadly but against Stavin he was vulnerable.

"Lower your weapon," Bormick commanded.

"I am not yours to command."

"You always have been."

Narrowing his eyes, Stavin forced Bormick back a step.

"No more. You choose that lying wench over our alliance, then I'll rule without you behind me. She tricked us both. She wants one thing and one thing only—power. You knew that in the beginning. The agreement was to use her until we grew bored. Remember?"

Her heart pounded. They'd had their own agenda as well. She couldn't blame them, but she'd still thought she'd had control the entire time, and it irked her that she hadn't.

Bormick glanced back at her, and a wave of need swept through her. Even with the fear present, it was there. The claim he had on her was strong; the hold on her one she couldn't deny.

"Do you see her for who she is, Bormick?"

She noticed the tension in his muscles loosen, Bormick's doing the same before both men lowered their weapons.

"Good, now step aside and let me kill her. Then we'll find a new woman."

Bormick met Crimson's eyes again, searching them.

"I'm yours, Bormick."

"Not all mine," he returned, his eyes hardening again.

She couldn't argue. Her mutual claim with Pete was too

strong. Nothing could undo it. Her heart was his, but she thought perhaps it had made room for Bormick. She knew the truth, no matter how she told herself it was only physical.

"Then you do it," she said. "Let it be your blade."

"Fine by me. Just get it over with. I haven't had a good fuck in days and I'm ready for one," Stavin grumbled.

Bormick stood over her, bringing his sword up.

She didn't flinch, only held his eyes.

"It's better this way," she said, giving him a small smile. "It's okay, Bormick. You don't do love, remember?"

She closed her eyes and awaited her death. Her mind filled with a lifetime of misdeeds, cruelty, punishments, abuse before it went to Pete. The thought of him calmed her and as her time with Bormick flashed through her thoughts, she waited. She was at peace, she'd loved and been loved and now she would spend her eternity with the Death God, knowing she'd had two men who had given her life meaning. Something she'd always craved but never found. Until now.

"Dammit,." she heard Bormick mutter.

There was a strike of metal against metal, and Stavin cursed. Opening her eyes, Crimson saw the two were fighting. A myriad of emotions berated her. As her body relaxed with relief another thought occurred to her. Bormick's defense of her may have spared her harm, but it may have put him in danger. Her body tensed with the fear of losing him.

"She has bewitched you, fool!"

"You're not killing her."

"Then I'll kill you first. I'm tired of being your puppet, anyway. This is my kingdom, not yours."

The blows were heavy, the sound of steel striking steel piercing her ears. She scooched back to avoid their feet, holding her breath each time Stavin struck. She knew that she couldn't lose Bormick. It would hurt too much. The thought squeezed her heart so tightly it ached.

The horses she and Bormick planned to ride were shifting their hooves as the two men increased their attacks, their blows heavier. She could see the tension in both. Bormick's arms were taut, the muscles bulging with exertion. They shifted closer to her, and she scooted back further as Bormick put Stavin on the defensive, Stavin's swings losing their force.

The horses shifted again, one fleeing, the other rearing its legs, bringing its hooves down on the ring she'd forgotten about. Portal magic flared to life, the horse fleeing. Bormick's attention turned to it, and Stavin took the moment to strike him hard. A scream fled Crimson's mouth as the sword sliced his chest, his hand dropping his own weapon. His eyes looked to her as Stavin jammed the sword through his falling body.

Her scream was endless, her heart ripping in two.

"I'll leave you alive while I kill her, then I'll end you, traitor," Stavin grumbled, oblivious to the portal that had formed behind him.

He put his foot on Bormick's chest and yanked his sword free. Crimson stared at the blood that was dripping from it. She started to crawl toward Bormick, her mind a panic that she couldn't stop.

The portal was glimmering with its magic, but Skye hadn't come through. No one had come through to help her and her mind raced in fear trying to figure out why they were leaving her to die.

"Now it's your time to die," Stavin said, grabbing her neck and bringing her from the ground before she could get to Bormick.

"It's a shame. You're a good fuck. I enjoyed it while it lasted."

She didn't struggle, knowing there was no use. Half of her soul felt shredded at the sight of Bormick's limp body. She'd lost Pete, now Bormick, and there was nothing left worth living for. Her heart was wrenched in ways it never had been.

She braced herself for death, but a movement caught her eye as Stavin drew his sword.

"Pete," she said in a whisper as she saw Pete walk through the portal. She must have died and not realized it. He'd come to collect her soul, Derrant sending him as punishment. She closed her eyes and waited for her soul to bear its rightful place in the Death God's hands, her lovers both torn from her, leaving her no reason to cling to life.

PETE

A portal had appeared in the middle of the training field as Pete and Skye practiced. She'd been training him for what seemed like hours. They'd gone through portal formation, a grueling experience until he realized the differences in his magic let him form portals with greater ease than she could. His shadows seeped out to create them so that by now he was faster than she.

Skye had just playfully hit him with a bolt of black she'd gleaned from the long riding boots she was wearing, her blue eyes sparkling with humor. Those boots had caused his mind to go places it shouldn't have when she'd strode out in them. They were coupled with the tight brown training pants that left little to the imagination and under which he'd surmised she wore nothing; it had been harder than normal to keep his mind on his training. He was actually looking forward to training with Mark afterward. Being constantly knocked on his ass by an Elite was preferable to fighting his overactive imagination and the resulting tent in his pants.

The portal yanked his attention from her eyes, and he turned to stare at it. Reality whooshed back to him. Once again, a doorway that led to an unknown stood before him. Only this time, that unknown involved his relationship with Crimson. He didn't know what he would find when he emerged on the other side. None of the possibilities assuaged his nerves.

"Skye!" Mark came running, Noah and a few other Elite behind him.

"What is that?" Courtney asked, she and Bo having come out to observe the training.

"Crimson," he said.

Mark barked orders to one of his men who went to gather the Elite.

"I thought you said you were sending mages to her?" Pete asked.

"No longer. They came into our land and stole a mage. Now she gets an army."

"If she has the mage, why would she summon us?" Skye asked, the concern heavy in her voice.

"She's in trouble," Pete said, running to the portal, all fear of what he would find gone with the thought of her in trouble.

"Pete!" Skye yelled. He paused and turned back to her. "Don't rush in there—"

"I have to, Skye. No matter what lies on the other side, she needs me."

He stepped through, hearing her mumble a complaint behind him.

He emerged to an unexpected scene. His eyes met Crimson's, fear transforming to surprise in her sage eyes.

"Pete," he heard her whisper as he quickly took in the scene.

A wounded man lay on the ground trying to reach her, but Pete's concern was the man holding the sword raised to strike her. Without hesitation, he grabbed his dagger, the only weapon he had on him, and threw it, landing it square in the middle of his back.

The man grunted, dropping Crimson and looking back at Pete.

"You're her rescue? And you think that will stop me," he said, turning back to Crimson and reaching for her. She hadn't moved, her eyes wide with disbelief.

Skye emerged next to him, Mark by her side. He was going to make a comment about buying time for Skye to kill him, but there was no need. The dagger expanded with a force that exploded through the man's chest, blood splattering over Crimson as she let out a scream. His dead body collapsed where he stood.

"Holy shit," Mark muttered. "I did not see that happening."

"Mark, we have company," Skye said as guards poured from the castle.

Mark gave a signal, and his men piled through the portal, running to meet the influx.

Pete couldn't take his eyes from Crimson. She looked vulnerable and torn.

"Noah, check that one. See if he's still alive, then take him to the dungeon for quick execution."

"No!" Crimson yelled and Pete saw things clearly, her hesitation confirmation that she'd fallen for one of them.

She looked between the two of them, and Pete turned his eyes to the man who'd taken her heart from him. His blue eyes met Pete's, a moment of understanding passing between them. He saw the hurt in the man's eyes before the pain overcame it. Crimson made her choice, running to the man's side.

"Don't kill him, Mark. Skye, please. Please don't kill him," Crimson pleaded as she laid over his body.

Fighting against his own heartache and the desperation in Crimson's voice, he asked, "Is it something a novice mage can heal?"

"Possibly," Skye answered.

"He's a wanted criminal. He needs punishment," Mark argued.

"It's Crimson's kingdom, and she clearly doesn't want him killed," Pete replied.

"And you're fine with that?" Mark asked him. Pete was the fool in everyone's eyes, Mark's tone giving no other indication.

"I don't have a choice, and I don't want her hurt."

Mark shook his head. "You're a better man than I am. Noah, take him to the infirmary. I want him heavily guarded, understood?"

"Got it."

They took him from Crimson, leaving her there, looking broken, too broken. He turned from her, observing the fighting that was now occurring. Her forces were strong, but they were no match for Mark's Elite who were fascinating to watch, the magic in their weapons glowing a brilliant blue.

"Crimson, you need to do something about that," Skye said. "Get up and take back your kingdom. I don't care what mess you got yourself into, you are their queen. Remind them who you are before my Elite slaughter them all."

Crimson's eyes fell on Pete. The sadness and guilt he found in them was palpable so that it gutted him. She didn't move, focused only on him, like she was waiting for him to do something. He thought of her past, the last times she'd messed up. The Death God had punished her for her actions, then punished her again when she'd fallen for Pete. She expected punishment. But he couldn't do that, he loved her too much to hurt her more.

He walked over to the dead body, gripped the handle and pulled his dagger out, wondering how it had returned to its original size. Then he walked to Crimson.

"Mark?" he heard Skye whisper.

Standing over her, he saw her flinch, sadness passing through her eyes. He sheathed the dagger and held out his hand. Her eyes held surprise, and she hesitated before reaching up and taking it.

The moment she was in front of him, his world became her again. Everything, including the betrayal, fell away. He leaned over and ripped a piece of her torn skirt and gently wiped the blood from her face. As he lowered his hand, she grabbed it, holding tight.

"You're really here," she said, her voice quivering.

He nodded, unsure of what else to say.

She brought her fingers to his face, tracing his jawline. Her expression was full of wonder just before her eyes grew sad. "I'm sorry."

"I know. Now go claim your kingdom."

She reached up and drew his lips to hers, his heart bursting and breaking at once. Slowly, she drew back and walked away, her hand lingering in his until distance separated them.

His mind was a tangle of confusion. She had layered the kiss with the love she felt for him. He couldn't deny it, yet she had fallen for another man. There was no question on that.

Shaking it off, he watched her demeanor change, her posture straightening, an air of authority coating her like an aura.

"Enough!" she called in a booming voice that commanded respect.

He watched as she took control, demanding her troops stand down.

"Anyone who does not swear allegiance to me may continue to fight at your own peril. I will not protect you."

Most of the remaining guard kneeled. The Elite drew back, weapons ready. A few men pressed forward, oblivious to the fact that their battle was lost. Crimson glanced at Mark. He gave the order, his men quickly cutting them down, their bodies falling to the ground in the graceful wake of the Elite weapons.

From the castle, a man emerged holding something in his hand. He was running toward Crimson, his head low in deference. An Elite took a defensive stance in his path.

"No!" Crimson cried. "He's my servant!"

The Elite stepped aside, and the man ran to her. He handed

her a crown of onyx with sparkling red rubies. She studied it before she placed it on her head.

"Our queen has returned," he bellowed, the field raising their voices in cheer.

Pete turned, catching Skye's eyes. They held worry and uncertainty as she gave him a sad smile. Calling his Shadow Magic, he created a portal; the shadows licking its edges. He glanced back at Crimson once more before stepping through the portal, leaving his queen behind with the pieces of his shattered heart.

CRIMSON

The room was quiet, save for the shuffling feet of the novice mage healers. No other patients were present. The Elite had cleared the room of any other patients, their presence stoic behind and across the room from where Crimson sat holding Bormick's lifeless hand. She'd lost track of the number of days, staying by his side, refusing to leave. Leaving Hentrom in charge of her kingdom in her absence, trusting Skye and Mark to help. Hentrom was loyal. He'd been with her since her childhood, soothing and caring for her after her first time with the Death God. He'd done the same after she returned from the hands of every loyal man her father had forced her to entertain. He'd stayed by her side as she'd hardened from the free-spirited quiet girl she'd been to the sexually charged weapon they'd made her.

He knew how she worked, knew the workings of her throne, and would no doubt have everything prepared for her return. A return that was still uncertain. A future she could not begin to fathom. Allies with Kantenda, the queen she'd once despised, plotted to overthrow, not to mention what she'd done to Mark.

She wasn't ashamed of her past. She was who she was, but she did have regrets. One of which she didn't know how to face: Pete.

She lowered her head, closing her eyes. Pete, who held her heart, who was like a breath she couldn't exhale. She wanted to go to him, to see him, touch him, feel his lips against hers, but she feared seeing him. She'd seen his eyes, read his expression, sensed his pain. Pain she had inflicted. Pain she couldn't undo or even correct.

She didn't know what to do or how to approach him and so she'd satisfied her need to stay by Bormick's side until he woke. There she'd remained, watching each rise and fall of his breath, feeling the warmth of his skin, the color as it returned to his face.

She reached a hand out and touched his cheek, the solid, strong jaw that led to his delicious mouth. Tracing her fingers over his parched lips, she wondered what his reaction to her would be. He might forgive her but there was a chance he would kill her and even try to kill Pete. She'd seen the look that had passed between their eyes, the knowledge they had both shared. She didn't want to lose him. Gods, she didn't want to lose either man.

Closing her eyes, she pushed back the tears that threatened to fall.

"You are a queen," she remembered her father saying as he'd removed his belt, hiking her skirts so the leather could meet her skin, his hand pausing too long on her soft flesh. "Queens don't cry."

The feel of the belt upon her skin seared through her, as if he were in the room with her. He'd reminded her of that fact every day, beating her any time she failed at her duty, even when she was older. Sometimes letting his prominent friends join before he whored her off to them.

She'd had her revenge, helping quicken his death when he'd fallen ill, then one by one, seducing and murdering his loyalists—some of the first kills she'd allowed Stavin to exact as she'd tormented them with the body they'd used for years. She was as close to a living sex demon as anyone could be, murdering them as they climaxed and watching their euphoria turn to horror as Stavin's blade slit their throat.

"Squeeze his hand any harder and you'll push him to the Death God's arms," she heard Skye's voice.

She looked up suddenly, releasing her grip on Bormick's hand, not realizing she'd been holding it so tight.

"Everything all right?" Skye asked with a raise of her brow.

"Just lost in thoughts of the past. Memories better left behind."

Skye studied her but didn't question. She came closer but didn't sit, choosing to lean against the wall instead.

"Pete is ready to leave."

Crimson's heart dropped. "No."

"He's ready. He has a future to claim. One you have yet to discover because you've been here instead of by his side."

"I can't leave Bormick," she said, touching Bormick's wrapped wound.

"Do you love him?" Skye asked.

"I don't know how I feel about him. I just know that I need him. Something about him calls to me, like I need to have him by my side, or I will cease to exist."

"And when were you planning to tell Pete? The man who loves you and freed himself from a curse to get back to you."

"I don't know how to tell him, Skye."

"It's not fair to him if you don't. Don't be selfish, Crimson. Just tell him you no longer love him."

"That's the thing," she said, looking into Skye's deep blue eyes. "I do love him with every fiber of my being that Bormick has not claimed. I need them both. It's like the claims they have on me are intertwined, running through me, calling to my blood on a level I can't ignore. If I do, if I'm forced to live without either of them, I won't be able to live. My being will shatter."

Skye pursed her lips, a flash of knowledge passing through her eyes, followed by a strange pensive look as if she were figuring something out.

"Talk to him, Crimson, before you lose him." She looked at Bormick. "They really do resemble each other, don't they?" she said with that same look before turning her eyes back to Crimson. "Talk to him, tell him how you feel because right now, he's crushed. His heart is broken, no matter that he tries to hide it."

She turned to leave.

"Why do you care? All those years you visited me. You helped me regain my kingdom. You're helping me now. Why after all I did to you and Mark?"

She turned, her eyes a rich shade. "I don't know, really. Something draws me to you, Crimson. I don't know if it's Eliana's blood that runs through us both or if it's something more, but I feel a connection to you, a damaged, warped one, but a connection nonetheless."

"You can't resist me. One day you'll be back in bed with me," she said with a wink.

Skye laughed. "Keep dreaming."

"I'm sorry."

"No, you're not."

"Well, maybe not all of it. Mark is quite a good fuck."

"Don't make me kill you here. I'd hate to make a mess for the novice mages."

"You love me," Crimson said as Skye walked away.

"Something like that," she shouted back before the door closed behind her.

She shook her head, thinking on the strange friendship she and Skye now had. Their friendship had developed over years of small talk and twisted remarks, banter that had slowly turned from malicious to teasing. They shared a past, one that Crimson had scarred like Skye had said. The woman Crimson had envied so much that she'd sold her to the Death God in exchange for her husband, a man who would hold his grudge until his dying breath, unlike his wife.

"You fucked the Mage Warrior and her husband?" she heard Bormick say with a gravely throat.

Her adrenaline rushed through her like wind on a fall day.

"Not at the same time," she replied with a sly smile.

"Damn, you are something, aren't you?"

He tried sitting up, then dropped back with a groan. "That bastard Stavin stabbed me, didn't he?"

"Yes."

"Did you kill him?'

"No," she answered hesitantly, "Pete did, to save me."

His sharp blue eyes searched hers. "Hmm, I suppose I'll have to thank him later."

"I suppose," she whispered.

That pull was tugging at her core, calling her to move closer to him, to touch him but she remembered where she was, unsure of his thoughts.

"So, you need me?"

"Yes," she replied.

"But you love him?"

She nodded, not sure what to say.

"Damn, I told you...dangerous. You cost me a friend, a dick, but a friend. Cost me a crown, an army, and I'm left with what? A battle scar?"

"I need you, Bormick."

"Need, but you love him. I should have left you that day you told me about him. Cursed cock refused to let you go."

"I thought you didn't do love."

"I don't, but that doesn't mean... Fuck, Crimson. You do something to me that I don't understand. Something I can't control, something no other woman has done to me."

He brought his arm out and pulled her body over him, wincing as her weight hit his healing wound. His fingers fell through her hair, his eyes watching as the strands moved with his touch. "I should hate you. I should strangle you right now or break your neck before those guards realize what I've done," he whispered against her mouth.

"But..." she said breathlessly.

"But all I want to do is kiss you, then take you right here with all of them watching."

"Well, you can't take me," she teased, running her fingers through his thick hair. "But you can kiss me."

"Who says I can't slip my hands down that dress of yours and make you burn from the inside out?" She felt her arousal at the thought. What this man did to her with just his words.

"Your nurses, the novice mages, would have my head if I damage the work they've done."

"Hmm, but my hand would be happy thrust far inside of that dampness I know is waiting between your legs."

The air slipped from her lungs; her need rising. "Does this mean I'm forgiven?"

"Damn, don't go ruining the mood, Crimson."

He pulled her head forward, his mouth pressing against hers. His tongue searched hers out as his fingers dipped below the edge of her dress to tease her fully erect nipple.

"You undo the work we did on you, and we will let these guards take you to the dungeons where they can fester," a harsh voice scolded.

Crimson didn't pull away quickly as a young girl would. She was a queen, and this was her man, one half of her soul.

Finally, she separated from him, her eyes falling to the bulging erection below the sheets. She met the novice mage's eyes, their irritation evident. Her arms were crossed tightly, and she wore a scowl.

She glanced down to where Crimson's eyes had drifted.

"Serves you right for risking more injury."

"Care to join us?" he teased. "I'm sure I could loosen you up a bit."

She blushed and huffed away, muttering for them to behave, or she'd have Crimson removed.

They talked the rest of the day. She told him the truth about everything, all the way back to why she'd disappeared and how she'd met Pete. He listened intently, never showing any judgement. It was the first time they had truly talked. Their bodies had been too needy in the past.

As night fell, she knew she had to see Pete. Bormick was alive, awake, and breathing. She could leave his side now without the worry of returning to an empty bed, and the fear that the Death God would claim him in her absence. She kissed him goodbye, promising to return when she had things worked out with Pete.

As she left, she wondered if that would even happen. Bormick seemed to accept her feelings for Pete, but they'd had a mutual agreement to begin with. There had been an understanding that it wasn't about love; it was about the sex. Glancing back at him, she wondered if that was still the case. He had worked his way into a sliver of the hold Pete had on her heart. She didn't know if it had been the same for him. He kept his feelings so guarded.

Whatever hold he had on her, she knew she couldn't let him go, couldn't take that piece of her heart back from him. Bormick may have accepted that she would not give Pete up, but she didn't know if Pete would be so accepting about Bormick. There was only one way to know. She took a deep breath and for the first time since the day this part of her journey had begun, she went to find Pete, the owner of the other half of her soul.

PETE

A hush had fallen across the land, the moon above ensuring the world slept. Pete had come to appreciate this time of night, the peace it offered. His body had yet to acclimate to a normal schedule, the night retaining its hold on him.

He heard the soft movement of the door and quiet footfalls. He was no longer in the mood to talk. Skye had tried persuading him to stay. Courtney as well, but he was determined to go. It was clear Crimson didn't want him here. Four days had passed.

Four long days and nights where he'd waited for Crimson to come to him, to assuage his doubts, to at least explain what had happened, but she'd never come. She had made her choice, and whatever he'd felt in that kiss, he'd imagined, grasping for some thread of what they'd had.

He'd been a fool to fall in love with a woman he didn't know —a seductress who had pulled him under—and he'd paid the price. He'd barely had time with her. What he'd felt couldn't have been love. Or at least that's what he told himself. The problem was it hurt too much not to be love.

He had half a mind to storm into the infirmary and take her, force his claim on her, but that wasn't his way, and it would do nothing but cause her to hate him.

"The nights here hold a calm they never held in your world."

His heart sputtered at Crimson's voice, but he refused to look at her, remaining quiet.

She moved beside him, the pull to her igniting instantly. He gritted his teeth against the need to take her in his arms. She'd made her choice, and he hadn't been the one.

"I'm leaving in the morning," he stated firmly.

He heard the intake of her breath, wondering at the reaction.

"Please don't leave," she whispered.

He turned to look at her, the beauty of her crushing him. Her red hair cascaded down her shoulders, the green in the dress she wore accentuating her eyes, the candlelight shining in them. He'd never really seen her in more than the moonlight, and she was magnificent. Her lips were the kind that screamed to be kissed, forming a natural seductive point that he longed to run his finger along, followed by his tongue.

Focus, Pete, he told himself.

"Why would I stay?"

"Because I love you," she replied, the honesty in her eyes leaving him confused again.

"You just spent the last four days by another man's side. I freed myself of that curse to find you and in four days, you couldn't leave his side, not even to say goodbye to me?"

"I couldn't—"

"I know you couldn't." His voice was rising, the anger he'd kept quelled finally surfacing. "Do you love him?"

"I don't know how I feel about him."

Pete ran his hand through his hair. "You don't know how you feel about a man you've relentlessly stayed with after you've spent weeks in his bed?"

"I'm being honest, Pete. I don't really know what it is. All I know is that I need him."

Her words cut him, like an incision slicing away the last of his heart.

"Then you've made your choice. There's no need to coddle me with your lies about love. I'm not a child, Crimson, I've been through breakups before."

None that have even come close to hurting like this, he thought.

"I'm not lying, Pete. I do love you. That hasn't changed. You claimed my heart—"

"And you've given it to another man. It's just a word, like I claim the last piece of pizza. It's meaningless."

She looked confused, then hurt. Running his hands across his face, his frustration mounted.

"It's not just a word. Maybe in your world it is, but it's not here. Here it marks you, it means we're mates, it goes very deep, spiritual even. It's not just a word. Do you not love me, Pete?"

Mate? He was feeling like he was in some paranormal book, although this entire experience had been like that.

"Dammit, Crimson. Yes, I love you, against every good judgement in my mind. I love you and I even meant it when I claimed you. You were mine."

"I'm still yours."

He raised a brow. "You're choosing me?" His heart began to heal with hope.

"I can't choose. I need you, Pete, but I need him, too."

"Well, you can't have us both."

"Then I'll die because you both call to something deep within me. It's like you call to my blood and without one of you, I will cease to function. You both have this hold on me and it's one I can't remove, even if I wanted to."

"Are you asking me to share you with another man?" He laughed as he said it, but her expression remained steadfast. "Jesus, you are. Are you insane?"

"No, I'm quite lucid... Well, most days."

Searching her eyes, he looked for any sign of doubt. "Crimson, I can't share you. I want all of you."

"And I can't give him up—"

"Then go to him, and I'll stay out of your life."

"And I will still wither away because without you I'm not complete."

She was serious, and he had no words.

"It will kill me to lose either of you. I feel that deep within my soul. Both of you are part of me now, a part I cannot live without."

Sighing, he walked away from her, unsure as to what to do. He should send her away, go on with his life. He stopped pacing and looked at her. The idea of leaving her killed him. He wasn't sure he could. Her green eyes were large with expectation, a glint of desire flashing through them as they met his. He didn't think he could walk away from her. He had spent weeks without her, but it had taken the distraction of another woman to get through it. He thought of Ash. He hadn't innocently waited to find Crimson. He'd indulged just as she had, but he hadn't fallen in love and no matter what Crimson told herself, she loved this other man.

The need to leave her, to walk away and turn his back on her was strong. But he didn't think he could without regret. Without thinking of her every day. But if he stayed...if he stayed he would have to share her. It seemed an odd thought, one he wasn't certain he could live with, but he knew he couldn't live without her. She was too far ingrained in his being. His blood did call to her, the blood ritual all those ages ago ensured he couldn't turn from her.

He sighed again and walked back to her, bringing his fingers up to push a strand of hair from her face. "Neither of us has been faithful. We both indulged while we were apart. I didn't know my claim on you was so binding or I would have refrained."

"Did the souls play with you?" she asked, the broken woman slipping away, replaced with the one he knew so well.

"A little but the sex demon the Death God sent me kept me

occupied most of the time," he answered, letting his finger trace her cheek.

"You had sex with a sex demon and lived to tell about it?"

"She was a test from the Death God to see if I was worthy enough to break the curse."

Her eyes glinted. "And you passed, then took a prize?"

"Doesn't that bother you?"

She let out a beautiful laugh. "No, it makes me crave you more. To tame a sex demon is a feat a rare few achieve. Even their mates have a hard time. Did she return to you?"

He gave her a cocky smile. "Yeah, night after night."

"That's impressive. I once shared a sex demon with the Death God. They are good at what they do. There's a reason they claim that name."

"You had a threesome with the devil?"

"Oh, no, he's not ours. The Death God. Get them right. Derrant does not like to be confused with his brother."

He didn't think he'd get it right. The gods were entirely too confusing.

Her smile faded. "I want you, Pete. Take me."

He groaned, all resolve he'd had fleeing. "Are you forcing me to share you?"

"I'm not forcing you to do anything. I'm just telling you, I can't live without you, and I can't live without him. Right now, I want you inside of me so badly that my thighs are burning and my chest—"

Kissing her, he brought her against him with such force that he felt the breath flee from her. The idea of sharing didn't matter anymore. He couldn't live without her. That knowledge was one he understood at a level that went deeper than his consciousness. A primal one.

He pushed his tongue through her lips, engaging hers in a dance that matched perfectly as her hands pulled at his shirt, their kiss breaking for just that moment. Her hands skimmed his muscles as he fumbled with her dress.

"Damn," he muttered against her lips, then drew his power to remove it, the material disappearing.

She jumped back, her eyes wide again, staring at him. She was fully naked, and he took her in—every inch of her beautiful soft skin, his pants pushing painfully against his hardened need.

"How?"

He brought her back against him, his hands feeling her curves.

"Shh," he said. "Let's just say there's a lot about me that you don't know. A lot has happened since Derrant separated us."

Her eyes narrowed. Her fingers followed the lines of his tattoos, and her touch stirred him.

"Gods, I wanted you before, but now..." She gripped his bulge, eliciting a grunt from him. "Now I need you to ravage me."

Grasping his hand around her neck, he pulled her to him, kissing her with the emotion that he'd been carrying for too long. If he had no choice but to share her going forward, he was going to take her over and over this night.

She worked his length free, and he pushed against her, the warmth of her skin inviting him. Moving her closer to the bed, he paused, and she took the moment to drop to her knees. His dick twitched in anticipation. Her tongue ran the length of him, and he closed his eyes at the velvety feel of it. Embedding his fingers in her thick hair, he moaned as she enveloped him. He was always surprised at how much of him she could take. He wasn't close to an easy mouthful by any means, but she took him with no effort. Her hand wrapped around his base as her head moved along his length in a rhythm that threatened to break him. She dropped to his full depth, eliciting a grunt from him. With only minutes of pleasure from her mouth, his legs were already shaking. Digging his fingers deeper in her hair, he resisted the urge to dictate her motion. It had been a long time since he'd had her, and nothing he'd had with his tree nymph had come close to how Crimson made him feel. He felt himself thicken with the rising desire, and it threatened to drown him as her motion quickened. His climax built fast, rising to its peak then thrusting him over the ledge. He held tight to her head as he came, filling her mouth with uncontrollable lurches of his pelvis. She welcomed him, her mouth sucking each stream he sent to her until there was nothing left to give. He loosened his grip in her hair, his knees quivering. With a final swipe of her tongue around his tip, she rose, seduction filling her eyes.

"Gods, I missed that taste," she said, pulling his head down to kiss him.

He slid his hands over her curves, realizing how much he'd missed touching her body. Ash had filled his void for her, but Crimson was who he'd craved. She was the only one who could truly satisfy him.

"My turn," he mumbled against her lips.

Walking her to the bed, he forced her down and crawled over her. She looked up at him, those sage eyes seeing right into his soul. They were brimming with the love she had for him. He let his hands skim along her breast, circling her pert nipple and coaxing it out further. Her mouth parted with her sigh, and he couldn't resist kissing her again. His lips traced her neck, making their way to her breast where he sucked the same nipple into his mouth. Her skin tasted sweet and as he took her nipple between his teeth, he slipped his hand between her legs, feeling the wetness that beckoned him. The warmth of it caused his dick to harden, and he dropped his head against her chest, biting back the groan that was building.

Rising above her, he dragged his fingers from her and brought them to his mouth. He licked the sweet taste from them one by one before returning his fingers to her clit and massaging it. Her head fell back with a moan, and he relished the expression of euphoria that her face held. Unable to resist tasting all of her, he stood and yanked her legs to the edge of the bed. Dropping to his knees, he took in the beauty that lay between her legs, spreading them and dipping his tongue in. Her groan caused his body to lurch in expectation, his full length ready to be inside of her. He sucked on her clit, his fingers slipping along her in caresses that had her squirming. Bringing his tongue back, he plunged it deep into the warmth of her. A cry slipped from her, and his dick pulsed as her hands pulled at his hair. He continued to torment her with his tongue, savoring the taste of her arousal until she was begging for release. Obliging, he sank his tongue in deep and wicked until he felt her break, her scream of pleasure filling the room. He licked the juices that flowed to him, relishing the quake of her body against his mouth.

He was so hard, so turned on that he rose quickly, her body still quivering below him, and penetrated her, watching with satisfaction as her back arched. Needing to be deeper, he pulled her closer, closing his eyes at the feel of her. Her legs were still draping over the edge of the bed, and he brought one up, pushing himself further into her depth.

She felt so fantastic that he didn't want to ever stop. Her breathing was growing ragged, a sound that only further intensified his arousal. She brought herself up, and he wrapped his arms around her, holding her close so that her breasts pressed against him. The softness of them called to him, but he couldn't drag his lips from hers. As her kisses grew more desperate, her body clenched tighter around him. He knew she was growing close again, but he wasn't ready for her to lose herself to him yet. He wanted to be lost together, to fall over the cliff with her. As he slowed his pace, a frustrated moan escaped her. He couldn't help but draw back to look at her. She was beautiful. A flush of arousal touched her cheeks, and her eyes were heavy with her need for him to continue.

Kissing the sweat that was just glistening on her brow, he moved in a slow rhythm, noting how her face reflected the torment his pace was giving her. Dropping his head, he licked her breast, nibbling on her nipple as she pushed her pelvis into him. He lifted his mouth and met her eyes again, seeing the emotion, the need that matched his. The power in their shared look was like a stroke within him, one that sent the flames rising higher. He thrust back into her with a force that caused her to cling to him. There was no return as the flames tore through him. Her body clasped tightly to his, her pelvis thrusting to meet his until the flames engulfed him and he joined her climax. Her muscles spasmed around him, coaxing him until there was nothing left, and he collapsed into her arms.

They lay there, their bodies as one, and Pete knew there was no other option, no leaving her, no matter the sacrifice. He needed her with a hunger only she could satisfy. There was no other choice for him but her, and he would do whatever it took to keep her.

PETE

The Elite nodded in deference as Pete made his way through the halls. He'd asked Mark and Skye to make this journey on his own, and they'd obliged. As the sun began to descend, he'd left Crimson, something that hurt to do, but it was time to face the next step in their relationship.

The night she'd come to him, he'd taken her repeatedly and throughout the next day, soaking in all that she was, all that he'd missed and hungered for. For two days he'd kept her, exploring a deeper connection to her, a level he'd thought they'd achieved before the Death God had taken her from him, but one they'd now fortified.

He'd assented to let her visit Bormick before they left for her kingdom. She needed to be to be in her realm, leading her people. Needed to prove to them that she'd changed but not so much that she was any less of a queen than she had been. Any chance of an uprising needed to be squashed with her presence and her claim to the throne that had always been hers. Three days had passed since then and she'd acquiesced to his wish that she stay with him, that he get his fill of her before they took the next step.

He had a kingdom to claim. A kingdom she'd granted back to

him, knowing they'd rule both their realms together. He had a new power that he was still grappling to understand as it continued to grow in him, and he had her other lover to deal with.

He thought back to that morning, after she'd come to him, her words circling his head like a vulture circling its prey. Her blood called to him, just as it did to Pete. Those words wouldn't leave his mind until he'd finally asked her as she'd snuggled into his arms, "Is Bormick from your kingdom?"

He'd dreaded the answer, knowing instinctually what it would be.

"No, he's from Digremile. I guess that means he's from your kingdom," she'd said, he having told her all that had transpired while they were apart and she doing the same, even the details he didn't want to know.

Bormick was from his kingdom. Her answer had affirmed his suspicions And as he made his way through the dungeon, where Mark had moved the man once he'd been well enough to be moved, Pete saw the truth of those words, the realization hitting him square in the chest.

He nodded to the guard to let him in. Bormick was sitting on the floor. His head rose slowly, bright blue eyes studying Pete through narrowed slits. Pete leaned against the cell, folding his arms over his chest.

"So, she was right. We do look similar," he said, appraising the man who'd stolen a piece of Crimson's heart from him.

"So, you're the one who claimed her first."

"It would seem we've both claimed her, cousin."

Bormick furrowed his brow, confusion reflected on his face for just a moment before a scowl replaced it.

"I have no family."

"Perhaps not, but you did once. And long before they had you, our two families were one. Three brothers, one left as king, two punished for breaking a blood ritual which tied them to Crimson's line. My line punished to another world, yours destroyed, or so they've always thought. I suspect that brother had a bastard the Death God didn't care to find and so you and I are now the only surviving heirs of the Digremile throne."

"Throne?"

"Yes, and the two left to fulfill the blood ritual."

"Does Crimson let you drone on like this? No wonder she let me claim her. You talk too much."

Pete glared at him. "Crimson lets me do a lot of things to her—"

"Nothing I haven't done."

This is going to be annoying, he thought.

"Maybe I should take my droning back to our bed and leave you here to think about my dick in her instead of yours."

If eyes could kill, Pete knew he'd be dead, but then Bormick let out a bellowing laugh.

"Go on with your droning, *cousin.*" He emphasized the word cousin. "Wait, does that mean I'm a bloody king?"

"No, you descend from the third brother, which gives me first claim and the power that comes with it."

"Good," he said in a gruff tone. "I don't much care for politics or thrones. I do, however, like power."

"I believe the power is mine, along with the throne."

"Then why are you here, other than to tell me you're fucking my woman?"

Pete gritted his teeth. "Our woman." It killed him to say, but it was the truth.

Bormick raised a brow. "Our woman?"

"As much as I dislike the idea, yes." Crimson had not known his intent until he'd left this evening, nor had he shared his thoughts on Bormick's heritage until just then.

"I have a choice. I can leave you here and let the Elites kill you for all the crimes Crimson won't punish you for, but by doing so, rip a part of her soul in half and leave a shell of the woman I love. Or I can accept the fact that a damned blood ritual from ages ago has tied us both to her, accept that her blood calls to you as strongly as it does to me and that yours calls to her as strongly as mine does to her."

"And?"

"I want Crimson happy, and she won't be happy if I leave you to rot, no matter if I'm the sharing type or not."

"And who says I'm the sharing type?"

Now it was Pete's turn to raise a brow. "After all I've heard?"

"I don't mind sharing, and Stavin had his uses. He was a joke with his tongue, but his dick was big enough to do the job while I took care of the rest."

"Nice," he said, hearing the sarcasm that layered his reply.

"But I don't want to share Crimson, and I made that clear to Stavin well before that jackass tried to kill me. I heard you took the final blow to him."

"I did and you have no choice but to share her. She's mine. I claimed her before you entered the picture, and I can leave your ass here."

Bormick was quiet for a moment.

"She said you saved her, stopped Stavin from killing her?"

"I did."

"You love her?"

"I believe I said that already. Do you?"

He drew his fingers over the growth on his face. "I don't know what I feel about her other than I crave her, like no other woman I've had. In fact, I have no desire for any woman but her now."

"Because she calls to a part of you that you never knew existed, on a level that goes deeper than words can express and to be without her is like not breathing."

"Something like that."

Pete walked over and put his hand out to Bormick, who looked at it before looking Pete over.

"What happens if I take that hand?"

"I suppose we're stuck with each other."

"So I have to share her?"

"We have to share her."

"Fuck me," he complained, grabbing Pete's hand with a not surprisingly strong grip.

"Now that's something I can guarantee you I won't be doing."

Bormick laughed, slapping his back. "I may actually grow to like you. Prepare to see a lot of my dick in your face."

"Great, so many things to look forward to," he grumbled, walking out of the cell.

"I'm free?" Bormick asked, following him.

"Skye and Mark agreed to leave your sentencing to Crimson. Although Mark had a few choice words to say about her decision to pardon you."

"You know the Mage Warrior and her husband on a first name basis?"

"I know a lot more than you suspect." He nodded to the guards, then drew his hands up, forming a portal with the shadows.

Bormick stared at him. "You have magic? Who are you?"

"I'm the King of Digremile, and descendent of the Death God, just as you are."

"Do I get magic, too?"

"Afraid that's just for me. The Death God favored the second brother over the third."

"Oh, well, I'm better at killing with my hands."

"We'll need to talk about that," he said, stepping through the portal. Bormick followed, the shadows flowing back to Pete as his eyes fell to Crimson. Her naked body was sprawled across the bed in a way that left no question of what she wanted.

"Hello, boys, it took you long enough."

"Holy shit," Pete mumbled, his arousal rising with no hesitation.

"Yeah, I think I made the right choice," Bormick said, taking off his shirt. "Miss me, Crimson?"

She gave him a coy smile, lifting her knees up and dragging her finger between her legs, before bringing it to her mouth and licking it. He wanted her and he could feel Bormick's need for her, as if they were connected, their call to her equally ravenous.

"So, how does this work?" he asked, never having shared a woman.

"It's easy, just try to keep up with me," Bormick replied, moving to her and pulling her up to kiss her.

Jealousy gauged Pete and he almost walked away. But as Bormick's hand moved to her breast, he couldn't help the throb in his pants seeing how her nipple responded and her body arched into him. This would take some getting used to, but he could do it as long as it meant he had her.

"You want him in your mouth or inside of you?" Bormick asked.

"Inside of me while my mouth takes you, then you switch places, then... Well, who knows."

"I have a few ideas," Bormick said as Pete gave up the fight and tore his shirt off, making his way to her. He moved on top of her, kissing her after Bormick moved aside. Her hand undid the buttons of Bormick's pants as Pete ravaged her breasts, taking them into his mouth and feeling her squirm as Bormick groaned. He drew back, kissing her thigh, his fingers reaching into her warmth, then sinking into her.

"Damn, you're so wet."

"She's always wet," Bormick grumbled.

Pete looked up, unable to take his eyes off her as she took the man into her mouth, her tongue licking around his head before plunging down his shaft. He'd always felt how deep she took him but never seen it from this perspective. Bormick was large like he was, and she took him to the hilt. His hand was tangled in her hair as he pushed her further, the sight sending a flurry of flames through Pete's body.

She grew wetter, and Pete tore his eyes away, slightly uncomfortable with how turned on the scene was making him. He brought his mouth to her, licking her arousal, and hearing her hum against Bormick's length. He drove her crazy, sucking and licking until he felt her growing close, her body prone and waiting for him to bring her over the edge. Bormick was thrusting at a faster pace against her mouth, and Pete couldn't wait any longer to be inside of her. Rising, he ripped his pants off and entered her, driving as deep as he could. Her mouth released with her cry. He thrust into her as Bormick brought her mouth back to his engorged erection. Within moments, she fell apart, her climax sending him over the precipice. Bormick grunted as he came, Crimson's mouth catching every drop of him while Pete continued to grip her hips tight, pushing the last of his essence into her.

Bormick pulled away, dropping his head to kiss her, his hand wrapping around her neck in a forceful way. "And that's how it's done, cousin."

Pete leaned down and kissed her, tasting the other man in her mouth and pulling away.

"That's going to take some getting used to," he complained before he returned to kissing her.

She pushed him over, trailing her kisses down his stomach and took him in her mouth, licking him clean. His reaction was immediate. Bormick didn't hesitate. He climbed behind her and jerked her ass up, kissing her ass cheek before plunging his way into her, the force pushing Pete further into her mouth and eliciting a groan from him.

They continued through the night, taking turns pleasing her and taking her, both adjusting to their new group dynamic and quickly coming to understand it. He could live with this. She was with him. She was happy, and as he finally collapsed next to her, listening to the sounds of their breaths, he realized he was where he was meant to be.

"Sharing's not too bad, is it?" Bormick asked, his voice sleepy.

"No, I think I could get used to it."

"You don't have a choice," Crimson said.

"I did have a choice, but I chose to give that up."

"So just the three of us from now on, huh?" Bormick asked.

"Well, not quite," Crimson said.

"What does that mean?" he asked.

"You might want to make sure you've caught your breath before she tells you this," Pete said.

"I thought sharing with you was the worst part."

"I'm the good part," he replied. "You're not going to like this next part."

Bormick rose and looked at them both.

Crimson was quiet for a moment before saying, "I'm not the only one you have to share with."

CRIMSON

Crimson rose quietly, lifting Bormick's heavy arm from her and sliding from Pete's protective hold. They stirred slightly, but neither woke. She stood over the bed to watch them sleep, marveling at them. They were hers, and for the first time in her life, she was content. She'd never been content, always craving more, seeking out men to satisfy her needs. Although none ever could. She'd always brought herself to climax. Men either used her or she used them. There was never a time when they focused on her pleasure. But now she had Bormick and Pete. Her mates. And gods, what they did to her.

Tingles cascaded through her at the thought. She turned and rummaged through her wardrobe, pulling out a luxurious red dress that brought out her eyes and her hair. Then she quietly left the room, glancing back at her men once more.

As she made her way down the hall, she thought about the previous night. There had been hesitation there from Pete, a reserved feel to his moves at first. She knew there had been jealousy, had seen it there until he'd relaxed. And once he did, it had been ecstasy.

Before Pete had left, they'd discussed the implications to his feelings and to their relationship, if Pete allowed room for Bormick. That had been after he'd told her his theory. One that had left her speechless. He and Bormick were cousins, very distant, but blood tied them. The same blood that bound them to her. There'd been a reason she was drawn to them both, that they looked so alike. A blood ritual that made them hers, and they had both laid that claim again last night.

Her thighs quivered, thinking back on what they'd done to her. They'd brought her to climax so many times she thought she'd die of contentment. She'd shared men before, but it had always been demanding, and rough. Even what she'd had with Bormick and Stavin hadn't been like this. There was an intensity to Pete and Bormick together that she could only attribute to the blood bond.

The night had been about her, then about the three of them. The two men had found a rhythm as if they were brothers, switching off, bringing her to climax as one, over and over. And she'd repaid the favor, taking them, letting them take her.

She felt the dampness between her legs and scolded herself for letting her mind wander. She needed to be level-headed and certainly not wet when she did this or Derrant would take it as an invitation.

Maybe that wouldn't be a bad thing.

Once she was far enough away from Pete and Bormick, she hurried to her throne room. Considering she had just taken back her crown and was now risking it again to face Derrant, she thought it an appropriate place. She lifted her hair before biting her finger to draw blood. As the blood pulled, she touched it to the light outline of the birthmark she shared with Skye. She'd never told her. It was powerless, her tie to mage magic was simply a shell that filled temporarily when she syphoned magic from other mages. The mark only shimmered when she activated it. Only her father had known of it. Pete had seen it in the moonlight of the grove as he'd tasted her neck,

Bormick noticing it as he'd run his fingers along her neck one night.

They shouldn't have seen it. To others, it didn't exist, but now she understood it had been their tie to the Death God that had allowed it.

As her blood activated her connection to him, there was a tingle of magic upon the skin. She spoke the words she'd first learned as a child.

"Death God to whom my soul belongs,

Take your claimed and bring me home."

For a few minutes, nothing happened, and she wondered if he'd even listen to her. There was a possibility that he was still angry enough to ignore her call.

In time, the air grew heavy and as with each time he'd heeded her call, darkness encased her body as she moved to the Shadow Realm.

Derrant was not where she'd expected. Instead, he was sitting in his bed, the sheets lying precariously across his naked manhood, his lean but muscular chest exposed. His blue eyes glistened with power as they met hers, eyes she now saw matched Pete and Bormick's.

Next to him lay a gorgeous woman who resembled Skye too highly to be mistaken for anyone but Eliana. Crimson had never seen her. The goddess had been in hiding from Derrant before, and Crimson couldn't help but gawk at her as she rose from the bed. Her navy eyes were so like Skye's that it was eerie, save for the power they radiated. Her lithe form walked across the room, her eyes never leaving Crimson's as she donned a dark robe. Derrant remained where he was, a distraction he had no intent of removing.

"Crimson," he said, drawing his eyes from the goddess. "You have nerve summoning me when you have yet to win my favor back, no matter that you settled the bloodshed in your realm."

For once, she didn't know how to proceed. The confidence

she normally exuded had fled with Eliana's cold stare. Using her wiles on Derrant would bring no favor from the goddess, and from Derrant's expression, it wouldn't work on him this time. He knew her too well.

"I've come to beg favor."

"A favor?" Eliana asked, her voice painfully acidic. "You dare ask a favor after all you did to my daughter?"

Skye, damn. Part of her wanted to argue that Derrant had done his fair share to her, but she stayed silent.

"You will find no favor here," Derrant said.

"I want you to release Skye from her obligation to you."

Eliana's brow furrowed as Derrant let out a booming laugh. The goddess studied her and put a hand out for Derrant to stop laughing. Seeing the Death God bow to her command so easily was a strange sight.

"Why would you ask that?"

"Skye and I have made amends. She and Mark don't deserve that punishment. I owe it to them to free them of the obligation."

Eliana's eyes softened.

"The obligation stands," Derrant said. His hands were clenched, and she could feel the malevolence that rolled from his aura.

"I know, which is why I offer myself in her place."

There was silence, then Eliana moved closer to her. "I should hate you for what you've done." She put her hands on Crimson's cheeks and she felt the power that radiated from her as she kissed Crimson's forehead. "But you are of my blood as well, and just as Skye does, I see the true you." She said the last words so softly, and Crimson knew they had only been for her.

Eliana walked away. "Derrant, consider her offer. You've tortured Mark enough. My daughter has paid the price for Crimson's deeds."

She left the room, the soft click of the door following her departure.

Derrant was staring at her, his eyes narrowed in anger. Rising, the sheets falling to expose his unnatural size, he strode to her. Her eyes took him in, having missed the beauty of him. She noted the twitch of his rising manhood as he came closer to her. She met his eyes, which were shimmering with humor, a sly grin to his mouth.

"No tricks or seductions this time, Crimson?" he asked, standing before her.

"No, only my honest offer."

His finger traced the curve of her cheek, then continued along the length of her body. She couldn't help the wave of desire that washed through her. Derrant was sexy and powerful, and his claim on her called to her any time she was in his presence. His touch made her ravenous for him as it had since the first time she'd sought favor from him.

"You're not Skye," he said, drawing his finger along her hip.

"I know, but you know who I am and how satisfied I can leave you."

"She satisfies me just fine."

She bit back the sigh as he grazed her nipple.

"Unwillingly. Her heart is Mark's, and he will cling to her each time you take her," she said, trying to control the quake in her voice. It wouldn't do for him to see the effect he had on her, although she was certain he knew it.

He moved closer, his rising girth pressing against her stomach. His hand pushed her hair back so that his lips found her neck. Her sigh escaped as a low moan, and she cursed herself and what he did to her.

"You have two mates who cling to you."

"I have two mates who will share as they share me. There will be no pull for me while I am with you. I will be completely yours. They understand this and accept it. They know I'm theirs but that you hold claim as well."

He trailed his mouth to her lips, kissing her demandingly, a demand she answered. She'd spoken the truth, and he knew it. All three men had claim on her, one she could never sever, nor would she want to.

There was a fire to Derrant that only a god could bring, one that stirred the soul he owned. It was an inferno that simmered deep inside of her and blazed whenever she was in his presence.

Her dress fell from her, and he pulled her naked skin against his.

"I accept your offer. You will take Skye's place for the five days that my brother steals Eliana from me." His hand tightened around her breast, and he drew her nipple to his mouth. She cried out as he bit it. With his other hand, he spread her legs, and sank into the arousal she knew awaited him. Walking her back, he forced her against the wall, the impact expelling the breath from her. His mouth captured it before it was completely freed. Effortlessly, he picked her up and entering her. A scream of passion tore from her throat, and she threw her head back. Every thrust brought a mix of pleasure and pain that seared through to her very core. It had been a long time since he'd taken her and she'd missed the aggressive nature of him, one that rivaled Bormick's rougher moments.

His hands dug into her ass as he tilted her pelvis, and she wrapped her legs tighter around him while he continued to selfishly take her. She would find no climax here. This was about ownership. He was taking her back, marking her as his again, laying his claim.

His thrusts became more violent until, with a groan, he spilled into her, his body finally stilling but not moving from hers. He kissed her again, a brutal need to it that caused her heart to pound.

"I've missed you, Crimson," he muttered against her lips. "Yes, you will take her place, but instead of five days, you will grant me seven."

"Seven?"

"Yes, seven." He removed his lips from hers, his blue eyes intense. "The five my brother steals Eliana from me to stay with him in Hell, and two more of my choosing. You will come to me when I summon you and pleasure me with that mouth of yours," he bit her bottom lip, drawing blood, "and this body of yours."

"Yes, I agree." She had no choice, no way to refuse him.

"Good, then I release Skye and tie you to her obligation."

He dropped her, pulling away and leaving her with a rush of emptiness in his absence.

"Now go back to my sons. Peter has a kingdom to reclaim, and all of you need to prepare."

"Prepare for what?" she asked as she put her dress back on, her eyes drawn to him while he pulled his pants over his still erect manhood.

She licked her lips, eliciting a laugh from him. "That will wait. Trust me, I will fill that pretty mouth of yours."

"Good," she said, feeling more herself.

"Go, use those lips on my sons. Peter must have his kingdom settled, his powers mastered, and you must work with the mage kingdom. It is imperative that the realms are united, but more so for your three realms. Revina will be of no use, and she will burn for it."

His seriousness worried her. "What's coming, Derrant?"

"The world is bigger than you know, Crimson. There is a storm coming, one which will decide the fate of my children and Eliana's children. A storm that will change everything."

ABOUT THE AUTHOR

J. L. Jackola discovered her passion for writing in grade school when she wrote a short story that earned her a spot in a local writing workshop. She has been creating fantasy worlds ever since. When she's not weaving tales, she can be found logging miles in her running shoes, watching movies with her family, or curled up with a book. She resides in Delaware with her husband and three children.

To learn more, visit her website at
www.jljackola.com